EVA AL

THE VAMPIRES OF EMBERBURY BOOK 2

ISBN: 9798686790896
First Edition.

Editing services provided by E. Latoria.

We thank all the artists who created the fonts and images included in this book and its cover.

To the Ladies of The Coven

You know who you are.

Eva

Other books in this series:

THE VAMPIRES OF EMBERBURY

- **Book 1 • Stray Witch**
- **Book 2 • Witch's Mirror**
- **Book 3 • Witches Masquerade**

- **The Vampire's Assistant**: The Vampires of Emberbury Prequel: Julia's story.
- **A Winter's Cobalt Kiss**: A Vampire Christmas in the World of Stray Witch.

You can visit the author's website at:
www.evaalton.com

WITCH'S
MIRROR

Come, come, and sit you down. You shall not budge.
You go not till I set you up a glass
where you may see the inmost part of you.

Hamlet, Prince of Denmark

Chapter 1

Alba

If you want to see the ghosts from the past, there's nothing like staring into a mirror at night. With some luck, you might even get a glimpse of your own deceased self from the future.

Or at least, that's what my grandmother used to say: and I'd rather respect her opinion, because some claim she was a witch.

After standing for hours in one of the most expensive couture stores in the whole city, surrounded by at least five floor-to-ceiling mirrors, I had found the underlying truth in my grandmother's words: perhaps it was just a consequence of my long-standing exhaustion, but I had started to spot ghostly visions in the mirrors of the store, and I was getting worried.

Elizabeth had insisted I get a proper gown for the oath ceremony. It had been a couple of months since I started to work as an assistant for the vampires of Emberbury, and she was adamant about formalizing our pact in the old-fashioned way. I found the concept a bit outlandish—signed contracts were more widely used in the 21st century, after all—but I had to accept that a certain level of pliability was necessary when dealing with centuries-old vampires.

It was the least I could do for Elizabeth, who had been of great assistance during the ordeal my ex-husband had dragged me through during our divorce. I would always be grateful for her help: had it not been for her contacts and knowledge, I might be living in a cardboard box instead of standing in a marble-floored room, wrapped in yards of silk and surrounded by seamstresses who fluttered around me, showering me with ribbons and pretty trinkets, just like Sleeping Beauty's fairy godmothers.

Only, come to think of it, I wasn't Sleeping Beauty, but rather… the witch.

A *good* witch, hopefully.

An utterly useless, virtually incapable witch, but a potential one at least. An inept sorceress working for the most unexpected employers in a secret place called The Cloister, hidden beneath a graveyard where the last vampires of Emberbury led a peaceful and clandestine existence.

Now, these vampires had asked me to swear to forever abide by their five sacred rules. In their eyes, that would basically turn me into a loyal vestal of The Cloister. In mine, it was just an archaic formality meant to keep Elizabeth happy.

And in my eagerness to please our queen, I

probably underestimated the extent of the commitment I was about to agree to. Had I paid any attention to the lessons learned during the past months, I would have realized that, when dealing with vampires, it was never healthy to undervalue them and their fancies. But somehow, the whole business with the pretty dress and the logistics of my newly regained singleness had made me imprudent… and I was going to pay for that candor very soon. However, that evening, I knew nothing about it—not yet.

"Stay still, or I will prick you," one of the three seamstresses warned me.

By then, I was probably bleeding from at least three different spots, and the many-layered brocade dress was getting increasingly heavy and itchy. Especially the corset—had corsets been invented by the Spanish Inquisition? How did those women in The Cloister put up with them daily? Of course, it might help that they were already dead, or half dead… or whatever the right term was.

Alas, I was just a mortal girl, and my endurance threshold was consequently much lower than theirs.

"It must be a really exciting party you are attending in this gown," another seamstress commented. They were all giggly and enthusiastic, and I could see why: the purple, floor-length garment they had tailored for me was short of a marvel and—although I would never admit it, not even under torture—it made me feel like a fairytale princess… and I enjoyed that.

"You have no idea," I agreed, leaning backwards to avoid a particularly long needle aimed at my side and protecting my other flank with the antique diary I had been reading. It was a beautiful vintage piece, which had once belonged to yet another clueless, stray witch like me.

My phone rang, and Clarence's name appeared on screen. As usual, my heart skipped a beat with anticipation before I picked up his call. He had been traveling often—too often—during the past weeks, doing errands for Elizabeth in the most ridiculously remote places. What kind of business a bunch of vampires could have in the most remote island of Alaska, was well beyond my understanding.

Clarence was having lots of fun with his new phone and the rest of the toys I had provided the vampires with after sneaking an illegal electricity connection into their nest. Thanks to my otherwise useless engineering background, I had even got them a Wi-Fi signal and a couple of laptops to play with. He might never become a software developer, but he was doing quite well, at least for someone born in the Georgian era.

"Isolde," Clarence purred on the other side of the line. He must be in a good mood to call me that. "Non-dinner at *The Midnight Owl?*" he asked playfully. I was surprised he was offering to take me to dinner—or technically, to watch me eat while he talked—because we had managed to squeeze very few dates into his busy schedule after Mark's nightmare had come to an end. I tried not to dwell on the reasons for his continuous absences and frequent cancellations, and kept telling myself it was all Elizabeth's fault for giving him too much to do, too far from home.

"I'd love to," I said, "but are you going to cancel last-minute just like you did last time? Because I'm really tired today. I've been running around for hours."

"Oh, well," Clarence said, a tint of sadness in his voice. "I don't know…" *How on earth could he not know?* "Maybe you are right. Perhaps come to say good night before you go to sleep, would you?"

"I will," I grumbled, grabbing my bucket-sized cup of coffee and missing it due to my sudden bad mood. The cup slipped off my fingers, and I skipped back, horrified at the thought of pouring a whole mug of coffee over the unfinished gown. The seamstresses gasped, and all the girls rushed in my direction to stop the disaster.

Stretching my arm, I tried to grasp the handle as the cup flew in the air, but it was too far already. And then, miraculously, the cup stopped its trajectory and started to hover in the air, just a few inches away from my extended fingers.

Everybody in the store—me included—stared at the floating cup, which glided magically, in perfect alignment with its porcelain saucer.

Someone let out a gasp, removing me from my mesmerized contemplation.

"Oh my God!" I uttered into the phone,

willing my erratic magic to stop the random display at once—it didn't.

"Is everything alright?" Clarence asked from the other side of the line.

"No," I whispered so nobody else could hear me, as I tried to steady my shaking hands, "There's a flying saucer in the room. I'll call you later."

Ignoring Clarence's anxious questions and protests, I put down the phone. As soon as I did it, the cup plunged to the floor, spilling its contents mid-flight over the diary I had been reading. The pages turned all brown and damp, and everyone let out a collective sigh as the shards spread all over the workshop.

The seamstresses looked at each other, rubbing their eyes, and started to flutter around the coffee-sprinkled shards.

"Did you see that?" one of them asked me with consternation, bracing herself.

"No? I didn't see anything," I answered with feigned innocence, straightening my back and checking the state of the soaked notebook. It had already suffered water damage once, and the extra coffee shower hadn't done it much good.

"It's like time stopped," a girl said.

"No way," I answered. "I'm just… clumsy. And tired. I'm so sorry."

I retrieved the journal and wiped it with a napkin. Sadly, it was too late. As I rubbed off the coffee stains, the leather cover detached from the pages and they fell to the floor with a soft flapping sound.

"Dammit," I muttered. That diary was the only thing I had left from Julia, my predecessor and previous witch of The Cloister. She had written it during her years living with the vampires, and I had taken to analyzing each of her words in the hopes of discovering the missing piece which separated me from my anemic—and clearly unpredictable—magical abilities.

I knelt to pick up the fallen pages and noticed a mark on the inside of the cover. It had been dressed in a layer of gilded paper, which kept the binding in place. Now, the golden material had started to peel away.

"That thing was hovering in the air," a seamstress was saying. "I swear it. Like witchcraft."

"Nonsense," I answered sternly, suppressing the instinctive urge to start crawling to help pick up the mess, which would have ruined my almost-finished gown. "It must be the lack of oxygen. The air is getting stale here; you have the heating too high. We should open a window before somebody faints."

"Stand up, or you will ruin the skirt!" someone warned me, and they all started to swirl around me to check the state of the fabric.

"Ah," one of them said, rubbing her forehead with relief, "At least the dress is okay!" She caressed the skirt with longing, and the others smiled with relief. I hoped they would dismiss my little magical glitch, so I didn't need to ask Clarence to come and administer oblivion to everyone. It would not be the first time.

"That's great," I said, although my voice sounded more worried than I had wanted it to. On top of my existing concerns, now I would have to deal with the very real possibility of the rumor of a flying teacup spreading all over Emberbury.

The girls started to unbutton the back of my dress, and meanwhile, I flipped the journal cover in case it could be fixed. As I turned it around, I found a few words scribbled in a corner, under the binding.

Who could have put them there? Either the bookmaker had written the message before gluing the notebook together, or Julia had taken the journal apart later, written those words and then glued everything back to conceal them.

Why would anyone do that?

"I think we're done for today with the fittings, Ms. Lumin," the store owner told me. "Come back tomorrow for the last touches!"

"Thank you so much," I said, as the fabric slipped to the floor with a swish, and I muttered a hallelujah when they freed me from the corset.

I stared at the message: it was Julia's handwriting. I knew it because it was the same throughout the whole diary.

The text was brief and somewhat puzzling:

Don't trust E.
Ask F.

I could fathom who *E* and *F* may be. There

weren't that many vampires in The Cloister, after all. However, if my guess was right, Julia's message was trying to warn me about a certain vampire queen: and more precisely, about the one I was about to swear loyalty to for the rest of my life.

Chapter 2

Alba

Clarence was not in his chambers when I knocked on the door. Disenchanted by his absence, I searched for Francesca instead.

The music coming from the piano room led me to her. It was late, and gorgeous Francesca had already tucked my daughters into their beds before my arrival. I sat in the back of the room, waiting for her to acknowledge my presence.

An angel at the keyboard, she had a talent for soaking up scotch like it was nobody's business, which hinted at her true unrelenting—sometimes even ruthless—nature.

"Shouldn't you be with Clarence, pretending not to be in love with each other?" Francesca teased me, as her fingers kept flying over the keys. "He was looking for you earlier."

I disregarded the second part of the question.

"He's not in his suite," I moaned, trying to hide the disappointment in my voice—and failing.

"And he's been acting so strangely these days. I have barely seen him for weeks. If he's not locked in his room, he's missing or on his way to places with names as obscure as *Yesterday Island*."

"Yes," Francesca exhaled with impatience as she missed a note. "Sometimes he reminds me of a two-hundred-year-old teenager."

I closed my eyes. Men could be so simple and so complicated at times. Undead men, though—that was yet another level of tricky entirely.

"So, you came to keep me company," she said mischievously. "How thoughtful of you."

"Well, yes…" I clutched Julia's notebook against my chest and walked over to the grand piano.

What I found most baffling about Julia's secret message was how the rest of her diary was crammed with words of praise for Elizabeth. True, some pages were torn or missing, but the vampire queen had never uttered a single negative word about her previous assistant, and nothing I had seen or heard so far suggested any animosity between them. This made me suspect that Julia might have written that note in a passing fit of anger, possibly after an argument with the queen, and forgotten to erase it later.

"Is this about Julia?" Francesca asked, closing her scores and turning to me with a thick-bottomed glass in her hand. "I haven't forgotten my promise to point you in her direction. I was just waiting for you to ask. I know you have been busy."

Julia had appeared to me in a vision after a terrible accident, pledging to teach me magic if I sought her. It had taken me a while to recover and get into a routine after my rocky divorce, and now that things were finally settling down a little, I had no idea how to reach her—the fact that she had been dead and buried for thirty years didn't help, either. Still, Francesca seemed to know things I didn't, and back then, she had promised to help me. The note in Julia's diary seemed to confirm the need for further research into the matter.

"Look at this," I told her, showing her Julia's wretched notebook.

"You should start taking better care of your things," she scolded me in her governess voice, giving a reproving look to my neglected nails and the diary.

"I know." I sighed, peeking guiltily at my half-eaten nails. "But look closer."

Francesca took the diary in her hands, a puzzled look growing gradually in her blue eyes. When she finished reading the little inscription behind the cover, she let out a brief huff.

"I didn't know anything about this," she said, closing the journal and returning it.

I stood there, waiting for her to elaborate, but she just turned towards the piano and started to play again: this time, a very sad and slow melody.

"Francesca, do you intend to explain to me what this is about? Does this mean what I think it means? Is Elizabeth a threat, or…?"

Francesca leaned abruptly over the keyboard and hit all the keys hard with both hands, making the whole room shake and muffling the last part of my sentence beneath the rumble of the mistreated piano.

"Certain things can't be discussed in The Cloister," she hissed, her knuckles white against the glossy, black lid. "Vampire ears are much finer than those useless... *funnels* of yours, Alba."

Did she just call my ears *funnels*?

"Do you want to have both of us banished?" she growled.

"No, of course not," I said, biting my lip and mustering all the patience I could so as not to enrage the tiny vampire. "Then, where can we talk? I really need to know what I'm getting myself into."

"Meet me tomorrow after the ceremony," she said very quietly, her eyes glowing with a turquoise radiance. "We'll go somewhere safer."

***

I didn't see Clarence for the rest of the evening and woke up the next morning to bell chimes on my phone, alerting me of both lousy weather and the Winter Solstice. The beginning of winter meant holidays, which newly translated into leaving my daughters with their father for the longest period since our separation. As much as it pained me to entrust Mark and his girlfriend with my children, an unexpected thrill washed over me as I imagined the bliss of taking a few days off. This year had been just short of a nightmare, and I had frequently dreamed about a brief vacation away from everything and everyone.

As I made my way to the conference room, I decided to discuss my free days with Elizabeth, as our contract signing kept getting postponed because of the impending oath ceremony.

The vampire queen sat majestically, alone at the head of a large, antique table.

"Good morning, Alba. To what do I owe the pleasure? Eager to take your oath?" Elizabeth asked, without a trace of a smile, as she detached her eyes from the thick and dull-looking book she was reading.

"*Um*, yes, sure," I stuttered, remembering the warning in Julia's diary. I rocked my weight nervously from one foot to the other and told myself everything would be fine. That the ceremony was just a formality to make Elizabeth happy. Just a pretty dress and a vow.

"Did you have any questions?" The way she glanced back at her notes showed her tolerance toward inept witches was already starting to run thin.

"Well, now that you ask, I was here to discuss my vacation days," I said, tentatively. "We never got to talk about that. It would be good to clear this up before we sign anything."

"What vacation days?" she asked, her voice an affronted rumble. "You just disappeared without notice a couple of months ago, right after I hired you. Why would you need any more days off?"

Truth to be told, my work at The Cloister wasn't exactly exhausting. Mostly I just ran errands and met with Elizabeth or her business partners from time to time. But still, asking for a few days off didn't seem unreasonable to me.

"It's going to be Christmas," I said, crossing my arms. "I'd like to go and see the snow."

Elizabeth snorted. "Excuse me? The whole Emberbury is squashed under heaps of snow at the moment. Why would you need days off to see *that*? Can't you just step outside and… I don't know, open your eyes?"

I rubbed my temples. "Elizabeth, please. I'm just so… worn-out. I'm just asking for a short vacation; one week or two."

"Currently, there's no law in this state which would require me to grant you vacation time whenever you please."

"I'm just asking nicely. Everything will be closed, anyway. What is so urgent that it can't wait until January?"

"Everything is urgent when my businesses are concerned. Do you think they are going to close the stock markets just so you can throw snowballs and go sledding?"

I puffed in desperation. Elizabeth could be such a tough cookie sometimes.

"Please. I don't know what kind of agreement you had with Julia, but this is the 21st century, Elizabeth. Keeping me here against my will is reminiscent of slavery!"

My comment caused her to stand up in a fury, nearly overturning the table. She leaned on her elbows in front of my face and stared at me with flaming almond eyes. What had gotten into me to make me pronounce the taboo word in front of her once again?

"What would you know about slavery, you spoiled little witch?" she rumbled.

I averted my eyes, wondering whether my years with Mark would count from her perspective. *Probably not.* "Nothing. You're right."

"Very well, then." She stepped back, and I let out a sigh when she finally freed me from her formidable presence. "You have my answer. Anything else?"

I shook my head and stood up, defeated.

Elizabeth picked up a piece of paper from a pile and gave it to me. "Before you go, take this. I should have given it to you a long time ago. It might have spared us a few discrepancies."

It was a handwritten note with the five sacred rules of The Cloister. I was already familiar with them, so I just stuck the list in the back pocket of my jeans.

"Watch your words, mortal girl. Don't forget I'm your queen."

Technically, she wasn't yet.

"Make sure you memorize the rules. I will ask you to recite them in front of the audience."

After this, Elizabeth buried her nose into

her books and pretended I was already gone. That was how she typically sent people off.

"As you say, *my queen*," I mumbled through clenched teeth. "I'll see you at the oath ceremony."

Chapter 3

Clarence

As I came out of my suite that morning, an enormous mirror with legs walked by my door and grunted. I gazed at my missing reflection as my eyes set on that cowboy aberration called *jeans* which had—to my sorrow—substituted petticoats in modern times.

"Mirror, mirror on the wall," I said, lifting the golden frame with one hand in order to uncover a flushed Alba Lumin underneath it. "If it isn't the fairest of them all!"

"Oh, Clarence, quite the stranger, aren't you lately?" She raised her beautiful muddy green eyes and stared at me with a dash of sorrow.

I gave her a half smile and deliberately ignored the comment. "I'm certain Elizabeth is going to love your new acquisition," I commented. Our queen had never been thrilled about mirrors, since they reminded her too much of her true nature. And this one was particularly large. And heavy. I wondered how someone the size of Alba had carried that monstrosity into the catacombs on her own. She never failed to surprise me.

"It's for my room. She doesn't have to know about it. I need to get ready for the ceremony, and I'm fed up with using the camera on my phone to style my hair."

"Of course. I'm sure this is the smallest one they had in the shops." She motioned to take the mirror from my hands, but I stopped her. "Please, allow me to carry it for you. Just let me lock my room first."

I set the mirror against the wall of the corridor and searched for my keys.

"How was Alaska?" she asked, staring at me with a tilted head.

"Cold, barren and grimly devoid of lovely creatures with lopsided smiles," I answered.

"I don't have a lopsided smile," she complained, right as one corner of her mouth started to twitch, as if on cue.

"Of course you don't, my dear. Who said I was talking about you?"

The half-smile vanished as quickly as it had made its appearance, and she curled in on herself a little, her heartbeat speeding up audibly as she debated on her next question.

"What is keeping you so busy these days, Clarence?" she asked, standing on her toes behind me to peek into my room. "Why weren't you in The Cloister yesterday evening when I came to say goodnight?"

"Oh, I had some… pressing matters to deal

with."

Her eyes wandered meaningfully over the unfinished solitaire game of cards on my bedspread and the many discarded charcoal sketches scattered around my desk like autumn leaves, and I rushed to close the door before she saw anything else.

Alba twisted her hands uncomfortably and avoided my gaze as she asked, "Clarence, please be honest. Have you been… avoiding me lately?"

Her words felt like a silver stake through my heart, not only because I had been missing her company terribly, but also because of the truth they carried. For a second, I pondered what the most gentlemanly answer would have been. A white lie? Or rather a sour truth? After a glance at her disheartened countenance, I opted for the former.

"Most definitely not!" I said with contrived joyfulness, but my slightly cracked voice betrayed me. "Which reminds me, I had been wishing to ask you if you'd allow me to escort you to the ceremony this evening."

"Well, it's not like the venue is too far, but sure, I'd love for you to," she said wearily. "Unless you are too busy painting… or whatever you've been doing all night."

Painting, she said.

I pressed my lips in a tight smile, overwhelmed by the memories which surfaced at the mere mention of that word.

If only she knew it had been a painting that had brought doom upon me a long, forgotten time ago.

***

London, April 1834

I didn't hear the lady approaching, her steps muffled by the rumble of passing carriages in the foggy night. She was slight and dressed in elegant widow's weeds, and her voice startled me as I stepped out of the mortuary and into the muddy London streets.

"Excuse me, Sir," she said from under her dark mourning veil, "are you Doctor Auberon?"

A well-bred lady would have never roamed the streets on her own, particularly not at night. But the way she stood and spoke, formidable and compelling, spoke of an aristocratic background. A fascinating occurrence indeed.

"My apologies, madam, you must have mistaken me for my father," I said, trying to discern her face under the dense net as I tipped my hat. Her voice sounded foreign, perchance Prussian. "I am just his humble assistant."

"No, I am quite sure it is you I have been looking for. I am not in need of a trained physician at the moment. A gentleman well-versed in human anatomy will do just fine for what I had in mind."

I stared at the lady blankly. In my thirty-something years of bachelor life, I had been propositioned by ladies more times than one would expect. Ladies seemed to be fond of physicians—even though, despite my age, I had never become a proper one. Most requests were discreet and dully appropriate, but from time to time, I would meet a lady with more unrestrained philosophies—those were the ones I usually took an interest in. Widows, particularly, had a way of overlooking social rules when faced with a man they may consider a decent pastime—or a marriage prospect, depending on their financial status.

"If you'd be so kind as to join me in my carriage, we could continue this conversation in private," she whispered, and extended her gloved palm upwards, "it's starting to drizzle, and humidity tends to ruin my hair."

After yet another day full of horrors by my father's side, I was on my way to induced oblivion anyway, so I decided to accept the widow's indecorous invitation and climbed into her lavish coach, which was waiting on the other side of the street.

She sat down in front of me with a graceful, almost childish hop. Once we were in motion, she lifted her veil, revealing high, bony cheekbones and the mesmerizingly pale countenance which was usually a tell-tale sign of consumption. In the years assisting my father, I had seen so many people die from it that I didn't even need to be a real doctor to diagnose her.

The lady produced a snuff box from under her coat and passed it to me with a sly smile. I smiled back and accepted it with curiosity, admiring the carved bone surface. The image of a skeleton decorated the lid, but I noticed a few ribs were missing—how unsystematic from the cutter.

"It lessens the ill effects of reality, doesn't it?" the lady said after I took a pinch. She sniffed the ground tobacco from afar and put the box back without using it herself. "Although I was under the impression that you might need something stronger after a day at the morgue… or am I mistaken, *doctor*?"

"You seem to know me well, madam, yet I don't even know your name," I said, closing my eyes as the heady scent of snuff filled my nostrils. I had always loathed the smell of operation theatres and the stench of rotting humans which accompanied my father's profession. He hated me for my weakness and my inability to become his successor, and kept dragging me to the most gruesome visits in a vain attempt to harden me. But after I had surpassed the thirty-year mark, it had become clear to him that I would never be more than a mere physician's assistant. At that point in my life, frustration had turned into resignation to the career someone else had chosen for me. Meanwhile, snuff, opium and alcohol had become my most trustworthy companions, together with my secret affair with paint and brushes.

"My name is Anne Zugrabescu," she introduced herself. "It's a pleasure to finally meet you, Doctor Auberon."

I bowed, ignoring her insistence in calling me by my father's title, and tried not to frown at her unpronounceable, exotic surname.

"The pleasure is all mine, Mrs.—" I strove to

say the word, but I just tripped over my tongue clumsily and she laughed, making the round, dark mole on the left side of her face stand out. Only then, I realized how young and fine-looking she was, with narrow shoulders and full, red lips. She had pitch black hair and snow-white skin.

"Zugrabescu," she repeated, almost licentiously. "It's Moldavian."

"You must have come a long way to seek advice on your condition here in London," I ventured, increasingly intrigued by the beautiful foreign lady.

"Oh, but I already told you—" She blinked, just once. "I didn't come here for medical advice, doctor. I am in very good health, thank you. What I'm searching for is a fine artist."

A horse neighed, and the carriage stopped to a halt. I narrowed my eyes, wondering how she knew about my little secret. I had always kept my artistic tendencies hushed to avoid upsetting my father any further.

"I beg your pardon?" I said, baffled.

"I need someone to paint a portrait. Not just anyone." She scrutinized me from head to toe in a forthright, overly intrusive way which I had never seen before from a refined lady.

"Excuse my audaciousness, Mrs. Zugrabescu," My pronunciation must have been wrong, because her lips curved upwards with mischief once again. "But shouldn't you be inquiring about artists at the Royal Academy, and not by the gates of a Dead House?"

"I certainly tried that first, but all I found were proper and prudish portrait artists who blushed when I expressed my wishes," she said with a mysterious smirk, "so I headed to the place where I knew I would find what I needed."

"Fascinating," I said, as we waited for the coachman to open the door of the carriage. "And what kind of artist did you expect to find at a mortuary, if I may ask?"

She gave me a slow, sly smile before she answered. "A deeply tormented one, hopefully."

Chapter 4

Alba

"Behold, the rising sun," Clarence said when he picked me up at the door of my room that evening. Stuffed in the uncomfortable purple gown Elizabeth had chosen for me, and slightly oxygen-deprived due to the tight corset, it took me a while to realize he was actually referring to me and not to the yellow star in the sky he mustn't have seen for hundreds of years.

"You don't look too bad yourself," I commented. His dark hair was deliciously unruly, and the sparse silver strays sparkled like steel threads in the dimly lit halls. He was wearing a black tailcoat and a white silk cravat, and I kept to myself the fact that he looked so dazzling that gawking at him must be, without a doubt, sinful. Clarence was conceited enough as it was and by no means needed further encouragement.

"Ready to become a vampire tonight?" he said casually, as we strolled down the hall and toward the ballroom where everyone was already waiting.

I halted abruptly, frozen on the spot, and stared at his flashing maroon eyes in horror.

"What did you just say?" I asked, or rather shrieked, as I elbowed him away from me and leaped back, calculating how long it would take me to reach the exit.

Would he be able to catch me?

Of course he would.

Clarence smirked and reached me in just two strides, then kissed the tip of my nose.

"I was teasing you, my Isolde. I just wanted to see your reaction." He shook his head. "In all truth, I didn't expect such a heated response."

He rubbed his side where I had hit him, pretending to be hurt. I let out a deep exhale and pursed my lips as I took his arm once again, not before throwing him several distrustful, sidelong glances.

"That wasn't funny," I snarled, nudging him in the ribs again—just gently this time.

"Oh. I had always hoped you would let me bite you one day." He sighed ruefully and lowered his eyelids in that sensual way of his. This time, I couldn't tell for sure whether he was being serious or not.

I was spared the need to answer because we reached the ballroom, and Jean-Pierre opened the door for us with a genteel bow.

"Ms. Lumin," he greeted me formally, "Clarence. Do come in."

Lillian—who otherwise hated me—had put

her artistic talents to use and filled the underground ballroom with hundreds of pink and crimson carnations, whose fragrance was so intoxicating that it made me sway.

All the members of The Cloister were sitting in the room, with Elizabeth on a stage at the front, posing proudly on a gilded armchair. Next to her there was a gigantic vase of flowers and a chair reserved for me. The others sat in two short rows in front of her, and a long, black carpet led from the entrance to the stage.

"May I have the pleasure?" Clarence said, and started to walk me down the short aisle ceremoniously. Anxiety started to throttle me as the situation suddenly reminded me of my wedding to Mark a decade ago. With some luck, this wouldn't end up at the top of my list of unwise life choices, too.

I shook my head and took a deep breath, trying to dissipate the grim memories and telling myself that this oath was just a formality. I had been working in The Cloister for months, and I knew those people well—or so I thought. If this was so important to Elizabeth, who was I to deny her this little satisfaction? After all, she had offered me shelter when I needed it most, plus a salary, and many other things I would have never found anywhere else. It was the least I could do for her.

My daughters, Katie and Iris, were sitting next to Nanny Francesca, and I kissed their heads as I reached them. The children were extremely excited about the party: probably much more than I was. We had bought them matching lavender gowns and dwarf rose wreaths to wear on their golden, curly heads, and they clapped their little hands when they saw me.

"Be good and listen to Francesca," I whispered, patting their backs as I passed by.

I took my seat, and Clarence retired to the background. Jean-Pierre struck a metal triangle with a small beater, and everyone fell silent.

"Dear members of The Cloister," Jean-Pierre said, addressing the small group with his best priestly tone. He had been a monk in a previous life, and it showed. "Let's begin."

Iris squealed, and Francesca hushed her.

"*In nomine Patris, e Filii…*" Jean-Pierre said in a low singing tone.

Everyone stared at each other in confusion, until Clarence cleared his throat, interrupting the former monk.

"Mercier…" he hissed, eyeing him with an amused expression. "Wrong speech."

Jean-Pierre slapped his forehead and crossed himself with a sincerely embarrassed expression. "Oh, please excuse me… *déformation professionnelle.*" He shook his head and took a deep breath. "Let me start again."

Katie giggled, and Elizabeth rolled her eyes.

"Dearly beloved friends," Jean-Pierre said this time, "we are gathered here tonight to pay homage to the sacred rules of The Cloister, by which our newest member, Ms. Alba Lumin, will swear faithfulness to our clan for the rest of her mortal life."

I stirred in my seat with unease, as Jean-Pierre went on to talk about Julia and praise my college education, and finished by thanking me for bringing the gift of electricity to The Cloister. During the whole speech, Elizabeth alternated between mild scowling and looking bored out of her mind.

Once Jean-Pierre's discourse was over, Elizabeth stood up.

"Now please recite the five rules for us," she commanded.

I stood up and held out the paper she had given me the previous day as I declaimed the five rules:

Thou shalt not spread the curse,
Thou shalt not speak our name,
Thou shalt not kill gratuitously,
Thou shalt not stand before a looking glass,
Thou shalt not engage with outsiders.

After that, everybody applauded, and Jean-Pierre congratulated me with a handshake. Slumping back on my chair, I sighed with relief that everything was over, and the vampires started to talk in a soft murmur around me.

"Can we eat cake already?" Katie asked, but Elizabeth grunted and raised a hand, asking for silence once again.

"We are not done yet," she said, taking a sharp knife from the table next to her.

To cut the cake, hopefully.

Francesca gasped, and the puzzled expressions of the others suggested that nobody had expected a follow-up, either.

"To conclude, let's proceed to the blood oath," Elizabeth said, lifting the knife over her head like a priestess about to perform a sacrifice ritual.

My hands started to sweat as I gawked at the gleaming blade Elizabeth was holding.

"*Er…*" I pointed at the knife. "That was just a metaphor, wasn't it?"

"Elizabeth, is this… is this really necessary?" Jean-Pierre stammered, as he stepped between me and the queen, twisting his hands.

Elizabeth pushed him aside and leaned toward me.

"Kneel down," she ordered with a chin nod.

Suddenly glued to my chair, I eyed her blankly, as my knuckles became white over the armrests.

"No," Clarence said, joining Jean-Pierre on the stage to create a barrier between the queen and me. "Elizabeth, I beg you."

But Elizabeth's eyes were bloodshot, and she didn't seem to be listening. She shoved both men aside in one clean move and pointed to Alonso.

"Hold her," she commanded him, and the mustached vampire sauntered toward the stage with a smug smile on his face.

"Don't you dare lay a hand on her," Clarence growled at Alonso, but the other vampire just kept grinning with arrogance by my side. "Francesca, will you please take the children outside?" Clarence added, without turning around.

Francesca stood up, took Katie and Iris and forged a tight smile. "Come, children. Let me show you the pretty flowers Lillian has brought from the graveyard."

Once the children were out of sight, Elizabeth addressed Clarence, "Will you please allow Alonso to fulfill his duty? Unless you would prefer to restrain the witch yourself?" She had started to tap the floor with her foot, driving me insane with the repetitive sound.

"Elizabeth, please," Clarence's voice was ragged, almost desperate, "what you are proposing is a barbaric, obsolete act. Don't make Alba go through this. She has proved her loyalty to you many times in the past."

"Has she, really?" Elizabeth raised a questioning eyebrow and licked her lips. "One can never trust witches completely. See what she did the last time. We need to make sure of her compliance."

"Will anyone tell me what this is about?" I shrieked, standing up to hide behind Clarence's tall figure. "Clarence? What's going on?"

He put his hands on my shoulders and stared into my eyes.

"*Nothing* is going on. Not while I'm here with you."

Elizabeth puffed with irritation and rolled her eyes once more.

"Clarence, dear," she said, stretching to tap on his shoulder, "I think you might have forgotten your place. Remember why you are here? Remember why you are alive at all? Remember… your own oaths?"

Clarence's eyes became somber, and his hands hardened, fingertips turning into claws over my shoulders.

"You do remember," Elizabeth said with a nod, "good. Now, if you are not going to cooperate, then I would kindly ask you to retreat to the audience, please."

Desperate, I tried to meet Clarence's eyes once more, seeking reassurance. But he just detached himself from me and stepped back, seething. He was shaking, and his jaw was so tense that he resembled a bomb about to explode.

"I will not be an accomplice to this viciousness," he said and to my horror, left the room, slamming the door.

"Clarence, wait! Don't leave me here!" I cried, but Alonso was already pulling at my arms and forcing me on my knees. "Jean-Pierre?"

Jean-Pierre avoided my gaze and ignored my call, his attention fixed on a large vase full of pink carnations.

"And now, the true ceremony," Elizabeth stated.

Dressed in a black gown, the vampire queen was daunting. An esoteric aura surrounded her, making her beautiful, terrible, and compelling at the same time. She stood over me, holding the blade over my head as if about to kill me.

I tried to resist against Alonso, but there was no way I could break a vampire's grip. Lillian joined her hands with visible excitement, while Elizabeth took my left hand and started to speak in a rumbling voice.

"I, Elizabeth Swamp, Queen of The Vampire Cloister of Emberbury, before my faithful subjects, accept you as a member of our secret circle. I swear to protect you from whatever darkness may lurk upon you, and I expect your everlasting loyalty in return. As proof of your faithfulness, I now call upon my right to drink my servant's blood and forge a lifetime bond between us, which will only be dissolved when you draw your last mortal breath."

My entire body quivered, with the corset making it hard to breathe. Elizabeth's silhouette started to fade around the edges.

She lowered the knife over my arm and slowly sliced a clean cut on my wrist. I let out a gasp, too dazed to feel the pain, and Clarence's muffled screams thundered in response, coming from the other side of the catacombs.

When my blood started to trickle, Elizabeth wiped it with her free hand and licked it off her fingers, ghastly slurping sounds coming from her lips.

"Now your blood runs through me, and you are mine to command," she said.

Her eyes were glowing red, and dizziness overcame me. I didn't feel my limbs anymore. After that, Elizabeth started to drink blood directly from my wrist. I caught a glimpse of Jean-Pierre, whose face was buried in his hands.

When Elizabeth finally let go of my arm, the monk let out a deep sigh. The pain and degradation must be over.

"Welcome to The Cloister, Alba Lumin," she said to conclude. "Now you are one of us."

Alonso released me, and the last thing I remember was the coolness of the stone floor as I collapsed on it with a soft thud, gasping for air.

Chapter 5

Alba

I woke up in a room which wasn't mine and smelled of roses. Shifting around in the bed, I tried to make out where I was. A lonely candle burned in the corner, and I stirred, trying to get used to the darkness. Francesca's slight figure was leaning over a book in an armchair, her long, blonde locks falling languidly over the pages.

"Francesca…" I whispered, pain darting through my forearm. I lifted my arm where Elizabeth had cut me: somebody had carefully bandaged the wound with clean, white gauze. It hurt, although not as much as my shattered confidence.

"She can be ruthless sometimes," Francesca murmured, looking at me with pity.

"What was all that about?" I asked, sitting up on the pillows and trying to remember how I had ended up in Francesca's bed after the ceremony. "And why am I in your room?"

"Clarence brought you here and asked me

to dress your wound." She lifted a brow. "He didn't even want to look at it. I think he was too embarrassed. With good reason, if you ask me," she added in a flat tone.

Clarence.

He had just left me at Elizabeth's mercy right after promising to protect me against her.

"Where is he now?" I asked, exhausted, still unable to understand his behavior.

"Who cares," she said, brushing a stray lock of hair off her eyes. "How is your wrist? Did I do a good job? I didn't think licking your cut was permissible, under the circumstances. So I did my best with what I had."

I flexed my fingers. The pain was sharp, but the gauze was clean and dry. At least I wasn't in imminent danger of bleeding to death.

"I'm fine. But I wish somebody would have told me about these quirky customs of yours… in advance."

"Nobody knew she was planning a blood oath," Francesca said, standing up and rummaging in a drawer. "This custom hasn't been practiced for centuries."

"Did she do the same to Julia?"

Francesca shook her head. "No. She never doubted Julia. You, on the other hand…" She clicked her tongue. "I think you upset her when you ran away this summer."

"I thought that matter was closed already," I grumbled, my mind starting to race.

"Closed?" Francesca blinked. "When was a

loyalty matter closed for a vampire?"

I shrugged, not knowing what to answer.

"Vampires tend to be spiteful," Francesca said with a shrug. "Forgiving is for the weak; forgetting… for the dead."

I rubbed my temples and let her statement sink in. As I wondered where Clarence's loyalties lay, a pang of anguish hit my chest, and I had to remain very still until the wave of sadness abated.

"Where are the girls?" I asked after a long silence.

"I put them to bed. Don't worry, they didn't see anything. You can tell them you cut yourself slicing the cake. If they are to live here, it's better if they don't hate Elizabeth. Or even worse, fear her."

"Will she do that again?"

"I don't think so," she answered, but it sounded like there was something else she wasn't telling me.

Silence fell over the room, and Francesca sat down on the edge of the bed, watching me intently.

"Now I realize that the diary was trying to warn me about this," I stated. "You should have told me why Julia wrote that message. To be honest, we should have talked about all this a long time ago. It might have saved me a lot of trouble."

"I was waiting for you to ask. You never came to me until yesterday, and I didn't expect Elizabeth to do this."

"Life got in the way, I suppose." I sighed. I had been so busy putting my life in order after Mark that I had pushed everything else to the background. "So, what happened to Julia?" I lowered my voice as much as I could, knowing that Francesca would hear me anyway, but she frowned anyway, visibly annoyed. "Francesca, I need to know already. I'm sick and tired of so many secrets."

She put a finger to her lips and scowled. "Not here."

"Okay." All this secrecy was starting to get annoying. "Where, then?"

"I'll ask Jean-Pierre to take care of the children's breakfast. Take a taxi to Saint Emery and meet me at the cemetery in three hours. Do you think you can walk? Or are you still lightheaded?"

I stood up. Someone had opened the back of my dress, and it sagged inelegantly over my shoulders. But it didn't squeeze my lungs anymore. I took a deep breath.

"I'm fine," I said, taking a few tentative steps around the room. "I'll meet you there. Let me just change and get my wallet."

***

The taxi driver was pulling up by the gates of Saint Emery's cemetery by the time I woke up. It must have been nearly four in the morning, and my wrist was throbbing, just like the growing wrath inside my chest. Sorrow had given way to anger: anger at Elizabeth for treating me worse than a slave; anger at Clarence for turning away in front of such humiliation, and most of all, anger at myself, for being naïve enough to believe that working for vampires was going to be a pleasant, harmless task.

What on earth had I been thinking?

As I got out of the vehicle, memories of my last time in St. Emery flooded my mind, and a knot started to tighten in the pit of my stomach. My first visit to Julia's tomb had earned me a police detention. I trusted Francesca wouldn't desert me in that same graveyard for a second time.

When I reached the gates, Francesca was waiting for me on the other side. She climbed atop the fence with the dexterity of a spider—long skirt and all—and offered me her hands as a stirrup. Then, the tiny vampire picked me up and effortlessly deposited me on the frosty ground, just like a gardener rearranging her flowerpots.

"Can we talk now?" I asked impatiently, wrapping my coat tightly around my shoulders. "Is this far enough from Elizabeth?"

Unlike Francesca, I had changed into a pair of jeans and a woolen sweater and coat, but I was freezing nonetheless, and I still didn't know why she had made me go all the way to St. Emery.

"Wait and see," Francesca said with a mischievous smile, then knelt in front of Julia's tomb and started to push the stone aside with all her strength. A slight frown appeared on her terse forehead, and she let out a soft grunt.

Startled, I looked around frantically, worried the custodian would hear us. Nobody was coming. When the stone gave way, it revealed a dark cement pit under it. Francesca skipped into the opening with joviality and offered me a hand. I cringed.

"Your turn," she said sweetly.

I stood by the open tomb and hesitated. There was nothing I wanted less than jumping into Julia's grave. Except, maybe, jumping into *my own* grave.

"Come on, Alba. We have no time to lose," Francesca said, crossing her arms.

She probably had some, immortal as she was, but I decided not to argue.

Sighing deeply, I sat on the rim of the opening and let my legs dangle over it without much enthusiasm. I scanned the hole for decayed coffins, but there were none. There must have been an urn somewhere, and with some luck, I wouldn't step on it and sprinkle Julia's remains all over my shoes.

"Do I really have to jump in?" I whined, watching Francesca crouch inside the dark, macabre hole. She started to scratch the dirt of the bottom with her bare fingers, and I winced.

"No, it's fine, I already found what I needed," she said, holding a large metal tin, like the ones my grandmother used for homemade cookies. "Look," she said, handing it to me.

"Julia's ashes?" I ventured, wondering why Julia's ashes would rest in a Danish pastries tin and what I was supposed to do with them. Should I use them instead of fairy dust?

Francesca let out a brief, ironic laugh.

"Ashes? Of course not!" She waved around herself. "This tomb is empty. Neither Julia nor her late husband are here. Never have been."

The sound of steps startled me, starting a slideshow of memories in my mind: memories of a night spent in St. Emery's police station, after hopping over the fence of that same graveyard.

"Someone is coming," I whispered, my heart in my throat.

Francesca tilted her head and nodded.

"The custodian," she muttered. "Quick. Jump in!"

Oh, no.

The whole thing felt like *dejà vu.*

Running was pointless. He would see me anyway and accuse me of trespassing.

Again.

Closing my eyes, I gave in and let myself slip into the pit. A second later, Francesca pushed the tombstone over our heads, hiding us from sight.

Darkness engulfed us. Only one narrow slit of light filtered through the rim of the stone, just enough for Francesca to slip her fingers through and reopen the grave later.

This must be the stuff nightmares are made of, I thought grimly, as the scent of mud and mold reached my nostrils.

The steps approached, and I tried hard not to think about the fact that I was sitting inside a sealed grave. Next to a vampire. A few hours after someone had feasted on my blood.

I pressed my eyelids together and counted three deep breaths.

This night was on the right track to

becoming one of the worst ones of my life.

A flashlight seeped through the narrow slit, creating eerie shadows inside the grave. I hoped the custodian wouldn't notice the small opening and the misplaced stone.

A dog barked. I still remembered those glistening teeth from the last time.

After a few eternal minutes, the man walked away, and I let my shoulders fall back.

He was gone.

I waited, desperate to get out of the hole but worried the custodian would come back. A bug crept up my leg, and I slapped it with disgust, trying not to think what the creature might have had for dinner. Francesca, on the other hand, seemed very comfortable sitting in the dark cavity. She had curled up in a corner, with her arms around her knees, and was enjoying the cemetery scent with her eyes closed and a blissful expression.

"Francesca…" I murmured. "Would you be so kind as to get us out of here?"

"*Mmm*," she hummed. "Isn't this a nice place? It's always so quiet."

"I'd really like to get out now. *Please*?"

"Fine," she said, sounding disenchanted, and she stood up with a rustle of skirts.

To my relief, she slid the stone slab open with a few dexterous moves, jumped out, and helped me climb onto the ground.

I shivered on the icy grass and waited for her to put everything back into place.

"What's in the tin?" I asked, trying to open

the cold metallic box she had given me.

"I will answer all your questions in due course, but dawn is about to break," Francesca pointed out, and her eyes flashed with a dash of amusement. "And I'm sure you, too, would prefer to watch the sunrise from a different location."

At least on that we could agree.

Chapter 6

Clarence

The broken paintbrush had a dark brown stain on its splintered end. A rusty smell of mortal blood—*my* former, mortal blood—still lingered on the raw wood. Sitting at my desk in The Cloister, I stared at the painting utensil and wondered why I hadn't used it to stake Anne's heart when I was given the chance.

That would have saved me decades of grief and many unpaid debts. Tonight, the chains of the promises made to Elizabeth at the rock bottom of my second existence were heavier than ever.

I wiped my face with a handkerchief: Vampire tears were a rare occurrence. Of course, I was not crying. It must be the dusty draught.

As I sat in my room and waited for Alba to rise, I fought the burning sensation in the corner of my eyes. Alba's dress had been soaked in blood when I had found her. It had taken all my self-control not to defy Elizabeth; but I knew she was older and stronger than I, and she was correct when she claimed I was alive because of her charity. Still, I was a coward and a failure for not having been able to spare Alba such needless suffering. I had to question the reasoning behind my long-held loyalties.

I twirled the brush in my fingers, feeling the scar on my palm. It was still there, after all that time. Sometimes, Anne's memories were so vivid that I almost expected the wound to start bleeding again.

She had been the spark that kindled the destructive fire inside me. But the fuel had been there already.

Thanks to her, I had witnessed many wonders which would have been denied to a mortal; but the wound caused by that humble paintbrush still hurt from time to time.

What would my life have looked like, had I never climbed into that carriage in April 1834? Anne would have doubtlessly killed me in a dark alley, without flinching, just like she did with the rest of her victims. Possibly thrown me into the Thames for the fish to feast on.

A grim end but not an unwelcomed one.

Conversely, I would have never flown over the ocean, nor witnessed the birth of countries, cities and innovations we could only dream about at the time of my second birth.

I would have never met Alba.

Thus, did I hate Anne?

I wanted to, but I could not.

Hating myself was so much easier.

The pain of leaving Alba to her fate in that ballroom would accompany me always. Just like the pain of watching Anne disappear every night with a different man. Back then, I hadn't understood why. Funnily enough, I could sympathize with Anne's needs so well now.

At least, Alba knew where I went after dark. But that never diluted the guilt, nor the memories.

***

London, May 1834

"What happened to Mr. Zugrabescu?" I asked, dipping the paintbrush in a glass of thinner as I wiped my hands on a white cloth.

Anne was lying on a divan, her ample black skirts spread over the brocade upholstery and her hair held up in a puff with ribbons, a couple of shiny onyx strands falling over her naked ivory shoulders in lazy, wavy locks.

I had been working on her seminude portrait for many nights, in a room of her house in the outskirts of London, and we had become relatively close during those friendly soirées. She loved posing almost as much as making veiled advances toward me, although she had never allowed me to lay a finger on her, leaving it clear from the beginning that our relationship was to be exclusively professional. Which I found simultaneously maddening… and bewilderingly arousing.

"He passed away in our home country," she said, stretching herself like a cat after a prolonged modelling session.

"My sympathies," I said, taking a seat in an armchair next to her, reluctant to leave. She took a bottle of brandy from the side table and served a glass for each of us. It must be my fourth one, but that was of no matter to me. She seemed to find pleasure in blurring my mind as much as possible during my visits, and I never found a reason to stop her.

"Oh, it's more than fine," she said, licking her lips. "It was a long time ago, and he had the joy of dying in my arms. A much sweeter death than he deserved, if you ask me."

It couldn't have been so long ago: she looked barely five-and-twenty. I squinted at her as she stood up and headed toward the half-finished canvas.

"It's not finished yet," I cautioned her. I never showed my work to anyone before it was done, but she was starting to become impatient.

She ignored my objection and walked over to the easel. "I'm aware of that, but I believe I have waited enough. Let me see."

Anne stared at the canvas, and her face contracted into a dreadful frown. She remained silent for a while.

"Hold on—" I started to say.

"Mr. Jameson said you were the right connection, but I am starting to doubt his word."

"Mr. Jameson?" I blinked with surprise.

"You never mentioned you were acquainted with him."

The last time I had seen Jameson, he had been reclining on a floor pillow in a filthy opium den. He had tried to become a fine artist for a long time, but his eye condition had always caused him trouble with proportions and perspective. When I had finally agreed to show him my amateur paintings, he had been aghast. Jameson had offered to introduce me to Mr. Martin, whose imposing works had always been a source of inspiration for me. But I had declined the tempting invitation: my place was next to my father—who had instilled into my young mind that art was not a real career. Art, according to him, was the road to immorality for any God-fearing, honest man.

In hindsight, he might have been right.

Anne started to smudge the paint with a finger. "This is surely below my expectations." She pursed her lips, those enthralling lips of hers, and ruined the depiction of her eyebrows.

"I beg your pardon?" I stood and tried to direct my irritation toward the brushes: I stirred them, splattering paint on the wall, then started to dry them systematically, one by one. She had just destroyed hours of work in one single swipe. "At the risk of sounding presumptuous, I daresay this portrait is my best work so far."

"This?" She pointed at the rosy cheeks in the portrait, then at the delicate collarbones of her alter ego. "This is absolutely mediocre. Not what I'm paying for."

Paying? Her words were so offensive that my temper flared. The paintbrush I had been holding split in two, and its sharp end stabbed the palm of my hand. I tried to fix the damage Anne had caused to the painting, but ended up smearing the canvas with traces of my own blood.

Blood had always made me nauseous. That was one of the reasons I never became a good physician, and yet another cause for my father to despise me.

Anne stared at me with sudden enthrallment and swayed as the tip of her tongue wandered over her upper teeth. She was enjoying my display of indignation.

"We never discussed a monetary exchange," I growled. "You know well I have other sources of income, and I'm not doing this for the wages."

"Then what for?" her eyelashes batted slowly, making her resemble a porcelain doll.

I averted my eyes, unwilling to answer.

She knew why.

We both did.

"I fear I shall need to find someone else," she said, and started to walk toward the door.

"Of course not," I said firmly, seething with fury under her disapproving stare. "Allow me to finish it."

She glared at me with disdain, motioning to leave the room.

Something exploded inside me, and I turned around abruptly to grab her arm. By the look in her eyes, it was clear that she hadn't expected me to touch her. Despite our unusual familiarity and my first impressions about her, touching Anne had always been off-limits. But I had had enough.

"You are so cold," I said, taking in her state of partial undress.

Anne took a deep breath, then tugged at my arm, clasping it with surprising strength. She gazed at me with half-closed eyes and lifted my palm to her lips. Slowly, she started to lick the blood off my wound. I remained still, watching her. I was enthralled; hypnotized. There had always been something eerie about Anne. Something I could not grasp. Something which attracted me to her like a moth to a flame.

"Anne," I murmured, enjoying the sound of her name, with that soft, humming *n*. Her mouth started to climb up my sleeve.

Suddenly, her nails sank into my palm, sharp as knives. I winced, startled by her unexpected display of violence.

She released me and pushed me against the wall with inhuman strength.

"I must leave," she said abruptly, rearranging her dress. "And if you value your life, you should go, too."

"I do not," I said calmly, straightening my shoulders.

"Well, you should. I must go out now. You cannot stay here."

"The streets are no place for a lady at this hour. Allow me to escort you."

"I never pretended to be a lady," she said with a soft laugh.

That much was true. From the first moment, she had posed as a widow in search of an occasional liaison. Even though she had yet to welcome me to her bed, her behavior during our encounters had been far from prudish.

"Go, Mr. Auberon," she commanded. "Leave now, before I do something I shall regret."

I nodded slowly, misunderstanding her reasons. In my obliviousness, I thought she was worried about me compromising her honor if I stayed. But then, no honorable lady would spend her evenings alone in her house with a single gentleman, not to mention go out on her own after midnight. Only women with dark secrets trod those poorly lit avenues in the wee hours of the morning.

Still, what kind of mysteries could Anne be hiding? Another man? A disreputable addiction? Where else could she go every night after our painting sessions were over?

The marks of her nails were clearly visible on my skin. I stared at them, tired of wondering. Tired of hoping.

I put on my hat, and I bid Anne farewell with a bow. But I did not leave: instead, I stationed myself round a corner and waited for her to go out.

When her slight, black figure appeared, swathed in the dense, nocturnal fog, I followed her surreptitiously into the darkness. Later, I learned that she had known I was there but pretended not to see me. Anne had a morbid sense of humor; I just didn't know it yet.

She headed toward the docks, and I went after her, believing she could not hear me. First, she stopped to talk to a grim-faced man. To my shock, she disappeared with him into a dark alley, regaling him with smiles and giggles that made the veins pulse in my temples out of sheer anger. When she reappeared, less than fifteen minutes later, she was alone again. But she did not stop there: after the first one, there were two more.

Later, I learned she had been amusing herself at the expense of her imprudent voyeur. On an ordinary night, Anne would not claim more than one victim: however, on that occasion she made an exception just for my sake.

Clenching my fists and dying of jealousy, I spied upon her as she made her way back home. By then, I was aghast and sick with resentfulness. I believed I had finally discovered Anne Zugrabescu's best kept secret. My logical conclusion was that she had become a woman of the night in order to keep afloat the extravagant lifestyle she had led before the death of her husband. In my naiveté, I told myself there was no way she could enjoy such an existence. How could she?

But how could I have fathomed what she really was? How was I to know that she was cursed with a relentless lust which made her seek warmth in perfect strangers as soon as dusk fell?

Her recklessness did not discourage me: on the contrary, her apparent brokenness woke up the dormant knight in shining armor inside me. My soul was wrecked after my profession had presented me with more death and sickness than most human hearts could bear. Finding yet another broken soul felt like the call of destiny.

I thought Anne must have been sent to me so I could *save* her. So I could change *her* life.

Fool.

During the following weeks, visions of Anne kissing other men haunted my nightmares, but I kept obsessing over her.

After many days of torture, I finished her painting.

Little did I know that her fate would soon become mine, for she was a lady of the night indeed, just not the kind I had assumed.

I never succeeded to change her life as I had set out to. Instead, it was she who changed mine one damned night shortly thereafter.

Nevertheless, even after Anne was long gone, I never quite forgot the pain of being a mortal in love with a predator.

For how could a human love such a creature without succumbing to sheer madness?

How could a lover watch his dearest wander into a stranger's embraces to quench a perpetual, morbid thirst?

They say life goes in circles, and two centuries later, I would stand in Anne's shoes, wondering how to look into Alba Lumin's eyes without being consumed by the guilt of my gruesome nightly undertakings.

Chapter 7

Alba

"Alba," Clarence said, rapping softly on my door. "Let me in. I brought wine."

I groaned, sticking an arm out of the warm duvet to check the time on my phone: it was half past eleven in the morning, and I must have slept less than three hours, after a merry night of jumping into graves with Francesca.

"Go away," I growled. "I don't know about you vampires, but normal people don't drink wine for breakfast."

"But it's almost midday," he protested.

I rubbed my eyes, and the gauze around my hand reminded me of the past night's events. A wave of fury shook me, and all my muscles tensed with rage. With a snarl, I wrapped the duvet around my half-naked body and opened the door just enough to stick my nose out.

"I don't want to talk to you," I spat, trying to close the door again, but he didn't let me.

"But Isolde," he said softly, setting his hand

in the narrow slot between the door and its frame, "I came to make amends. Please."

Clarence was standing in front of me with a dusty bottle of wine possibly older than me, annoyingly pristine in his favorite frock coat and silk cravat. He stared at me with such innocent eyes that, for a second, I entertained the thought of allowing him to enter. There had to be some truth about the stories of vampires being able to enthrall women, even though he kept denying it.

I shook my head, and I reminded myself of how he had been avoiding me for weeks without an acceptable explanation and, even worse, how he had deserted me in front of Elizabeth the night before. All of a sudden, all the wistful thoughts vanished.

"No amends," I said sharply. "And don't you *Isolde* me. I'm not in the mood."

Clarence sighed and stepped back. "As you wish," he said, his shoulders slumping. "I understand. I just wanted to let you know how awfully sorry I am."

***

Elizabeth spent the rest of the day treating me like nothing had happened. The only clue about the torture she had inflicted on me the previous night was that she refrained from admonishing me when I appeared in her office ridiculously late and wearing a reindeer sweater in protest.

She handed me two binders of paperwork to sort and blatantly ignored my wounded hand for the rest of the day: the way she acted, one would have almost thought that stabbing an employee and drinking their blood was totally acceptable business behavior. Maybe it even was—among vampires, perhaps.

I was lethargic and absentminded most of the morning. I kept daydreaming about Clarence and how rare it was to find a man capable of apologizing as earnestly as him. But there were things one couldn't just solve with a kiss and a glass of chardonnay. When I wasn't feeling guilty for sending him away with his dusty wine in tow, my mind kept wandering to the contents of Julia's tin.

"Elizabeth," I said, once she dismissed me, "have you reconsidered my free days?"

She frowned but didn't answer right away. "How many days?" she blurted—to my utter surprise—after a brief consideration.

"Two weeks," I answered, as firmly as I could.

"That's preposterous."

"I don't feel well," I said, waving my bandaged hand in her face.

Elizabeth let out a deep sigh. "Five days," she said finally. "More than enough."

"Fine," I mumbled under my breath. "Better than nothing, I guess."

***

Francesca was nice enough to take care of the children in the library so I could rest after lunch. Clarence joined them for a game of pick-up-sticks, clearly hoping to meet me and possibly soften my upset heart a little. I watched them play from the corner of the room, with my arms crossed as I tried to evoke the deepest and scariest frown I could. They offered a peculiar—but equally endearing—sight: two vampires in their elegant period frocks sitting around a carved wooden table next to a four- and a six-year-old in frilly unicorn pajamas.

Francesca threw the sticks on the table, and they started to pick them up in turns, trying not to move the rest as they did so. When Iris' turn came, she started to whine, complaining it was too hard for her.

"Here, let's do it together," Clarence said to her, gentle as always, his eyes glued to mine as he tenderly placed his hand on hers and started to pull at one of the sticks. "Things are easier when you work as a team."

The last part was obviously directed at me, so I frowned a bit harder to show him I was still mad.

"That's not fair," Katie protested, "Clarence has skillful vampire fingers. If the two of them team up, I'll have no chances of winning!"

Her innocent mention of *skillful vampire fingers* threw me off my angry pose and probably made me blush the color of ripe cherries. I turned toward the wall, wishing Clarence hadn't noticed.

After a while, the pile of sticks became more and more unstable, and even Clarence looked distracted, staring at me most of the time instead of paying attention to the game. I saw he was having doubts about the best stick to tackle next. When he finally selected one at the bottom of the pile, I knew well before he touched it that his decision would make him and Iris lose the game.

"Wrong choice," I muttered to myself, somehow failing to remember that he could hear even the breathing of a fly.

"Why is that?" he asked, his face beaming with expectation. He seemed delighted I had addressed him, after giving him the cold shoulder for the best part of the day.

"Well, isn't it obvious?" I grunted. "If you knew something about engineering and structures, which is clear you don't, you would realize right away that the stick you have chosen is going to make the whole pile collapse."

He lay his chin on his hand with interest.

"Really?" he said with a naughty smile. "And which one would you recommend I pick up, my dear?"

I pointed haughtily at one toward the left, and he squinted at me with mischief.

"Well, thank you," he said with playful defiance, "but I'll stick to my stick."

"As you wish," I retorted with a shrug.

I was right, and he lost.

In retrospect, he probably did it on purpose,

just to make me feel better.

"I told you," I said triumphantly. "You should always trust the engineer, unless you want things to start collapsing."

***

I left the library and decided to take advantage of the free vampire nannies to lock myself in my room and open the tin we had retrieved from Julia's grave. Inside it, I found a few sheets of yellowish paper torn from a journal. A journal I already owned. I was aware that a few pages were missing; now, I finally knew what had become of them.

Most of them were dedicated to Julia's somehow feverish ramblings about a man called Ludovic, who seemed to have gone missing and whose presence in The Cloister she missed terribly. But two of them were different, and those were the ones which immediately caught my attention.

The first one was a map, drawn in a hurry in quick pencil strokes and marked with a thick, black cross. It was dated after Julia's death—but the few existent captions were in her handwriting. The city was not mentioned, but the names of the streets were visible and scribbled in Italian. It might be possible to find the place with a bit of effort… and Francesca's help.

The second one was even more exciting, because it looked like a spell. A *summoning* spell, it said. It started with the following notice:

"Light three white candles in front of a mirror and chant thrice before slumbertime in order to summon another witch's astral projection. If the witch accepts your call, she will come to you in due time."

To my utter surprise, this page was addressed *to me.* Not by name, but by title: *"For my witch successor,"* it said.

My hands shook with excitement: I had just got hold of Julia's esoteric telephone number. Only better, because I might be able to reach her even in the afterlife—or wherever she was.

That night, I put the girls to sleep early and set out to work. There was no shortage of white candles in The Cloister, so it was easy to find three and arrange them in one of the many silver candlesticks the vampires had lying around.

In a low, trembling voice, I read the spell three times as directed. Then, I sat in front of my new mirror and waited.

The grandfather clock in the hall kept striking every quarter of an hour. It chimed eight times, and I started to feel sleepy.

I started to lose faith.

A greenish light appeared in the center of the mirror, and I pondered whether I had fallen asleep or not. A current of wind swept the room, and it carried to me the echoes of a voice I had heard before.

"It's nice to see you again," it said, as lightning ignited the room.

***

A black cat materialized inside the mirror. I knew that cat: my daughters used to call it Miss Jilly. I suffocated a scream, not wanting to wake the whole Cloister up.

"Julia!" I whispered with incredulity, twisting my hands as I sat up. "It's you! The spell worked!"

The cat curled up in a tight ball of fur and stared at me with its bright purple eyes.

"You are right," she said. Her mouth didn't move, but I heard the words clearly in my head.

"Why do you always look like a cat?" I asked, extending my hand to touch her. My fingers passed through her body like it wasn't there and landed on the duvet. "An *incorporeal* cat."

"It's easier this way," she answered, lifting a semitransparent hind leg and starting to lick it. "I live far away from here, and it takes less energy like this. My vitality is running dangerously low at the moment: that's why I'm going to need you."

"You need me?" I asked, blinking in confusion, "I thought you were going to *help* me."

"We both have something to gain," she said mysteriously.

"So you didn't come to teach me magic?" I asked with disappointment.

The cat—Julia—sat on its hind legs and tilted its head before answering, "I will mentor you, just not now," she said. "How has your magic been doing since last time?"

"Terrible," I answered with a sigh. "I keep having unpredictable glitches… jars popping open, appliances stopping working as I pass by… but whenever I really need it, the energy is just not there. I think I'm hopeless."

"You are not. You just need guidance, and I could offer it to you if you came to me. But I'd like you to do something in exchange."

"Sounds fair," I conceded. The green light around Julia was becoming gradually softer. "Tell me about it."

"I'll tell you everything, but we need to meet in person. Astral projection takes a hefty toll on my energy, especially to places as far as this. I can't practice it indefinitely. Moreover, there are things I need to show you and places I'd like you to go."

"Meet in person?" I stuttered. "But I thought you were…"

"Dead?" she interrupted me, and her tone was somewhat mocking. "No, no. It's a long story. For now, please take my word for it. One day, when things calm down, we can discuss my life over a cup of coffee. Or over a cauldron of toad brew, if you prefer."

The air shook with something which vaguely resembled a chuckle. Julia's green aura had become thinner, and now it barely spread a couple of inches around her body.

"Where should I go?" I asked, wondering whether she was about to disappear.

"Northern Italy," she said. "If you managed to call me, you must have my map, too. Meet me on the marked spot at noon, on Christmas Eve. I have something to show you. I'll be expecting you, but please don't be late. I won't have much time."

"Julia, wait… did you just say *Italy*? Italy*, the country*?" I asked, then realized I had been talking in a loud voice. Luckily, my daughters were sound sleepers and didn't even flinch. Julia nodded. "No. I can't go to Italy now. Elizabeth won't allow it."

"Elizabeth doesn't own you," she pointed out.

"I can't promise you anything," I said, shaking my head. I wasn't even sure Elizabeth didn't own me, after the blood oath.

"Then don't. Just come."

Julia started to fade, her body becoming more and more translucent. I knew she would soon be gone, and I opened the tin, frantically searching for the map to confirm with her the location of our meeting. But I was drowsier by the seconds, and my hands moved in slow motion. When I found the piece of paper, Julia wasn't more than a slim puff of green smoke in the mirror.

I woke up, startled, with a strange pain in my neck after sitting in an uncomfortable position for too long. It was too early to get up, but too late to go back to sleep.

The mirror was empty, and the candles had burned out. The tin was still resting on my lap, open. I took the first piece of paper from the small heap and studied it closely: on the hand drawn map, a green cross which wasn't there before had appeared, and over it now I could clearly read the words *Città di Como*.

Chapter 8

Alba

The next day, I headed to central Emberbury to drop the girls at Mark's place after lunch. Before that, we stopped at a clothing store, because the children always seemed to run out of clothes whenever they spent time with their father—I presumed Mark just threw away dirty underwear instead of dealing with such plebeian things as doing laundry.

After choosing enough garments to last them for a couple of weeks, we continued to the checkout. On our way there, I saw a man talking into a mirror, which almost caused me a heart attack—it reminded me of my conversation with Julia the night before, and for a second, I thought it was sheer witchcraft. Upon closer inspection, I saw the label on its silver surface: *"Hello. I'm your virtual shop assistant. Ask me anything."*

Ah, technology. Always lagging behind magic so badly.

"Show me blue casual t-shirts," the man was

saying.

"This is the *Cote d'Azur* model," the mirror answered. A photo of the man appeared on the glass surface, wearing a photoshopped blue t-shirt. "You'll find it in aisle number four, men's section."

The customer said thank you to the talking mirror and went his way.

"How fun! Can we try?" Katie asked with a wide, gap-toothed smile.

"Why not?" I said, counting the pairs of socks to make sure they would be enough.

"Show me purple dresses," Katie asked the mirror, skipping with glee.

"Showing you children's fashion," the mirror answered, and started to show frilly dresses over my daughter's photo.

"Wow, this gadget is smart!" I said in admiration. "How does it know you are a child? We didn't even say it."

"I've been trained for human shape recognition," the robot voice answered.

"What if I'm just a tiny adult?" Katie asked, squinting maliciously.

"Okay," said the robot voice. "Showing you dresses specially tailored for people of short stature."

"Impressive!" I declared, fascinated by the talking mirror. "What else do you know about us just from our pictures?"

The mirror's voice became lower and deeper, and it said, "I know your name is Alba Lumin, and there are two witches who want to talk to you. They are waiting outside the store right now."

A lump formed in my throat as the image of two middle-aged ladies flashed in the glass for a split second. It was a good thing there was a rack of men's shirts nearby to lean against, otherwise I would have fallen on my rear.

"*Eh*… excuse me?" I said, rubbing my ears/funnels to check they weren't full of wax.

"Showing you toddler dresses," the machine answered like nothing had happened, and started a slideshow of children's fashion.

I blinked in confusion and looked at my daughters. "Did you see that?"

"Yes, I like the one with the seahorse!" Iris said, running in circles and pretending to ride a horse.

"No, I meant the picture of those two ladies?"

"What ladies, mommy?"

"Never mind."

***

"Do you want the hangers?" the cashier asked me. I could hardly understand her, because her mouth was so full of chewing gum that I could even guess the flavor—melon, no doubt.

I eyed the wire hangers pensively and remembered the mirror's revelation.

"Yes, please," I said, probing the metallic end: it wasn't very sharp, but better than my nails in case the need for self-defense arose.

As soon as we stepped outside, I spotted the two ladies the mirror had shown me. They were standing on the other side of the sidewalk, next to a tall and narrow stand full of pamphlets and with their faces covered by woolen hats and scarves. Swallowing hard, I took courage and walked toward them, followed by my little girls. What could those women do to me in a crowded, public place, in broad daylight? I wrapped my arms tightly around my daughters and approached them, making sure to remain in the store security guard's line of sight.

"You must be the one seeking incubus banishment spells," one of the ladies greeted me, handing me a brochure.

I took the paper with two fingers, pressing the children against my legs. There was a large, bold title on the first page:

> *"Unexplained morning weakness? Don't disregard the benefits of proper vampire slaughtering! We are here to help!"*

"What is an incubus?" I asked, eyeing both women with suspicion—for some strange reason, they seemed to be laughing behind their scarves.

"Don't mind Sarah," the other woman said. "She has a twisted sense of humor. But we have a message for you."

"For me?" Even though I had suspected it,

I couldn't help but be astounded.

She lowered her head and talked from behind a pair of greasy, pencil-drawn eyebrows. "It's from The Witches of the Lake," she whispered. "They would like to meet you."

I took a deep breath. It seemed so many witches wanted to meet me lately.

"Who are you? And who are The Witches of the Lake? Are *you* The Witches of the Lake?" I asked, grabbing Iris's hood to prevent her from running after a creepy balloon seller.

"We are just honest Salem witches," she answered. "We want nothing to do with those European *prima donnas*. They think so highly of themselves." She sighed. "But, as sisters, we sometimes agree to carry messages for each other. Basic manners, you see."

"Okay…" I said, shaking my head. "So, what's the message?"

"They asked us to relay their address to you, so you can get to know each other." She took a hard binder and retrieved the vampire slaughtering pamphlet from my hand. "There. I'll write it on this flyer, if you don't mind. It's a place in Italy."

"Italy, Texas?" I raised an eyebrow.

"There's an Italy in Texas?" The other witch snorted. "No, the real one. A small city called Como."

That was insane: it was the same city I was supposed to meet Julia in. A coincidence? I didn't think so.

The woman handed me the paper. "You

keep it. And have a good look at our services, we are very affordable." She winked. "In case you change your mind about the incubus."

"Change my mind?"

They hadn't even told me what the word meant yet.

"Well, read it first." She tapped my forearm, just like my grandma would have done. "Our number is printed on the back, in case you need anything. Silver bullets, graveyard dirt… you know, your basic everyday staples to deal with the bloodsuckers!"

"*Hmm*, yeah… thanks?" I said, wincing as I stuck the pamphlet in a pocket of my coat.

A raven flew by, and Iris pointed at it.

"Look, mommy, Clarence came!"

The witches frowned and looked up at the black bird, who was hovering right over our heads at low height.

"I think we should go," I murmured through gritted teeth, suddenly worried about Clarence's wellbeing near those women. I turned to the kids and pulled them toward me. "Daddy will be angry if we're late."

***

Since the divorce, Mark had moved into a luxurious loft apartment in the city center, closer to his attorney's office than our previous residence. He was now living with a woman called Minnie, who had been his lover for a year or so. I didn't like the idea of Minnie's existence, but she was kind to my children, and after all, she was crazy enough to live with Mark willingly: a woman with such nerve definitely deserved my admiration—and perhaps my pity, too. She also made me feel less apprehensive when I had to leave the children at Mark's place.

My relationship with my ex-husband hadn't been the best during the past months, but I tried to behave as normally as possible for the sake of my girls. Whenever possible, I messaged Minnie and avoided contact with him. That seemed to keep his yelling and arguing at bay, at least most of the time.

The girls and I crossed the vast lobby, and I nodded at the well-dressed concierge. He greeted us, and we entered the elevator. Katie and Iris trotted cheerfully behind me, obliviously happy to see their dad again.

I always found it fascinating how forgiving little children could be.

I squared my shoulders and tried to look as smooth as possible before meeting the devil. *Today I'm going to behave in a civilized way*, I vowed.

I am calm, confident and self-assured. I am a well, and I seek for calming, fresh water in the depths of my soul, I repeated, mimicking the soothing voice in my self-help mp3's.

Minnie opened the door, dressed in an extremely thin and short chemise. Unlike my vampire housemates, who had no trouble with cold spaces, Mark and his girlfriend never bothered to save on heating.

"Hi, Alba, how is work?" she uttered out of

thin air.

The woman always had the strangest way of greeting people. I feigned a smile and let her kiss my cheeks, shoving the girls into my ex-husband's luxurious new quarters.

"Oh, it's going great, thank you," I answered, wondering what was wrong with good old-fashioned *how are you.* "My dream job."

Okay, maybe I overdid it a little bit.

"I bet she won't last until the summer," Mark shouted from the living room.

I rolled my eyes. "Hi, Mark."

He came out in his briefs and greeted me with a twisted lip. "Haven't you noticed the pattern yet? Everyone gets rid of you, sooner or later."

My heart sank at the truth in his words: he had a talent for making me feel terrible in the blink of an eye.

"Isn't that skirt too short for someone your age?" he commented, as my eyes traveled in confusion toward his new girlfriends' *missing* skirt.

She was younger than I, her skin effortlessly rosy, plump, and luscious. I was ancient next to Minnie. Which reminded me that soon I would look *truly ancient* next to two-hundred-year-old Clarence. In a couple of years, people might start to mistake me for his mother. Perhaps he had already thought about that, which would explain why he had kept himself so busy lately. The thought made my knees falter, and I had to steady myself against the doorframe.

"Come on, Marky," Minnie said, tousling his

hair in a way he would have never allowed me to. "*I am aloof as a rock*, remember?" She smiled innocently. "We have a new life coach. From London! He's working wonders on darling Marky and his temper, isn't he? Can't you feel the difference already, Alba?"

"*Err…*" I hesitated. The way Mark was scowling at me, he was going to need many, many sessions for the effects to become noticeable.

I wasn't happy to leave my children with Mark, but standing at his doorstep for the rest of the month of December wasn't ideal, either. I hugged the girls as tight and long as I could without looking deranged and then turned to Minnie, ignoring my sullen ex-husband.

"Take good care of them." My voice trembled. "I bought them lots of underwear, and new ski jackets. Make sure they're not cold, will you? Iris has a drippy nose. Check her temperature in the evening." Even though I wasn't a fan of Minnie, she always did as I said and sent me messages and photos every day, explaining everything they did together. In a way, I was thankful for her. "I'm going abroad for the holidays," I added, "so I might be hard to reach by phone from time to time. But don't worry, I'll read everything eventually."

"Oh, how cool! Where are you going?" Minnie asked, clapping her hands.

I paused. Could Mark use this information against me? I decided that most probably not.

"I was thinking about Italy," I said casually,

then I got a naughty idea. "They say it's romantic. I'm hoping to find a decent man and stay there *forever.*"

Minnie arched her eyebrows and started to giggle. "We're glad you are overcoming the divorce," she said, emphasizing the *we* part, like *We, Mark and Minnie*, was a consolidated concept already. "It's good for you."

I often felt bad for secretly hating Minnie. At the end of the day, not only did she have to sleep in the same bed as Mark, which was horrible enough, but she kept trying to be nice to me. Too nice, almost.

I kissed my girls once more, realizing bitterly that this would be our last kiss until the New Year. That made me feel weepy, so I left the building as quickly as I could.

This was going to be our first Christmas apart. Would I ever get used to sharing them? At least they wouldn't have to spend the holidays watching me and their father throw glittered ornaments at each other. I told myself that this must be an improvement, even if a small one.

I repeated my mantra, but it became hazy in my mind. Mark might be *a rock*, but I was supposed to be a well, and wells had a right to weep.

I am a well, and I draw up fresh water from the depths of my soul to keep myself calm and collected.

I am a well, and I draw up fresh buckets of sorrow and envy to keep myself in the worst mood possible…

Wait, what?

No, scratch that. That wasn't right.

I am a well…

And I'm going to need a larger bucket to survive the holidays.

Chapter 9

Alba

It was dark and wintry when I stepped on the street again. The air smelled of smoke and caramel apples, and the sound of Christmas carols seeped out of the still open stores.

I ambled absentmindedly along a busy promenade flanked by trees, thumbing through my phone and searching for affordable plane tickets. Clarence's voice came out of nowhere, breaking my concentration.

"Alba, how lovely to see you here."

I could have sworn he wasn't there two seconds earlier. He had a talent to materialize out of thin air, and right now he was right beside me, sitting peacefully on a concrete bench under a tree.

"Oh, Clarence, you startled me," I gasped, pushing my bag against my chest while my breathing went back to normal. "Please don't do that on the street. Somebody could notice!"

"Sit down, please," he said with a half-smile, seemingly unconcerned. But I knew him too well by then to be fooled by his soft manners: there was something going on under the surface.

The concrete bench was freezing cold, although he probably hadn't noticed. I sat on the edge, divided between feeling guilty for sending him away with the wine or angry at his behavior during the oath ceremony. He wrapped a shy arm around my waist and started to flip through a brochure with extreme interest.

"I was reading a very informative document while I waited for you," he said, pointing at the leaflet he was holding. "If I'm not mistaken, you should fill one of my socks with graveyard dirt or stab me with coffin nails while I sleep." He winced. "I have been quite sleepless of late, so… which sock would you prefer, the left one or the right one?"

He rested a foot over his knee and started to untie his shoe, staring at me with a daring smirk.

"Clarence!" I blurted, realizing it was my brochure he was holding—the one the witches had given me. "Where did you get that?"

"It was in your pocket," he said innocently.

I felt the pockets of my coat and, sure enough, they were empty. I had no idea when it had gone missing.

"You really have to stop snitching my stuff!" I said, slapping his arm in admonishment.

He looked amused. "Now you wear no rings anymore, what else was I supposed to steal to draw your attention?" As he spoke, I rubbed my bare hands. Mark had requested I give him back the wedding bands. "When I saw you talking with those witches, I got sticky fingers again… and it ended up being a very edifying opportunity, as well. Did you know you can buy corpse water by the gallon? And it's cheaper than Port wine!"

"Corpse water?" I grimaced with disgust. "Why would anyone want that?"

"To fend off vampires, of course!"

I looked around cautiously, concerned someone might have heard him. The street was crowded. Most of the passersby were carrying shopping bags and nobody seemed to be paying attention to us.

"Clarence, stop," I hissed, trying to take the brochure off his hands. "What's the matter with you?"

We tussled for the piece of paper, but he was too fast for me. In the end, he held my wrist and pulled the leaflet—and me after it—toward his chest until our lips met. In an impulse, I snuggled between his arms and embraced him in surrender. It had been weeks since the last time we had been so close. To be precise, it had been weeks since the last time we had kissed at all. Cold radiated from his body, firm and strong like a marble statue. A very handsome and competent marble statue with a talent for leaving me light-headed.

"I have missed you so much," he said, breathless, holding me with such strength that I had to gasp for air.

I stared at him, remembering I should be angry at him, not kissing him. "*You* have missed *me*? You have been away so often that I don't even know what we are anymore, Clarence. If we were ever *anything*," I said in an offended puff. His rusty taste was still on my lips. "Nobody forced you to go all Houdini on me!"

"In all fairness, as much as I vow to, I can't stay away from you, my Isolde." He shook his head with dismay.

Then don't, I wanted to yell. It wasn't me who had started that odd hide-and-seek game of his.

"Clarence, you have been behaving in such a strange way lately. I don't understand, and you never give me any explanations. One day, you are all smiles and kisses, and the next, you disappear and leave me to my own devices when I need you the most. It's becoming really hard for me to live like this, you know? Please don't get me wrong, but I thought you… I thought we…" I trailed off, hoping he would finish the sentence for me.

Instead, he slouched a little and let his hand fly to a small red stain on his shirt. He was wearing normal, twenty-first century clothes, as he often did when he went out in public. He tried to scratch off the blotch with a brooding expression.

"Do you know what this is?" he asked in a listless tone.

"It's a stain," I answered bluntly.

"That's inaccurate." He shook his head, took my hand and started to caress it.

"Of course it's a stain. I'm a mother of two: it's not the first one I've seen, trust me. Not even the most disgusting one."

"It's a *blood* stain, Alba," he murmured, scanning my face with those maroon eyes of his.

"Then I'd recommend soaking it in hydrogen peroxide. I have a small basin I could lend you, and there's warm water in my room..." I started to ramble, because I knew where the conversation was leading… and I didn't want to go there.

"Do you know whose blood it is?" he asked patiently.

I lifted my eyes and observed his cheeks were oddly flushed—he had been so pale lately, but now the pallor was gone.

"No?" I answered with hesitation.

Please. Don't tell me.

"It's another… *person*'s blood." His voice sounded ragged, infinitely pained. "Could also be another *woman*'s blood."

An invisible wrecking ball hit the pit of my stomach, and the floor crumbled beneath my feet.

"Did you…" I ran out of air. "Did you…? With her…? Before you…?"

I couldn't even bring myself to finish the sentence.

He had been so absent, after all.

I was going to age and die, wasn't I?

It all made sense now.

"No. No! Of course not!" He raked his fingers through his raven hair. "But still."

I exhaled. I was aware of his feeding habits, even though we both preferred not to discuss them. The sudden image of his lips on a stranger's neck made me nauseous, and he noticed my unease.

"Can you see it now?" he rumbled. "I will never be able to offer you a normal life—a happy life. The one you deserve. It would be selfish to keep you for myself in these circumstances."

I buried my face in my hands. Was this some sort of extremely polite goodbye? The vampire version of '*it's not you, it's me*'?

"Clarence, please. I've known what you are… and what you *do*… from the very beginning, and I never blamed you for it. Never said a word."

"The fact that you don't say it doesn't make it disappear," he pointed out. "As much as it troubles me, I know I will always fail you: I can't help it. Even if you don't talk about it, your anger is like a cloud hovering over us."

"No," I said. "Well, yes, I'm angry at you. But not for *that* reason."

"I know, my dear." He nudged my cheek with his icy nose. "And you have all the right to be. You don't have to justify yourself. I understand."

As if on cue, my wounded wrist started to throb. He watched me, wordless. It was too excruciating to stay like that for so long, so I broke the silence.

"I'm thinking of going to Italy for the holidays," I said, hesitant.

"Italy?" He scanned the vampire hunters' brochure with worry. "Is it because of this? Are you…?" He left the sentence unfinished.

"Leaving you? To join those witches?" I

laughed bitterly. "Of course not! You know well that my encounters with other witches haven't been exactly great so far."

"Why then?"

"It's Julia. You know, I had a very nice chat with Francesca the other day. Inside Julia's tomb, to be precise."

He blinked, his mouth wide open.

"I beg your pardon?"

"Did you know Julia is not resting in her grave?"

"I didn't know," he said, "but it makes sense, given everything that happened while she lived in The Cloister."

"I think Julia is alive." When I said that, he looked at me like someone calculating a complex mathematical formula. "She has asked me to meet her in a city in Northern Italy. I suspect all of this—her non-death, the secretiveness of it all—has a lot to do with Elizabeth, to whom I just swore lifetime loyalty a couple of days ago."

Clarence shook his head. "I can't believe Francesca knew all that and never told me."

"That last part I heard from Julia herself. I summoned her into my mirror last night."

"Did you? Well, your magic seems to be improving. Congratulations," he said ruefully.

"It's not, really. I think the merit was mostly hers. But she promised to teach me a few things if I visited her. She said she's not able to come here. She wants to show me something." I pursed my lips. "You know, the other day in that store, I made a teacup hover in front of at least four strangers. This is getting out of control. I really have to take matters into my own hands before something terrible happens."

"Does Elizabeth know about your travel plans?"

"She gave me five days. I can go wherever I want."

"Five days!" He gasped. "That's barely enough to get there and back!"

"Well… my flight might be delayed," I shrugged. I had been thinking about possible ways to extend my European vacation. Surely, Elizabeth wouldn't chastise me if my airline had trouble due to Christmas. "Or even cancelled, who knows."

"But, Alba…" He tried to grab my hand once again, but I squirmed out of his grasp. As much I craved his touch, it made it hard to think straight. "Now is not a good moment. You don't have enough time. And lying to Elizabeth… that's never a good idea. You just swore loyalty to her. You can't just disobey her the very next day. This won't end well."

"I'm not planning to disobey her!" I complained, "I just said I might extend my vacation a little—if necessary."

"Don't do it. Please. Stay."

I shook my head. "No. I need to go. I need to see Julia. This might be a once-in-a-lifetime chance."

And I'm so confused about us at the moment that I desperately need to get away from this place. And from you.

He pressed his eyelids together. "Then let me go with you."

"You can't board a plane."

"That I cannot. But I could fly. I have done it before. It's risky, yes, and it would take me a long time, but it's doable."

"I'll be fine," I said slowly, my eyes fixed on that cursed blood stain on his shirt. "I think I need a couple of days on my own. A change of scenery."

"I understand." His shoulders slumped, and he put a hand over his heart. "And I respect your decision. But whatever happens, please remember… you are very dear to me. And will forever be."

Chapter 10

Clarence

"Merry Christmas, Clarence," Alba told me before leaving for the airport on that gray, foggy December morning.

Her tone was not particularly *merry* during our farewell under the mausoleum, and neither were my spirits. I hadn't celebrated Christmas for two-hundred years, as I saw no merit in commemorating the birth of a god who had given up on me a long time ago.

After she left, I stood on the landing of the stairs which led to the catacombs, sheltering from the bright sunlight reflected on the snowy graveyard. I wished she hadn't refused my company, for I was worried about her.

Then again, flying over the ocean would have taken me a few days: I would arrive just to watch her leave. Boarding a plane was out of the question, as well: the authorities might notice my forged passport, if I didn't burst into flames on a shuttle bus first.

And finally, there was Elizabeth.

Hopefully, Alba would be back after the agreed five days. But in case she was late, someone would have to appease our queen, and I had a talent for that.

How much more convenient it would have been if Julia could have remained dead just a little longer.

The Cloister felt empty without Alba. I headed to the library, hoping to find Jean-Pierre. I wasn't seeking clarity: I rather expected him to numb my mind with one of his lengthy and tiresome monologues about Plato or Aristotle.

When I got there, I found Francesca lighting candles with a fire steel and a tinderbox. Even though we were *blessed* with the miracle of electricity now, none of us vampires were too fond of the droning buzz it involved. Candles, on the other hand, were much gentler on our sharp eyes and let out blissful crackling sounds.

"She's gone," Francesca stated, then added with a loaded meaning, "Without you."

"We are not Siamese twins," I informed her. "She preferred to go alone."

"So, allow me to understand this," Francesca said, her teal irises following the candle flame. "She's traveling to the other side of the world, to a place we know is swarming with witches, and you don't mind?" She shook her head. "I don't know whether I should be proud of you for becoming such a progressive man after all this time, or deeply concerned about your mental stability. At any rate, I didn't expect you to watch her go so calmly when I sent her on her way to meet Julia. I am astonished." She threw me a condemning look as she rearranged the candles. "But I'm sure she will fend for herself quite well, won't she? What could a whole coven of powerful Old-World witches do to a lonely, clueless stray if they happened to track her down?"

Francesca lifted the chandelier and set it on a coffee table, admiring her work with satisfaction.

"What makes you think I watched her go *calmly*?" I murmured, swiping a stack of papers from Jean-Pierre's desk so I could sit on the edge of the table. He frowned at me from his chair and started to put the papers in order again, visibly offended by my carelessness.

"Wait. Is this about that old injury of your wing?" Francesca continued. "When the ex-husband attacked you an eon ago?" She stepped back and stared at me with distaste. "Are you afraid the after-effects of that wound will make you plunge into the ocean if you go after her? Because I doubt you could drown, even if you tried really hard."

"My arm is fine, thank you. It took a while to recover, but I have no problems at present."

She grabbed my elbow and studied it nonchalantly, feeling under my shirt all the way up to my shoulder with her tiny, sharp fingertips. Yes, it had taken longer than expected, but the blame was entirely on me. It could have healed in a couple of days, had I fed properly and spent the days slumbering, instead of taking on any single foreign mission Elizabeth had come up with and brooding about Anne Zugrabescu and how horribly similar I had become to her.

"How unusual that it took so long, don't you agree?" Francesca commented. "I have never seen a vampire heal as slowly as you." She grimaced with reprobation as she released me. "You must have been doing something wrong, Clarence. Have you fed lately? You look pale."

"He's doing *everything* wrong, *ma chérie*," Jean-Pierre said, appearing from behind an enormous pile of Greek books. "He thinks he can save the world by starving himself. How did he put it?" He continued in a mocking tone, "He now believes that behaving like a normal vampire and sinking his fangs into other mortals' necks is akin to… *unfaithfulness* toward the little witch."

Jean-Pierre burst into laughter and Francesca rolled her eyes.

"Ah." She sighed. "I always knew you were a bit impractical, Clarence, but this… this is quixotic, my dear."

"Says the vampire who feeds on rabbits and squirrels," I objected.

"Nobody forbids you to do the same." Francesca explained, in that slow and patient tone of hers. "Starvation leads to weakness… and loss of control. Is that what you strive for?"

I had tried to emulate Francesca's feeding habits. But it was unbearable: the stench was horrid, and animal blood never satiated my thirst properly. It was never enough, and certainly not meant to be: just like a human drinking from a foul water fountain when foodstuffs were required instead.

"The bloodlust is too strong: stronger than I am. It's perplexing that you can walk the streets at night, amidst all those sweet-smelling warmbloods, and not be tempted to pounce on them. If I fast for too long, I can't help it. Sometimes it gets so bad that I don't dare roam among humans in the open anymore."

"You were always weak." She shrugged. "Anyhow, there's nothing wrong with being who we are. I don't mind squirrels: I'm used to them. But if you can't stand the taste, there's nothing wrong with that. We are not humans. We needn't share their moral principles. This is starting to go too far, if you ask me."

"No, indeed I did not ask you. I just came here to talk about Aristotle, but you two had to give your unsolicited opinion, as usual."

I was trying not to lose my temper, but it was proving harder and harder.

"Our *helpful* opinion, Clarence," Francesca corrected, holding a strand of hair over a candle flame and watching it burn. It smelled of burnt flesh, and I flinched at the memories it recalled.

"Ah. Leave him alone. He will come to his senses eventually," Jean-Pierre said, taking Francesca's hand and bowing in a classical minuet opening as he hummed a tune. "Given that you are so committed to this illusion of loyalty to your witch, have you at least… tasted her?" he asked with no little sarcasm. "And, if you haven't, what are you waiting for?"

I did not bother replying. He knew the answer very well.

"Then what on earth do you do when you are alone? Are you a vampire or a damned forest fairy? What kind of relationship is that, if I may ask?"

"None," I growled with my eyes closed. "Unlike you, I don't believe there can be a true relationship where one only gives and the other only takes."

"You are so confused, my friend," Jean-Pierre said, and started to twirl Francesca around the bookcases, throwing me amused glances. "Until you bite her, she's not yours. Which means she's free for anyone else to take."

"Even for me?" Francesca giggled and winked at me.

"Oh, *ma belle* Francesca, did I tell you what an exquisite lady I met yesterday evening?" Jean-Pierre said conversationally, licking his lips and caressing his dancing partner's back as they twirled around the room. "Two-and-twenty. Such a glowing, succulent bosom; hair like golden waves of silk over a mantle of snow… and what fire! What passion! It's a pity you weren't there, she would have enjoyed those sweet lady-tricks of yours." He moaned exaggeratedly and turned to me. "What about you, Clarence? What did you catch yesterday…? A cold, perhaps?"

They started to cackle, and I pounded on the table.

"Enough!"

They stopped dancing, but the smirk on Jean-Pierre's face remained.

"Tell me, both of you, who seem to be so knowledgeable," I asked them, trying to hide the rage in my voice. "Were you ever in love with a vampire?" I paused, and they stared at each other blankly. "Did you ever share your affections with one of our kind when you were still mortal?"

Jean-Pierre waved his hand in dismissal, but Francesca lowered her gaze, her countenance suddenly grave.

"No," Jean-Pierre answered haughtily, "I didn't know any vampires back then. But let me tell you: I have been well-liked by many mortals in this life, even though none of them remember me anymore." He chuckled. "It must be my many innate charms. And, not to boast, but none of them denied me their blood, either; nor did they frown at my feeding habits. Because we are vampires, remember?"

He started to laugh again, but Francesca hushed him, looking moody.

"In that case, my dear friend, I doubt you will ever understand my misery," I said dryly, and left.

Chapter 11

Alba

I boarded the plane feeling excited and queasy in equal measure.

Possibly more queasy than excited, but I tried not to dwell on the lingering nausea which had plagued me since leaving The Cloister.

I was feeling terribly cranky after parting ways with Clarence with a kiss *on the cheek*. His eyes had betrayed how wretched he felt letting me go, but he hadn't repeated his offer to accompany me. Had he done so, I would have said yes. Panic was starting to creep in as I pondered all the possible outcomes of this trip. What would await me after landing in Italy? Had I made a mistake refusing his help? If nothing else, perhaps my absence would make him miss me. Maybe my constant availability had made him take me for granted.

Hence, here I was, sitting in a crowded Airbus and holding a vampire slaughtering brochure and an ugly old book with brownish covers which had come straight from Clarence's private library. *The Merry Adventures of Robin Hood*, first 1883 edition; probably worth hundreds of dollars by now.

I sat back in my seat, sipping airplane trolley tea which tasted like old socks brew, and started to read the bizarre leaflet the witches had handed to me on the street.

There was a man sitting next to me, and he kept reading over my shoulder. Feeling uncomfortable, I folded back the brochure and picked up an airline magazine. The first page was a dull-looking article titled *The Wonders of Northern Italy*.

Nonetheless, the neighboring man kept staring and making me uneasy. Finally, I gave him a discreet, sidelong glance, in the hopes he would get the hint. He must have been around my age, with dark blond hair like Mark's, although styled in a short, military-looking haircut. The way he clenched his muscular jaw made me suspect this man had spent half of his life being angry at the world. To my relief, he didn't sound particularly angry when he addressed me.

"First time traveling to Italy?" he asked with a cocky smile.

Oh no. Now *Fitness Man* wanted to do small talk, and I was trapped with him in a twelve-hour long flight. I was never one to enjoy talking to strangers, and even less so to those who looked like they spent 24/7 sitting in a chest press.

I could pretend to be absorbed in my magazine, couldn't I? *For twelve hours*?

"Aha," I mumbled, hoping that would stop him from asking further questions.

To avoid making the situation more awkward than necessary, I stuck the witches' leaflet deep into *The Merry Adventures of Robin Hood.* As I opened it, a black feather with red sprinkles fell out of the book. Hastily, I retrieved the feather from the floor and put it back into place. The page it had fallen from was dog-eared, and Clarence had underlined a passage with charcoal pencil:

> *"Robin whistled as he trudged along, thinking of Maid Marian and her bright eyes, for at merry times a man's thoughts are wont to turn pleasantly upon the lass he loves the best…"*

Oh, Clarence, nicely played.

My heart skipped a beat at the memory of him. While Fitness Man wasn't looking, I brought the feather to my nose, gave it a good sniff, and got lost for a second in Clarence's rust and evergreen smell.

Why did he have to keep confusing me like that? One day he stood me up, and the next, he sent me subliminal love messages. That vampire was about to drive me nuts with his shifting moods.

"Let me guess…" The man next to me hadn't stopped staring, and I quickly closed the book. I made sure the feather was safely tucked inside: I would need to sniff it again later. "You're going to Venice, aren't you?"

"No," I answered laconically, hoping he would leave me alone to agonize over Clarence for the rest of the flight.

"Smart girl!" he insisted. "The high tide is awful in December. I wouldn't go there either. It stinks of dead fish, and it's so overpriced! Did you know I paid *five euros* for a can of cola last year?"

"Appalling," I said in a flat voice.

"You have no idea!" He nodded and pointed at my wrist, which was still covered in bandages. "That must have hurt. What happened to you? An animal bit you?"

Quite close. If only he knew.

"I'm not a great cook," I said. It wasn't a lie.

"You won't need to cook while in Italy: the restaurants are awesome. What's your name, by the way? Have I seen you somewhere before?"

At first, I thought he was trying one of those cliché pickup lines. But, upon closer inspection, I noticed his face was familiar, too. Only I wasn't sure yet whether it was *good-familiar* or *bad-familiar.*

"My name is Carlo Lombardi," he introduced himself. Carlo Lombardi offered me a firm hand, connected to an arm which looked like the muscle dummy from a high school laboratory. I shook it weakly—it was warm and a bit callused. "And you? What's your name?"

"Alba," I muttered. My boarding pass was on the tray, with my name clearly readable on it.

"Beautiful name. Where is it from? Italy?"

No. From Introvertland.

"I don't think so," I answered.

"I see you are reading about Lake Como," he said, pointing at the magazine. He was scanning my face for a reaction, so I displayed my most professional poker face. I also turned on my antennas in case he had something interesting to tell me about the place I was visiting. "A friend of mine owns a small inn near the lake. If you haven't booked a place to stay, I can give you the address. I go there every year, and it's really cozy."

"Oh, don't worry. I already booked a room, but thanks."

"Really? Where?"

"Uh, it's called *The Trees* or something. How do you say *tree* in Italian?"

"*Albero,*" he answered, in a perfect pronunciation.

"Is that what your friend's place is called?"

Please, say no.

"Nope, my friend's place doesn't have the word *tree* in it. But, if you are staying near Como, I can pick you up some day and show you around. You are on your own, aren't you?" He looked around, like he expected a husband/boyfriend to pop out of my handbag. "I have lots of free time. I'm alone, too." He studied me with round, blue eyes framed by thick, light brown eyebrows.

"Oh, I've got a really busy schedule already. I doubt I'll be able to fit any more activities in."

"But what about Christmas Eve?" He insisted. "There's a singles' party in my hotel. Speed dating, drinking games… why don't you come? It will be fun."

I wanted to retort that I wasn't single, but I wasn't even sure any longer. Also, I had completely forgotten about Christmas and had no interest in joining any celebrations if my kids were not present. My plan was just to meet Julia, see what we could do for each other, then return home as quickly as possible. I should be back in Emberbury before the New Year.

"*Uh*… I don't know. I'm meeting some friends. I'm only staying for a couple of days," I said.

"Oh, Italian friends are the best, don't you think?"

"Didn't you just say you were Italian?"

"I am *half* Italian," he clarified, his elbow perilously crossing the tacit boundary of our shared armrest.

I rummaged in my bag and found a sleeping mask in an inner pocket. Popping it over my eyes, I yawned with exaggeration and said, "Time to get some beauty sleep, or we'll be too jet-lagged on arrival to enjoy the views."

***

Agroturismo Foresta Chiara was a fairytale country house built on one floor against a mountain slope overlooking the lake. Its pointed roofs shone under the bleak winter sun, surrounded by leafless vineyards. It wasn't far away from the famous Lake Como, but distant enough to avoid the hordes of tourists who stood in line, waiting for the buses which toured around the area all year round.

On my arrival, after a long taxi ride from the airport, I was greeted by the owner, a sprightly thirtysomething called Berenice. She assigned me a cozy Alpine room decorated with honey-colored wooden furniture, a vintage crochet quilt and paintings of women dancing in long, striped skirts while drinking wine off each other's cups.

"You should join me and the rest of our guests tonight," Berenice said. She was wearing a rainbow patchwork dress, which must have been sewn by an army of drunk fairies. "Is this your first time in Italy? Are you on your own?"

Was everybody going to ask me that?

"Yes, but I'm visiting some friends," I answered politely.

She winked. "You may like to hear that lots of single men have checked into our inn this week." Did I have the words *divorced and desperate* written all over my forehead? Judging by her mischievous smile, I might have. "Expect a very special Christmas this year. Love is in the air!" She wrinkled her nose mischievously, and I grimaced in horror. What had possessed me to check into this dreadful matchmaker's inn? "Don't forget!" she sang. "Dinner is at 8 PM."

I spent the afternoon channel-hopping in my room, trying to find a program able to capture my volatile attention. Meanwhile, I made up my mind not to attend Berenice's welcome dinner. An hour or so later, my cell phone started to flash with two incoming messages.

The first one was Minnie's. Mark and I avoided texting each other, because most of the important information ended up lost in a sea of bickering. Minnie was neutral ground, so we used her as an intermediary.

Iris and Katie wanted to show you their Christmas tree.

The text was followed by several photos of the girls hanging ornaments on a tree taller than Mark, wearing new dresses and beaming wide smiles. My heart constricted just a little, but I ignored the sinking feeling and wrote back a polite thank you message to Minnie.

The next message was Clarence's, and his deliciously archaic style—better suited for handwritten letters than plain instant messaging—automatically made me smile. He had grasped the use of technology surprisingly fast, but we still needed to polish his texting language skills a little.

I pictured him sitting at his desk, pressing the letter keys one by one with a stylus and with flashing vampire speed. He had to use a typing tool because, otherwise, phone screens didn't respond to his tomblike, cold touch. The message said:

My dearest, beloved Alba,

I hope this message finds you well. I am writing to inquire about the outcome of your travels. I hope you arrived safely to your accommodations and are enjoying your stay in Continental lands.

Please write back soon and take care.

Missing you already,

Your admirer and friend,

Clarence

I miss you too, I thought, hugging the phone against my chest. Only then I took a closer look.

He had signed himself as my admirer *and friend.*

And friend?

A wave of heat washed over me as my worst suspicions were confirmed. How could I have thought Clarence's affections would last forever? How many times did I need to fail to learn my lesson? Mark was probably right: not only was I too old for miniskirts, but I was also a disaster and bound to be rejected over and over until I ended up an ugly old witch with warts on my nose.

Dispirited, I sat on the bed and pondered over Clarence's words like a broody teenager. After lengthy—and fruitless—deliberations, I gave up trying to decipher the hidden meaning behind his message and decided to do something more useful with my life.

I remembered about the brochure the witches had given me and took it out of my bag. Seemingly, those friendly-looking ladies had a buoyant vampire slaughtering side hustle. The brochure included a test to check whether you had been an unknowing victim of vampirism and how close you were to becoming a bloodsucker yourself. I scored a whopping 95% probability of being a victim and an 87% likelihood of joining *The Dark Side* eventually. My answers went more or less like this:

> *Wake up tired?* Check.
> *Uncommonly pale, photophobia?* Check—I was living in a catacomb, after all.
> *Constantly followed by ravens, black cats or bats?* Check.
> *Incoherent talking?* Check, check.
> *Clouded thinking?* Triple check.

After that, there were a few do-it-yourself deterrents you could easily prepare with ingredients sold in their store. Just like Clarence, I loved the sock one. The leaflet also stated that throwing a fistful of rice in front of your doorstep would force any passing vampire to count each grain compulsively before entering—which would theoretically take them long past sunrise and therefore cause them to leave you alone. Maybe that was deterring Clarence from visiting my room more often? He could be quite pedantic sometimes, so it wasn't entirely implausible. I pledged to give a good sweep to the floor on my return, just in case.

According to the leaflet, if the vampire was really persistent and refused to leave you alone, you could also enlist the witches' services and get 50% off your first buy. Did the discount mean that they expected returning customers, or resurrected vampires? They boasted about owning a large stock of silver stakes and tungsten chains—seemingly, those were the most effective in restraining a bloodsucker, even better than silver, against popular belief.

I was *never* going to throw away that jewel of a brochure. If nothing else, I would wave it in front of Clarence's face whenever he got on my nerves.

Because we were still friends, weren't we?

I took a quick look at the words scribbled on the back:

> *Ask for Valentina Caruso at the Museum of Witchcraft of Como, or call this telephone number.*

Okay, I definitely wasn't going to call those vampire-loathing witches any time soon. But I would keep the leaflet for future reference.

I threw on a green wool dress—long enough for an Amish wedding reception, because Mark's words were still echoing in my mind—and headed downstairs, to the common living room where dinner would be served.

Berenice, the quirky inn owner, came by and brought me a plate of toast with olive oil, slices of cheese and tomato, which I accepted with great enthusiasm.

"Thank you, this is delicious," I said, taking a bite of cheese. I hadn't eaten anything since the plane.

"Glad you like it!" she answered, taking a seat at my table. "Is your room alright? Do you have enough towels?"

"Everything is great, thank you."

"If you need any ideas for day trips, I can help!"

"Oh, no, it's fine, I already have a few things on my to-do list. I found them on the internet. But do you know if there is a passenger terminal for boat trips? I'd like to explore the lake a bit while I'm here."

"Yes, great idea! I'll mark the spot on a map for you. Or, even better, I could take you myself. I have a small boat, and I can organize a trip for a couple of guests who were asking this morning. I would just charge you for the snacks. Are you free tomorrow?"

"*Hmm*, no, I'm going to Como tomorrow. But you don't have to trouble yourself. I'm fine on my own."

"No trouble at all! I'll see if we can change the date to the day after tomorrow. We sisters must help each other!"

I cleared my throat. *Sisters?*

"Oh, look who is here! My favorite guest!" Berenice turned around to greet a newcomer and the man from the plane walked into the dining room, a smug smirk all over his face. "Carlo!" she squealed and embraced him, hopping slightly to reach his shoulders. "Let me introduce you to Alba. She's new!"

"We know each other," he said, putting his hands in his pockets.

"Do you?" Berenice smiled. "Then you should sit together. I'm a bit short on tables tonight. Tell her about the places she should visit. And about Turanna's mirror. She said she's visiting the Museum of Witchcraft tomorrow, she shouldn't miss our finest piece."

No, I didn't say that. I just said I was going to visit the city.

Carlo sat in front of me, and I greeted him with an uncomfortable grin.

"Anything you need, just ask!" Berenice said, waving at us with a dishcloth. "Although I think you will be well taken care of," she added with a twinkle of her eye directed at Carlo. Then, she disappeared into the kitchen and left us alone to eat.

"*Mamma mia*, what a happy coincidence," Carlo said, as I choked with a tomato peel. He was wearing tight black jeans and a grey Cashmere wool sweater full of lint and dog hair. He helped himself to my plate of bread without even asking for permission. "I see you looked up the hotel I was telling you about on the plane."

It was probably useless to explain that I had made the reservation long before meeting him.

"You said your hotel didn't have the word *tree* in the name," I complained.

"And it doesn't. This place is called *Foresta Chiara*. Where do you see the word *tree*?" he sounded truly surprised.

"*Foresta* means forest! It's close enough!" I whined, and he laughed, regaling me with a direct view of the half-chewed cheese in his mouth.

I made a mental note to check the cancelation policies for *Agroturismo Foresta Chiara* right after dinner.

"Do you want me to drive you to the museum tomorrow?" he said, dragging his chair forward. "I have a rental car. I can give you a ride."

"I don't have time to visit museums, but thank you. And I like taxis, anyway. They give me a chance to interact with the locals."

"You can pretend I'm a local. I speak perfect Italian."

"So do I." It was only a half-lie. We had moved often during my childhood, which in turn had forced me to learn a few languages to survive. Italian wasn't one of them, but Portuguese and Spanish were close enough. Shame I could not remember how to say *forest* and *tree* in all possible European languages.

"Really?" he was asking in the meanwhile. "Are you a translator?"

Berenice left a wine decanter on the table and invited us to serve it ourselves. Carlo poured himself a glass, full to the rim, and drank it in one gulp. A soft burp escaped his throat, and I averted my eyes so he couldn't see me wince. He hadn't bothered to fill my glass, so I did it myself and refilled his.

"No, I'm not a translator," I answered. "Just a sort of… secretary." That was the standard, tinned response I gave to all strangers who dared to ask me about my job. "I work for a small company which trades in real estate and art."

"Sounds cool," he said, soaking in his second glass like a sponge. "What do you do exactly?"

"Nothing special. Just boring work," I said, hoping he wouldn't notice my unsteady tone. "You know, I take my boss's clothes to the dry cleaner's, post things, that kind of stuff." *Occasionally they use me as an appetizer, too.* "What about you?"

"Me?" he said casually, and stuffed his face with a piece of bread larger than his fist. "I'm in… law enforcement."

Something in the way he said it made it sound daunting.

"Oh." My mouth went dry with all the possible ways the evening could go wrong. "Really?"

"Yes," he extended his hand, like we were meeting for the first time, and gave me a squinting look. "Officer Lombardi, from Emberbury Police Department. At your service, madam."

Chapter 12

Alba

The next day, I woke up later than expected and with a massive headache, partly due to jet lag and partly as an aftereffect of drowning my sorrows in *pinot grigio* while listening to Carlo Lombardi go on about sports and fitness for hours on end.

Remembering I was supposed to meet Julia at noon, I dragged my sorry, jetlagged self to the breakfast room of the inn and ordered two cappuccinos at once, which Berenice brought to my table with a disproportionate smile.

"I have good and bad news for you," she chirped, throwing three brown sugar packets my way. "Which one do you want to hear first?"

"Bad first," I said, sinking my spoon into the heart-shaped coffee foam and checking the hour—I had enough time to eat breakfast quickly and hop on the shuttle bus which drove to Como every hour o'clock.

"Yeah, I always choose the bad news first,

too," she said with a sympathetic nod. "Thing is, I won't be able to take you on a boat ride tomorrow. The inn is fully booked for the first time in five years, and I won't even have time to pee."

"No problem," I said. With some luck, I would get Julia to manifest again, and there would be no time left for sightseeing.

"Now the good news!" Berenice clapped her hands with excitement. "There are three other guests interested in going, and one of them has a boat license, too. So, the trip is still on, and you're sailing off tomorrow morning!"

"Well, awesome!" I said, finishing my two coffees in a hurry. "Talk later, I must catch the bus to the city!"

***

The bus ride took around half an hour, which was barely enough time to answer Clarence's message: in the end, I sent less than two lines of text after writing and deleting different versions, some including Carlo, some not.

Why did it feel so awkward mentioning that encounter to Clarence?

Carlo and I had met once before at a police station, when I had been detained for trespassing into a graveyard, and he had been there just by chance.

Fine.

I had been wearing a soaked, transparent, mostly torn and uncomfortably revealing yellow minidress.

So what?

He had taken me for a necromancer.

Misunderstandings do happen, don't they?

I didn't see why any of this should be mention-worthy. Therefore, I left it out.

In the end I just wrote:

> "*Hi, Clarence. The flight was okay, it's cold here, I'm okay, I hope you are okay, too.*"

I finished off my utterly lame message with a lousy "*Take care!*" in the hopes of upsetting my admirer *and friend* as much as he had me.

***

The city was picturesque, full of narrow streets and historical buildings, which extended up to the edge of the lake and seemed taken out of the illustrations of a children's book.

I got off the bus near the train station. It was relatively easy to find Julia's address from there, with the help of her map and some Italian sign language. Once there, I learned two things:

1. Julia's house was clearly abandoned, and the doors were boarded up with derelict-looking wooden planks.
2. Julia's house was right next to the Museum of Witchcraft, the place I had categorically decided *not* to visit because it might be swarming with vampire-

loathing witches.

I sat on a bench in front of the museum and waited until a distant church clock struck noon. There was no sign of Julia anywhere.

I was slightly disappointed that the Museum of Witchcraft was a plain looking concrete construction, shaped like a grey cube with a sterile glass door, and not an eerie medieval prison. They must have demolished one of the older houses to build it.

After forty-five minutes freezing on the street in front of an abandoned town house, I decided to walk around the building and knock on the boarded-up doors and windows.

Nothing.

Desperate, I paced in front of the door, checking the time and cursing myself for traveling across an ocean just to be stood up by a ninety-year old witch.

After three hours I urgently needed a bathroom and didn't feel my toes due to the cold, so I gave up.

Grudgingly, I took the road back to *Foresta Chiara* inn, and hoped to be able to contact Julia again with the mirror spell.

***

Someone must have put a curse on that day.

I entered my room with one single thought in my mind: contacting Julia again, whatever it took. One didn't travel all the way to Europe just to be stood up like that. I made sure there were no smoke detectors in the room and attempted to repeat my previous success with the mirror spell. My suitcase was full of candles, which I had taken with me just for that purpose, and I lit two of them to perform the summoning.

I read the spell a couple of times, but nobody showed up in the mirror. Wherever Julia was, she had no interest in meeting me that day, or she could not come for some reason.

It was getting dark when I gave up on my attempts to contact my supposed mentor. I went outside and sat at the back of the inn to watch the sun set behind the lake. Leaning on a windowsill, I wrote to Minnie and asked about the girls, then checked for messages from Clarence. There were none, so I tried to call him to tell him about my awful day. By then, I had lost all my pride and was desperate to talk to someone remotely homey and willing to listen. To my disappointment, his phone was off. In the end, I wrote a brief message and asked him to call back when possible.

I felt like crying.

I was alone in an isolated inn away from civilization, with nobody to talk to and no idea how to reach Julia. Had I dreamed the whole mirror scene in The Cloister? Had I imagined everything and come all this way for nothing? Maybe I was going crazy. My actions as of late definitely supported that theory.

The stench of cigarettes preceded the arrival of Carlo and stifled the pleasant scent of greenery which surrounded the secluded mountain inn.

"Look who's here," he said, coming out the back door.

I sighed and did my best to wipe the tears off my cheeks. The last thing I wanted was Carlo's pity.

"Are you okay?" he asked, a flicker of concern in his eyes.

"Never better," I answered, turning away from him and swiftly changing the subject. "I went to Como. Cute little city."

He sat at the window next to me and tried to peek into the screen of my phone. Quickly, I locked it so he couldn't see Clarence's old messages.

"Did you get to see the museum?"

I rolled my eyes. "I thought I had told you—I was supposed to meet a friend, but something got in the way and she didn't make it."

"See? You should have gone to the Museum of Witchcraft. They have really fun torture devices there, and I think you can even buy some as souvenirs."

"*Hm.* I could put one or two of those to use if I had them." Next time I met Mark, for example. "Maybe I'll go, after all."

"They also have old spell books and haunted mirrors. I think you would like it."

I stared at him with suspicion. "Why?"

He snorted and threw the cigarette to the floor, putting it out with his combat boot. "I don't know. You strike me as the kind of gal who likes weird things. Like snooping into old tombs at night and such."

"Well, then I'm sorry to disappoint you, but whatever you might have concluded about me after that unfortunate first meeting of ours, I'm the kind of *gal* who likes normal things. The more normal, the better."

A small, dark bird crossed the sky above the clouds, and I watched it wistfully, wishing it was Clarence. But I knew it wasn't him—by then, I would have recognized him anywhere, no matter what shape he took. Carlo's eyes followed mine and he frowned, then started to tap nervously on his knee.

"What? You don't like black birds?" I asked, noticing his growing discomfort.

He shook his head and spoke in a somber tone, "No. Especially not crows and ravens. They are well-known thieves. As a policeman, my job is to catch them and lock them up so they stop harming people."

I forced myself to laugh at his joke. *Because it had been a joke, hadn't it?* But only a weak cackle came out.

"I'm tired," I said, "and I need to take a shower before dinner. See you later in the restaurant."

When I looked again, the bird had already vanished.

***

I picked up a daisy on the way to my room and twirled it between my fingers as I walked down the corridor of the inn. My door was unlocked. I didn't remember leaving it that way, but given my mental state, everything was plausible. I walked in and kicked off my muddy shoes, then threw my coat on the crocheted bedspread and dropped onto the bed, defeated.

Clarence hadn't answered my message yet. He hadn't answered any of them at all. I turned off the phone so I wouldn't check it every five seconds and stared at the daisy, then started to pluck off its petals, ready to wallow in my melancholy now that I was finally alone.

"*He loves me, he loves me not…*" I murmured absentmindedly, tearing at the flimsy white petals with abandonment.

"I didn't know you were still in high school."

The voice startled me, and the mostly bald daisy fell from my hands. The sound was coming out of my closet, soft and musical.

"Good evening." Francesca appeared in front of me and her chilly, delicate hand brushed my shoulder. I gasped in shock, my heart about to stop. "Calm down. It's just me," she whispered.

"For goodness sake, Francesca, aren't you vampires supposed to be invited in?" I took a deep breath, feeling the blood flow return to my limbs.

"Not really. Unless the windows are bolted shut, and we don't feel like breaking in." She sneered.

"What are you doing here?"

"The old English vampire was too proud to beg for your permission to come, but I thought you might be thrilled to enjoy your vacation with a fun girlfriend. Even though I see you were quick to make new acquaintances here." She raised her eyebrows questioningly.

"*Huh*?" I glanced at her sideways. "Are you talking about Carlo? He's no acquaintance of mine. We just met on the plane."

"Whatever you say; you know I'm not prone to judging others."

"I thought Clarence had said it took days to fly across the ocean and that the crossing was very risky. How did you get here so fast?"

"I always said Clarence was a wimp, and this just confirms it," Francesca said, blowing away a few strands of hair which had fallen over her eyes. "You see, men always focus on the obstacles. Women, on the other hand, are built to withstand miserable conditions and deal with them… or die. It's in our nature." She shrugged and exhaled with impatience. "As you see, I'm here. Do I look dead to you?"

She did, a bit, but I decided not to provoke her.

"I have traveled this route before, and so has he, by the way. I think your sweetheart is growing old."

"How is he?" I asked cautiously, as my eyes roamed to the discarded phone.

"I believe he's going through an existential

crisis," she answered slowly, "although Jean-Pierre doesn't agree entirely. In his opinion, he just requires proper refreshments and some more—" she studied me critically, "—never mind. You two will figure it out, if that fling of yours is meant to last."

I gave Francesca a sidelong glance and gaped at her. Some more… *what?*

"Anyhow, the sulking boy remained in Emberbury. But am I such a bad alternative?" She sat on the bed and spread her bulky skirt around her, making sure not to leave a single crease.

"No, of course not. I'm glad to see you. It's just… it's been an awful day. I was meant to meet Julia, but she didn't show up as agreed. Now I have no way to contact her."

"I see." She remained silent for a while, like she was considering several options. "And what is your plan exactly?"

"I'm not sure I have a plan. I was thinking about lying in bed and weeping for the rest of the night."

"That's pathetic," she said. "You should be thankful I'm here. Let me see, do you have Julia's address?"

"Yes, but the house seems abandoned."

"Let's go there," she said, jumping on the windowsill. "Maybe I'll smell something you missed."

Chapter 13

Alba

Francesca refused to change into one of my dresses for the taxi ride to Como. She insisted on keeping her exquisite—but very noticeable—gold-trimmed Renaissance gown instead. Never mind it had short sleeves and a square décolleté which nearly reached her navel. Plus, she was wearing no coat. *In December.*

"It's not who I am," she said, not a bit concerned. "That would be like wearing a costume."

"Yeah… speaking of costumes…" I whispered, nestling in the back next to her, "could you please tell the cab driver we're attending a masquerade party, so he stops glaring at us?"

Due to my heavily accented Italian, I had resolved to rely on Francesca to do the talking—she was a native speaker, after all. She gladly engaged in conversation with the driver, and I dozed off for a while. The next thing I heard was the driver's voice announcing our destination.

"*Museo della Stregoneria*," he said, stopping right in front of Julia's old house. "Do you want me to pick you up after dinner?"

"Yes, please. Could you be back in two hours?"

"Of course, *signorina*, I'll drive you ladies back home," he answered gallantly, and a second later, he was gone.

"So, this is where they lived," Francesca said wistfully, sniffing the air around the derelict house and caressing the flaky stone walls like she was searching for a secret lever.

"They, who?" I asked, inhaling deeply just like her. The only noticeable smell was a pleasant mixture of roasted meat, lasagna and pastries coming from the houses at the end of the street.

"Julia and my brother, when she first came here."

"You had a brother?" I asked. She rarely talked about herself, and it was hard to imagine Francesca having once had a proper family.

"I *have* a brother," she corrected, throwing me a steely look, "or so I hope."

"Is he by any chance called Ludovic? The man Julia keeps mentioning in her diary?"

Francesca nodded and a stern expression clouded her face. Then, with an impossibly quick leap, she disappeared into a side alley which led to the back of the museum.

"Hey! Wait! Where are you going?" I said, rushing to follow her.

I found Francesca perched like a gargoyle

on the stone wall which surrounded the museum's backyard. She reminded me of one of those Victorian child ghosts from horror movies, ready to throw herself at someone's throat. Maybe that was how she stalked her victims, come to think of it.

"I hear you are good at jumping over fences," she said, with a dazzling—and decidedly wicked—smile.

"Not again," I sighed with resignation but took the hand she was offering. That vampire girl was always around whenever I ended up trespassing. My late mother would have labeled her a bad influence.

"This must be the museum's garden," she said, depositing me softly on the floor. "I think we'll be able to get into Julia's house from this side."

We found ourselves in a small park with nicely groomed trees and bronze sculptures. One of them depicted a typical witch with a pointed hat, riding a black broom. Just like Carlo had mentioned, there were also a few torture devices, including a daunting, life-sized gallows and an iron chair covered in sharp spikes.

"Those are not comfortable, trust me," Francesca commented, frowning at the torture chair and the wooden scaffold next to it. "I have tried both."

I shook my head and tried to disregard the visions her words had just conjured up.

The gelid breeze brought the echo of a woman sobbing. Francesca put a finger over her lips and motioned me to stay where I was. I hid behind an enormous iron cauldron—which currently served as a flower planter—and waited.

Francesca crept, silent as a panther, toward the source of sound. I watched her from my hiding place, trying to get a better view among the brittle rose bushes.

A pentacle-shaped pergola stood in the middle of the garden. There was a circular bench inside, and it was occupied by a woman clutching what looked like a cello's skeleton between her legs. She had short hair, half white and half green, and was wearing a black leather jacket full of cinches and pockets. When she saw Francesca, she gasped and clutched her cello even harder with both arms, as if scared the vampire would steal it.

***

"Good evening," Francesca greeted the girl sweetly. So sweetly that I wondered whether I was about to witness a vampire having dinner.

"Did you come to take my life?" the girl sobbed, but she didn't recoil: instead, she let her head fall backwards in an offering gesture. There were thick ropes around her chest and legs which kept her tied to the bench. Her hands had been tied around the broken musical instrument in some sort of bizarre punishment. "I don't mind. Just do it fast, please."

"Of course not." Francesca approached her patiently, talking in her governess tone: calming, but commanding. "But I would like to sit next to you, if you'd allow me to."

The girl shrugged, and Francesca joined her on the bench, moving slowly, like she didn't want to scare her. Meanwhile, I peeked among the branches, wondering what Francesca was plotting.

"What is that?" Francesca asked, touching the strange, large object the short-haired girl was attached to. "Wait, let me help you."

With an effortless tug, Francesca got rid of the ropes, setting the girl free. The latter took off a pair of horn-rimmed glasses and wiped her teary eyes on her sleeve, staring at Francesca but never trying to flee.

"It's a…" she hesitated, watching Francesca warily. "It's an electric cello. But it's broken. My girlfriend broke it. On purpose."

She started to bawl her eyes out again.

"*Shh*," Francesca said, rubbing a loving hand against the girl's upper back. "What kind of person would damage a musical instrument on purpose?" she asked, with a disapproving headshake. Her voice was like a siren's, so charming and hypnotic that even I couldn't turn away from her. "That must have been a despicable person, indeed. You should find yourself someone better. Someone able to appreciate music and musicians."

She inched slowly toward the girl, gradually closing the gap between them.

"Stop trying to enthrall me," the girl growled, still sniffling, but sounding somehow braver. "I know what you are."

"I know you do," Francesca purred. "I can smell you, too, so I reckon we are even. And so that you know, vampire enthrallment is a myth. It's not my fault if I am so… charismatic."

"Why are you here?" the girl asked. Francesca offered her a frilly handkerchief, and she took it cautiously, like she expected it to be soaked in poison. "You are the third creature who appears here in less than a month. Which is weird, because we never had any before… like ever. You know what is also weird? None so far tried to bite me. But what about you? Are *you* going to bite me?"

"Bite you?" Francesca repeated, as if talking to herself. She licked her lips, and her eyelids fluttered sensually for a split second. She quickly regained her self-control and added, "I don't usually bite witches." She put her arms around the girl's strong body and kissed the top of her head. Her helpless target remained completely still, opposing no resistance. "But I'd so love to hear everything about those creatures you met."

***

"You can come out now, Alba," Francesca called, keeping one hand around the green-haired girl's waist. She kept talking to her like she was a small child, or a scared horse. "This is Alba, she's our friend. And I am Francesca. We are here to help you. Tell me, my dear, what's your name?"

I tiptoed out of my hiding place behind the cauldron planter and grinned at the bizarre couple.

I chose a spot to sit on the furthest end of the bench, still unsure of Francesca's intentions.

The girl introduced herself as Alice, the museum receptionist, and informed us that she had just been dumped by her girlfriend of two years and had no particular interest in staying alive after such a distressing event.

"I was supposed to fly to Rome with our band, but she wanted me to stay and meet her parents for Christmas," she explained between loud sobs. "When I explained I wasn't ready, she tied me to this bench and trampled my cello. She said I loved symphonic metal more than her."

"And you should." Francesca nodded. I strongly doubted she knew what symphonic metal was, but she sounded convincing enough. "As Plato said: *music gives a soul to the universe, wings to the mind and life to everything.*"

"Never heard that before, but it's quite cool," Alice said, in complete awe.

"We have more in common than you think," Francesca murmured, sniffing the girl's white and green hair.

"Do we?" Alice asked with a sigh, echoing my thoughts as Francesca rubbed the red marks the rope had left on her wrists. The girl leaned against the vampire's side, apparently enjoying the closeness to a fellow musician.

"Now tell me about those vampires you met," Francesca said softly. "Can you describe them to me?"

"Well, I think only one was a vampire. Not

sure what the second creature was. Our high priestess saw a vampire roaming the forests near the lake a couple of weeks ago. They managed to—" she hesitated and eyed Francesca warily before continuing, "—they managed to capture him."

Francesca nodded, unfazed. "Do you know his name?"

The girl shook her head. She had stopped crying and was now fumbling nervously with the pegs of her cello. "No, he didn't tell."

"Any remarkable features you remember?"

"Tight black curls, blue eyes. That's all I know."

"What happened to him?" Francesca asked. Her voice was soft and friendly.

"I don't know. Valentina, our high priestess…" she paused to assess whether Francesca knew what she was talking about. She did. "She said they would take care of him. I don't know anything else."

Francesca frowned for a second, but quickly recovered her loving expression.

"What about the other one?"

"The other one was… strange," Alice said cautiously. "I'm not even sure of what she was."

Francesca's eyes glimmered with interest, shining with a bright blue light in the winter night. "How is that?"

"She manifested herself today, around noon," Alice explained. All my attention turned to her. "The ground floor of the museum is undergoing renovations, and I was there, cleaning, when a woman appeared inside a mirror."

All my muscles tensed.

That had to be her.

"She called me *sister*, and for a moment I believed she was one of us. I thought, if she was able to do mirror projection, she must be a witch. But then… there was something off about her. We can sense other witches." She threw me a meaningful glance but said nothing. "I couldn't detect her scent through the mirror, but her face… her eyes… she looked odd. Ageless. I couldn't tell whether she was thirty, or fifty. Her eyes were much older than the features she was allowing me to see. So, I don't know. As far as I know, vampires can't astral travel, but she reminded me of one. She asked me to go outside and fetch a friend of hers who was supposed to be waiting on the street."

"And did you go?" I asked, knowing the answer in advance.

Alice laughed. "Of course not. It was probably a trap. Some powerful witches can even step out of mirrors and use them as portals. I wasn't going to hang around just to find out what she could do. I just covered the mirror with a sheet and banished her."

"Did she tell you anything else?" I asked, moving closer to Alice.

"As I was reciting the banishing spell, she tried to tell me something. A message for her friend." Alice squinted at me, connecting the dots. "It was you, wasn't it?"

"How do you know?" I asked with surprise.

"I'm good at reading people. Anyways, I remember her mentioning the name Carlo, if it rings a bell for you."

"Carlo?" I gasped. "Yes, it does. What about Carlo?"

"No idea. I sent her off too fast for her to finish the sentence."

"Shit," I muttered, balling my fists. I wondered what Julia had wanted to tell me about Carlo. Was he friend or foe?

"So, who and *what* was that woman?" Alice asked me, raising an eyebrow, which caused her oversize glasses to slide down her nose.

Francesca threw me a cautioning look.

"I'm not sure," I said, quickly reading Francesca's warning. "But I do think she was asking for me."

"Perhaps, if you showed us that mirror, things would become clearer," Francesca suggested, and Alice nodded obligingly.

***

"She's a stray, isn't she?" Alice asked Francesca as we marched toward the entrance. The vampire nodded. "I knew it as soon as I saw her. The energy around her is so scattered and irregular, it makes me queasy. I don't know how you can stand it."

I remained behind them, paying close attention to Francesca's antics. They walked holding each other, their familiarity too deep and sudden to be genuine. Francesca had somehow seduced the museum receptionist to extract information out of her; but I still wasn't sure whether there was something preternatural involved or just her natural charms, as she had stated earlier. Clarence had told me such a thing as vampire compulsion didn't exist. After what I had just witnessed, I was starting to doubt his words.

"Can you do mirror projection too, Alice?" Francesca asked, as the girl entered a code into the keyboard at the door. A loud beep greeted us and the glass door unlocked.

"Oh, no. That's really hard to do, unless you get hold of a haunted one. I can banish evil spirits and read cards, but moving things around, especially your own body… that's reserved for very gifted witches. Most of us can't even move a breadcrumb."

"Oh, that's a shame. But tell me about you, Alice. You mentioned a high priestess. Do you belong to a coven, perhaps?"

"Well, it's more like a book club. Mostly we check the phase of the moon, bake stuff and knit scarves. Nothing spectacular, really."

"So, no dancing naked under the moon? No talking to the dead?" I asked with disbelief.

"Not much," Alice said with a shrug.

I sighed, disenchanted. "But you can sense other witches," I said, remembering how she had known I was a stray right away.

"Oh yes, that's such a basic ability I can't

even believe you aren't able to do it!" Alice giggled.

As we walked, she turned on the lights and briefly showed us each of the museum halls. There were many interesting artifacts and paintings in each exhibition. According to the wall panels, most of those so-called *witches* had been just poor, ordinary women, forced to plead guilty for crimes they never committed.

"These two are my favorites," Alice said, pointing at an ink drawing depicting two screaming, long-haired girls in torn gowns. "Their names were Celeste and Maria. They were born in the late 16th century. Celeste's father arranged for her to marry an old, wealthy man. On the eve of her wedding, she ran away with Maria, her maid. But the villagers found them asleep in the forest, and they were accused of witchcraft. Burned together at the stake." She chuckled bitterly. "For loving each other. For being the Devil's mistresses."

Francesca cringed and stared at the drawings in a grim silence.

"I know, right?" Alice continued and, to my shock, she squeezed Francesca's hand sympathetically. "My thoughts exactly. I'm glad I wasn't born back then."

We entered a dusty room full of moving boxes and unidentifiable items covered in white sheets.

"This is the main exhibit, where we display Turanna's Mirror," Alice said. "We just hung it back yesterday after the workers left, although it's still a bit dusty in here. It's our most valuable piece, dating back to Etruscan times."

"This?" I asked, a bit disappointed.

Their so-called *most valuable piece* was an archaic hand mirror with engraved scenes of doves and dancing women in the nude. At first glance, it wasn't more than an old piece of junk. Had I found it in a dumpster, I would have walked past it, no regrets.

"It's not very reflective," I pointed out. It didn't even have any glass on it: just a roughly polished metal surface which might have been buried in a mudhole for centuries.

"Not anymore," Alice conceded, "but it turns reflective again when you wake it up. It's a powerful magic tool, if you know how to use it."

"Really? What can it do?"

"According to the myth, you can summon the goddess Turanna when holding it. If she hears your plea, you will see yourself clearly on the surface of the mirror. It can answer any queries your heart longs for, or take you any places you wish to be." She smirked. "Some say it can even trap your lover's soul for you, or show you the man you'll marry."

I stared into the greenish-brown piece of art, hoping it would give me some valuable—and needed—relationship advice. But the mirror ignored me, just like everyone else so far.

"I wish I could exchange a few words with this mirror," I said with a dreamy sigh. "Or ask it to take me somewhere far, far away…"

"It's enchanted, so anyone could use it,"

Alice continued. "Even a dud like you could pull it off, with the right spell."

"Well, thanks for the compliment."

"Just being realistic here." She picked up a rag and started to dust off the Etruscan piece, right after cleaning her glasses. "You would only need someone to teach you the incantation. Sadly, I'm not that person. But if you knew it, you could go just about anywhere, and take whomever you wanted with you, just by holding their hand."

"Wow," I said, glancing at the old exhibit with new eyes. "Sounds like those shoes in The Wizard of Oz, minus the sizing trouble."

"If you intend to stay there for much longer, I'd rather wait for you at the reception desk." Francesca said from the door. "You know I loathe mirrors. They trigger my anxiety."

"No, I think we should leave," I said, following Francesca to the exit. "I've seen everything there is to see. At least for tonight."

Alice locked all the halls, and we went outside, back to the wide strip of sidewalk in front of the main entrance.

"Your taxi will be here soon," Francesca said, wrapping a spidery arm around Alice's stout figure.

"What? Aren't you coming with me?" I asked with surprise.

"I'll join you later. I'm sure you will find a great way to enjoy this lovely, festive evening on your own."

Was she kicking me out in order to make

out with the receptionist, or was it just my imagination?

"Leave the window ajar, but don't wait up for me." Francesca kissed Alice's ear, and the latter let out a troubling moan I wished I hadn't heard.

After I jumped into the taxi, I watched them disappear in the distance. I crossed my fingers for receptionist Alice and hoped she would survive the night.

I arrived at the inn and fell asleep holding my phone, waiting for a message from Clarence which never arrived. I wished I had asked him to come. I wished it was him, and not Francesca, who had appeared, unannounced, in my room. But why would he travel half the world to meet me if I had made it clear that I didn't want him to? I, the clueless witch, the mortal woman who would soon be too old and decrepit for him, had sent him away. What did I expect now? He might be a vampire, but he could not read my mind.

And of one thing I was sure: he was better off without me.

Chapter 14

Clarence

She was better off without me: at least of that I was certain.

The night after Alba left, I allowed myself to go on a proper hunt. Giving in to the bloodlust, to the darkness inside, turned into a desperately needed and exhilarating release. Her absence made it easier. I had been on the brink of insanity after starving myself in the hopes of finding a better way.

There was no such thing as a *better way*.

As I returned to The Cloister, sheltered by the moonlight, I strove to keep the human fragments of my conscience at bay. Apart from the obvious pleasure of stalking and feeding off prey—because calling them *prey* made it easier to detach from the grim reality of our nature—recovering the ability to think rationally had been a very welcome outcome of the night's events.

So, here I was, wandering around Saint Anne's cemetery on my own, as I had done for decades.

Alone, but surrounded by ghosts.

Anne's was particularly buoyant tonight.

She kept whispering into my ear; teasing me with her bubbly laughter, simmering with obscure undertones.

"*We are so much alike. More than you care to admit,*" she teased me.

We shared the same blood, hence it would be absurd to expect anything else.

Perhaps Jean-Pierre and Francesca had been right all this time.

I staggered into my room, relishing the pleasant drowsiness of a good night's hunt, then sat at my desk to write Alba a message inquiring about her journey.

How long did it take to travel half the world on a plane nowadays? Probably less than I imagined.

Would she run the risk of seeking those Italian witches on her arrival? Or worse: would they sense her presence and try to find her? She had claimed not to be interested in them: only in Julia. But what did I know about Julia's alliances? She was a sorceress, after all. And one who should have been dead, as far as I knew.

I dismissed a sudden vision of Alba returning to The Cloister armed with a plentiful shipment of coffin nails and silver stakes. The thought of that slight, sprightly human trying to stake me in my slumber was as entertaining as it was disturbing, and it made me simper… although just briefly.

Coffin nails or not, I hoped she *did* return.

I would have no right to blame her if she didn't, given my erratic behavior as of late.

Anne's finished painting mocked me from the wall, her perfect eyebrows raising with derision. I must be blood-drunk. Francesca was right about the harmful effects of long fasting. There was only so much a vampire could tolerate before strange phenomena started to become a troubling issue.

Francesca had spent the whole day attempting to convince me to fly all the way to Italy. She believed Alba needed me; no, she had declared she *wanted* me there. But did she? How could Francesca be so certain?

Furthermore, there was the daunting issue of visiting the Old World again, after all this time. Once upon a time, I had promised myself—and in an indirect way, my father, too—never to set foot on the Old Continent again.

The canvas on the wall turned blurry, a thin mist arising from behind it. Astonished, I stood up from my desk and took it off the hook. After checking the back of the portrait, I concluded there was nothing amiss. The mist lifted, but left a lingering scent of smoke in the air. I set the canvas against the wall and took a couple of steps backwards.

What was wrong with this painting? Had I imagined the smoky fog, or had Anne made a pact with the devil, in the manner of Dorian Gray? Did she leave a final present for me, buried under the crumbling paint strokes? And, if she did, why had she chosen this, of all days, to set it free?

Perhaps she, as my sire, was still able to sense my unease from wherever she was. Unlikely, but with someone as singular as Anne, not impossible. I could imagine her scoffing at my chagrin concerning Alba: surely, she would have found it preposterous. Vampires and humans were never meant to associate. Not to mention *vampires and witches*. That was why I had hauled that painting back from the gallery and into my room: to remind myself of the proper world order.

Anne would have gladly stood up from her tomb—had she had one—just to ridicule my corroding guilt at touching other humans while thinking of the only one I couldn't—*shouldn't*—have.

I knew it; I understood it; and nevertheless, I could not prevent that feeling from consuming me like a house fire out of control. A fire just like the one which had devoured Anne… so many years ago.

***

London, October 1834

Even the consuming bloodlust intrinsic to new vampires wasn't powerful enough to fade my growing obsession with Anne.

She never asked me for permission before leading me to my undoing.

But I forgave her.

I always did, no matter what.

She remained my gas lamp, and I her ludicrous moth, up to the very last of her days on this earth.

It was demeaning, but I deserved every single torture she inflicted on me.

One of my last mortal days, as I was putting the finishing touches to my best portrait thus far, she bat her lashes at me and smirked as she said, "I can't wait for you to finish the painting, for we shall both become immortal once it is done."

Little did I know what kind of immortality she bore in mind for me.

However, in my naiveté, once she had achieved what she wanted, I still excused her. I believed that now we were *equal*, she would finally become mine.

I changed for her; left everything behind. Surely, that should be enough for her to love me, shouldn't it?

Young and foolish, as they say.

I couldn't have been more mistaken.

Even after she summoned me into the ranks of the undead, I never had her just for myself: not for one single night.

Anne was like fire: luscious. Relentless. Irrepressible. Wild.

I was a thoughtless romantic.

She was bored of returning from her adventures to an empty house.

We were a match made in Hell.

On the evening of October 16th, 1834, I saw

Anne Zugrabescu for the last time.

Her last kiss was passionate, as was everything she did.

Those days she had taken a liking to a member of the House of Lords, whose name was unbeknownst to me. She left the house right before nightfall, ready to fly into his arms just like every other night. I never minded her feeding on them—I was no better in that area. It was what happened before and after that haunted me. She stood by the parliament every night at sunset o'clock, and came back invariably sated, knowing I would be waiting for her, ready to be her pillow, her substitute lover, her patient ear and her reluctant friend.

But I had had enough of that.

That night I followed her, soaring along the Thames all the way to Westminster. Darkness had barely shrouded the city, and she shifted back into human form right behind the arcades surrounding the old palace yard.

She sauntered across the dusty square, brushing her shoulder against the stone walls; attempting to become invisible. The stench of smoke filled the air, but apart from that, nothing seemed out of place. I tracked her to the east side of the building. She knew I was there and, after a while, she finally deigned to turn around and look at me.

"I didn't expect you to follow me here, my dear," she said, stopping to grab my chin with both her hands as she often did. "You know I have an appointment tonight. I had better not be late, or I might miss the… *entrées*. But you are welcome to join us, if you wish." She smiled mischievously.

I considered her offer. I had joined before in her little ventures: they were inevitably sumptuous, almost always pleasurable; occasionally gory and deliciously depraved. Once her current infatuation faded and was replaced by a new one, her praying-mantis-self flared off and led her poor victim of choice to a dreadful end in a final—and gruesome—burst of fireworks. She found my remaining human scruples laughable, sneering at my ability to shed them for good. Oh, the irony of a physician's son squirming at her blood-spattered games.

"I was hoping for a change of heart on your behalf," I whispered, my hands shaking.

"A change of heart?" She giggled. "On what basis?"

I took a deep breath, a lingering human habit. A sense of dread filled me, an inner voice whispering into my ear, *It's now or never.* I needed to tell her, and it had to be tonight: I knew that for certain.

"On the basis that I love you, Anne, and I cannot stand here while you lay with him—with them—every single night; or else I will soon be out of my mind with jealousy. You made me yours, but you did not want me for yourself. Why, Anne? Why else would you do this to me? Why, if you never meant to have me?"

Anne laughed, a seductive laugh like a forest waterfall that made the birthmark by her lip tremble sensually.

"Oh, my darling, innocent Clarence. Always the artist, ever the dreamer."

She shook her head and patted my shoulder, like one would a dog's head, then turned around to leave.

"Stay, Anne." I grabbed her arm, but she shook my hand off. She was stronger than I; much older than I. "Please. Stay one minute longer and tell me the truth. Tell me you don't love me; release me from this servitude, and I shall never inconvenience you again."

She studied me with a condescending smile, which slowly turned into a sneer as she placed both hands over her chest. "My dear child, this heart of mine has not beaten for hundreds of years. Love is as foreign a concept for me—*for us*—as a sunrise. We are vampires, Clarence: the spawn of the Devil. We were not made for love, but pleasure is our prerogative. Our place is in Hell, not Heaven. The sooner you internalize these truths, the easier your transition to your new life will become."

Anne kissed me once more and took off, abandoning me to my grieving thoughts.

She almost certainly forgot our conversation long before she ran into the arms of her last nameless lover and straight into the flames that consumed her.

But I will never forget the ensuing inferno, nor the woman who cursed me with an eternity of darkness just to vanish forever shortly thereafter.

Not a moment had passed since Anne's

departure, when a giant flashover engulfed the parliament, and London's indigo skyline turned a sanguine shade of cerise, becoming an earthly replica of Hell: the place we should live in; the place we belonged to. An earthly Hell where Anne met her ultimate death, right before plummeting forever into Hades' embrace.

That evening, the House of the Lords burned to ashes: and with it, my first love.

The one who never quite faded.

The one who never loved me back.

Chapter 15

Alba

An hour or two before sunrise, the screeching of an old windowpane woke me. Francesca tiptoed into my bedroom with the guise of a drunk teenager sneaking back into her parent's home after an illicit after-hours party. She rummaged in my closet and got hold of a thick duvet and a couple of pillows. Then, she wrapped herself in a spring-roll manner and jumped feet first right into the closet, shutting the doors behind her.

"Pay me no mind," came her voice, muffled from the inside. "I'm exhausted after crossing an ocean, so I'll just stay here for the rest of the day, if it doesn't bother you. I'll try not to breathe, and you can pretend I don't exist."

"Oh, okay," I said, covering my face with the blanket. The room was chilly, and even chillier now she was there.

"One more thing—" Francesca added, peeking out of the closet and wrapped tighter than Ramesses II. "—don't go back to the museum on your own. It's crawling with witches, and too dangerous for you. Wait for me, will you? Find that man named Carlo. Get as much information from him as you can."

She disappeared back into her nook, and I attempted to fall asleep again. It wasn't an easy task—what with the vampiress using my closet as a coffin and my mind drifting back to receptionist Alice: had she ended up as Francesca's midnight snack? Had she really met Julia? What did Julia want me to know about Carlo?

Around eight in the morning, I was fed up with the endless tossing and turning, so I stood up, got dressed and left the room, taking good care not to allow sunlight in. Instead of leaving the key at the reception, I stuck it into my pocket: the last thing I wanted was a chambermaid finding "my" vampire while browsing for linens. It might not end well for either of them.

The inn restaurant was empty, and I sat in what I had come to lovingly call *The Leave Me Alone Chair*—a single armchair facing a wall, located in the darkest corner of the dining space.

Berenice came out of the kitchen, whistling and boasting a fantastic mood.

"Good morning, Alba. Did your mommy put you in timeout or do you enjoy the simple pleasure of staring at empty walls?"

I wanted to roll my eyes at her joke, but she was carrying a cup of coffee for me, so I smiled vapidly instead.

"Bad news first, is that right?" she sang,

placing the steaming cup in front of me. It was a cappuccino, and today she had even drawn a five-pointed star on the foam with cocoa powder.

"I guess…?"

"So, bad news—all the guests but one cancelled the boat trip. They are too hungover after yesterday's singles' party."

Oh, yes. Christmas Eve and that awful party. After Francesca's arrival, I had forgotten about it. Nevertheless, it seemed a pity to leave Como without visiting the lake. It could be nice to explore the surroundings on my own while waiting for Francesca to wake up. I would just take a taxi and go on my own.

"Yeah, okay," I said, somehow relieved I wouldn't have to spend the day in a boat full of strangers. "Never mind, I'll find something else to do. And the good news?"

"The good news: the only guest who didn't cancel holds a boating license, and you get a free private tour of the lake!"

"Really?"

I tried to sound excited, but my voice shook too much. Perhaps I could fake a sudden bout of diarrhea right after breakfast? I really didn't want to be stuck on a boat with Mysterious Sailor Man.

"That's not all!" She handed me a tray with bread, jam and butter, and my stomach clenched a bit.

"Isn't it?" I asked in fear, poking the butter block with my blunt knife to release some of my growing nervousness.

"You get to go sailing with Carlo!"

I exhaled, counting slowly up to ten.

Okay.

I had meant to talk to Carlo anyway. Not exactly while trapped with him in the middle of a large mass of water, but it couldn't be so bad, could it?

No, actually, it could.

He was pushy and a bit slimy.

"You know what, Berenice…" How could I put it nicely? She seemed to like the guy. "I'm not sure I want to go on a day trip with Carlo. I was thinking of…" I made up a quick alternative, "…going to Como and visiting a couple of churches."

Berenice's expression hardened.

"Why? What's wrong with Carlo?" She put her hands on her hips, waving a musty dishcloth like a whip ready to flog ungrateful clients.

"There's nothing wrong with Carlo; I simply don't want to be alone with him on a boat. I barely know him."

"What is there to know?" Now she was visibly affronted. "Why wouldn't you want to? I wish I could go instead of you, but the inn won't run itself. You get to spend the day with a good-looking, hard-working man, and you are complaining? If only you knew what he has gone through…" Berenice paused, her arms crossed over her patchwork dress.

I gave her a slight nod, inviting her to keep talking. She was daring me to ask, as it was obvious from her stance.

"Did you know his wife was murdered?" she uttered defiantly, then scanned my face with squinting eyes.

The last gulp of cappuccino got stuck halfway down my throat.

"*Murdered*?"

"Yes," she spat, "*murdered*."

"I'm… so sorry. What happened?"

"Ask him yourself."

All of a sudden, I wasn't hungry anymore.

"Did you know his wife?" I asked tentatively.

"Yes. They met in this inn, and he still comes back every year to mourn her."

"Oh. That's really sad," I said, suddenly seeing Carlo in a completely different light. "I'm so sorry for him."

"Well, seemingly you are not, if you are too busy to join him on a *pleasant* boating trip!"

I massaged my temples. *Poor Carlo*. I had been so mean to him during the past days. Why was I so reluctant to accept Berenice's offer? I was supposed to be talking to Carlo anyway: I needed to find out whatever Julia wanted to tell me about him. But, for some bizarre reason, something inside me was rebelling against it.

Berenice disappeared into the kitchen, and a vision of Carlo alone in his room, staring at a photo of his late wife, filled me with sympathy for him.

"Hey, Berenice," I said to the inn owner as she passed by my table, barely five minutes later.

"You know what… I think I've changed my mind."

***

When Carlo made his appearance at the parking lot, I was checking my phone for the *nth* time and wondering what the heck had become of Clarence. There was still no news from him, and whenever I'd tried to call him, his phone had been off. He was never very tech-savvy, but such behavior was a bit extreme, even for him. His radio silence could only mean one thing: Mark had been right all along about my age and my universal ineptitude.

Here I was, a divorced mother of two, and the only potential partner without relationship baggage I had found so far was a two-hundred-year-old vampire. Who, technically, was neither my age nor exactly without baggage. Nor was he interested in me anymore, judging by his erratic behavior.

But then, why did my thoughts keep drifting back to him like a barge washed away by the tide?

Speaking of barges, Carlo was staring at me and, judging by his expectant expression, he must have asked me something about the impending trip while I was mulling about Clarence. *Again.*

"Hey… hi, Carlo!" I grinned, putting the phone back into my purse—not before checking the notifications one final time.

"*Buon giorno, bellissima*!" Carlo greeted me with a pat on the back. I flinched at the familiarity.

For a grieving widower, he hid his sorrow very well. "Ready for the coolest journey ever?"

"Yay," I cheered without much excitement.

Carlo had rented a shiny red Alfa Romeo convertible. It was slightly larger than a matchbox, with enough space for two average-sized humans, a wallet and maybe two sandwiches. He spent the whole ride talking about himself and how they always tried to cheat him in restaurants. Unsurprisingly, all the anecdotes ended with him outsmarting all sorts of malevolent waiters and storekeepers. He didn't seem to expect any particular feedback from me, apart from regular nodding, so my mind started to wander yet again to Julia and a certain maroon-eyed vampire as I silently watched the rustic landscape reeling outside the window.

We found a place to park the convertible and strolled languidly to Berenice's boat. It was one of the smallest ones around, a simple sailing vessel with wide, white and blue stripes. It had a small cabin and enough space for six people to sit comfortably on the deck. Or for two, if one of them wished to sit very far apart from the other.

"So, you know how to steer this thing?" I asked warily, watching the boat rock perilously in the dark, cold waters.

"I've been on a boat since the age of three. I could sail this beauty with my eyes closed." He cast off the dock lines with his eyelids tightly shut, proving he was serious. "Just don't flash me your undies if a storm comes, and I swear by my *nonna*'s pizza that I won't let you drown."

I grinned uncomfortably at the mention of my undies and his *nonna* in the same sentence and headed to the furthest end of the vessel, pretending I hadn't heard anything.

"There's no rain in the forecast, by the way," he added. "So… you have free rein."

The lake was enchanting, and moderately crowded. The surrounding mountains started out black at the base and gradually turned pearly white towards the top, where they meshed at an invisible point with the overcast sky. Not far from the shore, the sun sparkled against the windows of the houses of Como, all white and red like drops of blood on the snow.

"Nice view," I commented, trying to dispel the uncomfortable atmosphere left by his uncalled-for mention of my unmentionables.

Carlo steered the boat towards the center of the lake. Once we were far enough from the shoreline, he disappeared into the cabin and brought Berenice's picnic basket to the deck.

"I love Berenice," he said, taking out two sandwiches and a bottle of rose wine.

"I think the interest is mutual," I said, remembering her heated reaction in the morning.

Carlo laughed. "I know! But no, she's not my type. Too garish."

I had no intention whatsoever to ask what his type was, for fear things got too personal too fast. But seemingly, his plans were different from mine, because he said, "I prefer shy, more discreet girls."

I grinned with awkwardness and handed him my sandwich. "I think I'm not hungry. Do you want it?"

He took it and ate half of it in one single bite, so large that a few breadcrumbs remained stuck to his lower cheek. I served myself a large glass of wine. I didn't feel like drinking, but I needed something inconspicuous to fidget with.

"It must be hard, being alone with two little children, working long hours every day," he said pensively, wiping the crumbs off his face in a very unstylish way. "Don't you crave a normal life sometimes? Just coming home to an honest man, going to the supermarket together, doing the things everybody else does?"

I choked on the wine, terrified of the feelings his words were evoking. "I'm perfectly fine. I like the way things are," I answered with false optimism. "And I'm not alone. I have a…" I hesitated, "a boyfriend."

"Do you?" He raised an eyebrow. "And where is he now? Why do you keep staring at your phone and crying in corners?"

I looked around, desperate to find a way out. But I was trapped in a boat with Carlo, and the only possible escape would have been to plunge into the ice-cold waters of Lake Como.

"This wine is making me sleepy," I said. It wasn't true, as I had barely drunk a couple of sips. "Would you mind if I go into the cabin to have a nap?"

"No problem." He rolled his eyes but showed me the way without saying anything else.

I lay inside for an hour or so, while Carlo watched sports on his tablet on the deck. Once I deemed it safe to step outside again, the personal tone of our conversation safely forgotten, I started a new, more neutral discussion by asking him about the New England Patriots. That was enough to entertain him for the following half an hour.

After that, I tried to slip a few questions about his job and interests, in the hopes of discovering the link between him and Julia. But nothing he told me seemed to be remotely related to the supernatural. Judging by his answers, he was just an ordinary man, perhaps not the brightest nor the most elegant one: just a relatively nice guy with an anodyne life who didn't seem to be related to any witches.

As it started to get darker, we sailed back. By the time we were nearing Como, all the lights of the city were twinkling, with added red and green garlands for the festive season. I was less than satisfied with my inquiries and decided Julia must have been talking about someone else. Carlo wasn't such a rare name in that region, after all.

Carlo docked the boat and approached me, an unreadable expression on his face.

"Thank you for this Christmas day," he said, settling himself between me and the access to dry land.

I looked towards shore and considered jumping over him to reach *terra firma*. I wasn't the worst swimmer, but getting wet in that weather didn't sound like a very enticing option, either.

"Yes, Berenice's picnic basket was awesome, wasn't it?" I said nervously.

When I tried to stand up, Carlo opened his arms and hugged me.

"Merry Christmas, Alba."

"*Um*, yeah, to you too," I said, wriggling subtly to escape his overly friendly bear hug.

Before I could stop him, he was kissing me.

A heavy-duty, stubbly and exceedingly drooly kiss which tasted of ham and cheese sandwiches. For the first five seconds I stood in shock, processing the situation. For the next three, I debated between biting his tongue or punching him. Finally, I shoved him away from me with both hands and wiped my mouth on my sleeve, which left a disgusting, foamy wet stain on my coat.

"Carlo, stop!" I shouted, cringing at the smell of his cologne on me.

Carlo's affable expression was quickly replaced by an offended scowl.

"What the hell?" he spat, still holding me with one hand. "You've been trying to seduce me since we met. What's wrong now?"

"Excuse me, what?" I blinked with incredulity. Me, seducing *him*?

I skipped over a coil of rope and tried to remind myself that Carlo was a rueful, lonely widower, and that Berenice had enlisted me to cheer him up, not to sink him into utter misery for the rest of eternity. I should be striving to be nice;

however, cheering him up was one thing, and going along with slobbery, unwanted kisses out of sheer pity was something else entirely.

"You are an awesome guy, Carlo, but…" I placed a hand on his forearm and racked my brains for the least painful way to reject his advances. "You know…"

Before I could finish the sentence, the unmistakable silhouette of a cloaked, dark man became visible in the distance. He was standing by the water, on a roof not far from the docks, staring directly at Carlo and me as his long cape billowed around him.

I opened and closed my mouth, unable to believe what my eyes were seeing.

That couldn't be.

My throat shrank as I imagined what he might have witnessed—and what he might be thinking at that very moment. I wanted to wave at him, but that would have alerted Carlo of his presence.

"We need to get back," I pleaded, my excuse unfinished. Carlo nodded grumpily; he crouched and tied up the boat in complete silence.

It took him a while to steady the vessel so we could disembark. When I finally stepped on the pier, I looked up to the roofs of the city.

By then, Clarence was gone; and with him, half of my heart.

Chapter 16

Alba

The car ride back to the inn took place in a maddening silence. Carlo's endless chit-chat had been replaced by a sequence of frustrating grunts and shrugs, which made the road seem much longer than the first time around. Meanwhile, my mind kept churning, desperate to discern whether I had imagined Clarence's figure looming over the lake in the half-darkness. His face hadn't been visible in the distance, but how many dark-haired, cloak-wearing men would climb on a roof after nightfall and stare at me being kissed by a stranger?

When Carlo and I finally parted ways in the hallway of the inn, I let out a thankful breath and sneaked into my room, desperate to talk to Francesca.

My sigh of relief was abruptly replaced by a choked gasp.

Francesca was lying barefoot on my bed, and next to her was Clarence, sitting against the headboard with his arms behind his neck and those maroon eyes of his glaring at me with a myriad of unspoken questions.

The two vampires fell silent, their conversation interrupted by my sudden appearance.

"There, speak of the devil…" Francesca said, springing to her feet noiselessly and tipping her head toward me as she stretched her back in an impossible back arch.

Clarence's face was an expressionless mask, but his eyes kept turning brighter—and *redder*—by the minute.

"Clarence…?" I ventured, hoping he would give me a hint about his unexpected presence in my room.

He stood up right after Francesca and greeted me with the most proper and impersonal bow, all while smoothing down his black cloak.

"Good evening, Alba," he said with calm poise, "glad to find you *so* well." A tired, dazzling smile flashed in his face for a millisecond.

"Yes, me too… what a surprise…" I answered sheepishly. His tone and posture—keeping his distance, like two strangers—were making me terribly uncomfortable.

"This room is getting crowded," Francesca complained, putting on her black, pointed booties. "Forgive me for depriving you of my delightful company so soon, but I have an unmissable appointment with a lovely cellist." She pointed at my open suitcase and the bundle of white candles inside of it. "If I spend a little more time with her, I might be able to find out what happened to Julia. I suggest you take the night off, Alba. You and Clarence can play spiritism with your candles and mirrors until my return. Or whatever it is you usually do when left alone. Anyhow… see you two at sunrise."

She jumped on the windowsill with effortless elegance and waved goodbye, just to change her mind and peek in once again. This time she looked just at me, pretending Clarence wasn't there.

"Oh, and please don't allow the Englishman to distract you with weather talk for the whole evening," she said, grinning. "You two lovebirds have some imperative matters to discuss, and hopefully without much blood shedding." She licked her lips meaningfully. "Because shedding blood is always a waste, when you could do better things with it."

She winked and disappeared with a soft sweep of her skirts, leaving behind her characteristic sweet scent of roses and carnations.

***

"How are your vampire slaughtering lessons going?" Clarence asked me in a hoarse, and distractingly deep voice, as he watched me with a tilted head from the heights of his tall frame. His tailored white shirt was slightly wrinkled, a mute testimony of the long journey he must have endured. "Judging by the scene I just witnessed by the lake, I reckon you reached the chapter where you practice staking my heart?"

I bit my lip and turned off the ceiling lamp. The small one on the nightstand, dimmer and less intrusive, was better suited for the delicate conversation ahead. I sat down on the edge of the bed, nervously tapping on my knees. His eyes followed each of my moves in a troubling, vampire-stalking-his-prey manner.

"*St… staking* your heart?" I stuttered, too wary to get any closer. I had cornered myself by the bedside table while he stood on the opposite side of the room. His eyes were now flaming rubies, giving away the turmoil boiling inside him despite his calm stance.

Was he angry at me?

Clarence had never been angry at me before.

This was entirely new.

Did he even have a right to be angry?

I was about to start explaining about the whole misunderstanding with Carlo's stolen kiss when Clarence materialized beside me with a sly, noiseless leap. Then, with a hand-flourish, he pulled a shiny, long object out of his sleeve.

A dagger?

"Clarence? What's that for? You are starting to scare me." His eyes flared in the dim lit room, casting bloodlike sparkles. I had forgotten how daunting he could appear if he wanted to. "Stop staring at me like that. It's like your eyes are about to burst into flames. Turn them off, please."

He half-smiled and bowed mockingly, handing me the knife by the handle. I took it with shaking hands: it was at least one foot long, with an ornate carved hilt and an extremely sharp blade. I gaped alternately at him and the dagger, holding the weapon without much conviction.

"So, what am I supposed to do with this?"

"I realized I had never gifted you anything," he said huskily.

"And then you went and bought me a knife?" I blinked and stepped backwards. "Maybe times have changed, but the custom nowadays leans more toward chocolate and roses."

"It does have a rose, if you look at it close enough." He slid his icy fingers over the handle of the knife, casually brushing them against mine as he went along. My stomach clenched under his touch. The mixture of emotions emanating from him was overwhelming; the electric current radiating off his skin excruciating. "And I did not *buy* it. It was given to me a long time ago, and now I would like you to have it."

I tried hard to gather my wits and focused on the dagger. It had the initials *C. A.* engraved on the hilt, which was shaped like two wings wrapped over each other. The pommel was a half-open, silver rose. It was Clarence's emblem: I had seen it in his visit card a while ago. His gift, though odd, was a perfect work of art and clearly a deadly one, too. Particularly in the hands of someone as clumsy as I was.

"This is going to be a great tool to make peanut butter sandwiches," I noted in a jittery voice.

"*Mm-hmm*," he hummed, then sat on the bed and wrapped his arms around me, covering my hands with his as he guided me to put the dagger back into its sheath over my lap: the last step was deliberate, daring and flirtatious all at once.

I felt suddenly limp.

"Are you cross with me for coming here against your wishes?" he asked in a taunting tone.

I grunted weakly. "No. But, in all honesty, I didn't expect to see you here tonight."

"I noticed that," he drawled, tracing with his fingertips the petals of the silver rose, which now rested on my calves.

"Clarence..." I let out a ragged breath. His ongoing teasing was making it hard for me to think with clarity, let alone explain to him the misunderstanding with Carlo. Who was Carlo, anyway?

"I was concerned about you," he whispered into my ear. "And I missed you *so much*."

A soft knock on the window startled me, making me spring on the spot. He held me tighter, his scent swaddling me like a delicious cocoon. Francesca's blonde locks stormed into the room, framing a smirking face.

"Oh, I see there's some improvement already! Nice, nice." She nodded with satisfaction. "Sorry to disturb you again. Just pretend I'm invisible. Keep—" she studied us through half-closed eyes, her eyebrows raising as she spotted the half-sheathed dagger on my lap, "—doing whatever you were doing."

She whooshed by, her dress sweeping the floor behind her, and opened the closet. I remained completely still, trying to guess Clarence's thoughts. Francesca rummaged through my clothes carelessly, throwing most of my stuff to the floor.

"Did you lose something?" I asked impatiently, lifting the knife like a dangerous viper in order to admire the delicate craftsmanship. I couldn't wait for her to leave, so we could continue our thorny conversation.

Meanwhile, Francesca kept tossing my best dresses in the air like dirty rags. Once the closet was almost empty, she plunged so deep inside it that only her perfectly round, silk-cladded buttocks remained visible from where I was.

Clarence let out a low, frustrated growl, which rumbled all over my back like a miniature earthquake.

Someone knocked again, this time on the door.

"Who is it now?" I barked, rolling my eyes and setting the knife on the bedspread.

"It's me, Carlo!" His voice came from the corridor. "Open the door, *carina.* I know you're there."

For goodness' sake. What was this, the Marx Brothers' crowded cabin? I disentangled myself from Clarence, who apparently knew just enough Italian to understand the word *carina;* he wasn't too keen to let me go. I stood halfway between the bed and the door, brainstorming for a way to send Carlo away as fast as possible, without arousing his suspicions.

"Can you come back later?" I shouted. "It's not a good moment."

"No, this can't wait," he answered, banging on the door.

"Okay, give me a second!" I yelled back, then turned to the vampires. "You two, into the closet!" I commanded in a hiss.

Francesca obliged tamely, squeezing her slight body into the wardrobe like an obedient bunny; but Clarence stood by the wooden piece of furniture with a deep, angered frown. I mouthed the word *"Now!"* holding his shimmering gaze.

"It will take me just one minute," Carlo said from the corridor.

"Yeah, coming!" I answered, slipping the dagger under the bedspread to hide it from Carlo's view.

I grabbed the doorknob and threw Clarence a fierce glance. Or, at least, what *I hoped* was a fierce glance. Reluctantly, he obeyed and folded his limbs tight enough to fit into the closet. He didn't close the door completely: instead, he left a narrow slit so he could peep into the room. As a result, his ferocious, glowing eyes were still clearly visible from the outside.

I *really* needed to get rid of all those unwanted visitors as soon as possible, so we could discuss in peace not only the incident with Carlo, but also everything else which was amiss in our relationship. If there was any time left, we might also address other subjects, such as stakes, vintage daggers, and their uses.

Impatiently, I leaped back to the closet, kicked the door into place and locked it. *There, perfect.* Now those smoldering eyes were impeccably concealed and taken care of.

I jumped over the heap of clothes and blankets Francesca had kindly left on the floor and opened the door of the room.

Carlo was waiting in the narrow hotel corridor, holding a sad-looking bunch of weeds and wildflowers in one hand. I offered him a tense grin, which was supposed to be an innocent smile.

"Hi, Carlo, I was about to—" I hesitated. "—take a shower," I said, mainly because *get the hell out of here* didn't sound like the kind of thing you would say to a grieving widower.

"I just came to apologize for… before," he told me, handing me the bouquet. "I picked these for you in the meadow. Take them as a peace offering."

"Yes, yes, *Namaste*," I said, snatching the flowers off his hands with little care. Half of them fell to the floor due to my sloppy handling, and the rest scattered all over the desk.

"What's this weird smell?" Carlo asked, sniffing around.

"I have no idea what you're talking about," I answered. Francesca's carnation perfume was clearly perceptible. If I paid attention, I could also discern Clarence's rusty, forest-like scent. And, for someone who knew what to look for, the very slight but lingering scent of blood was also noticeable—a telltale sign of vampire presence.

"Did you hurt yourself?" Carlo asked, wiggling his nose, "It smells like a… field hospital in here, kind of like… blood and flowers?" he peeked under the bed and made his way through the tossed clothes to the bathroom.

"*Whoa, whoa*, wait, what are you doing?" I stepped in front of him with my arms open. "This is *my* room. And no, I haven't hurt myself. I think it's your flowers. They are a bit rotten."

Carlo ignored my complaints and kept patrolling the place, checking the window handles and kicking aside the pile of clothes by the bed in order to open the drawers one by one. By then I'd had enough, so I grabbed the knob of the highest one to deter him.

"Will you stop already? What do you think you are going to find here?" I asked with exasperation.

He lifted an eyebrow. "You tell me. Given the gory smell I was thinking… a hiding burglar? Illegal drugs? Stolen weapons?"

I stopped him one second before he tried to sit on the bed, right on top of Clarence's dagger.

"You are joking, aren't you? I haven't killed anyone, if that's what you're thinking. Now please stop searching my room and leave." In order to make a stronger case, I added the best excuse which came to mind in a rush, "As you see, my clothes are all over the floor. It would be embarrassing if you happened to stumble upon, *um*, my dirty laundry."

The trick worked, just not the way I had expected it to. He *did* stop searching the room, but his face started to glare with mischief.

"Are you challenging me?" he asked, in a lustful tone which didn't bode well for me. "I *love* dirty laundry."

No. Just no.

A strong thump resounded from inside the closet, and I threw myself against it just in time to pretend I had tripped and fallen.

Carlo tilted his head and approached the wardrobe with crinkled eyes, ready to open it.

"Seems I'm all thumbs today!" I said with feigned cheerfulness.

Another thump interrupted me, this one impossible to conceal. Clarence was trying to get out. And he would in no time unless I did something to prevent it.

Meanwhile, Carlo was fiddling with the lock.

My heart started to race.

"Carlo, don't you dare touch my closet!" I shrieked, stepping between him and the wardrobe. "It's private!"

The wooden doors trembled, and the closet threatened to tilt and topple over us. Carlo stared at it with growing wariness.

"What the hell are you keeping in here? A wild boar?"

"Yes, sure!" I yelled, "I keep *two* alpine boars in there, happy now?" I glued myself to the wooden doors, my arms extended from one end to the other. "And now, if you excuse me, I need to go to the bathroom. Bye, Carlo."

I pushed him towards the exit with all my might and someway managed to kick him out of the room before he could ask any more questions.

After slamming the door shut, I inhaled deeply a couple of times and waited for Carlo's steps to vanish down the hall.

It took me a good deal of courage to fish the key out of my pocket and let the vampires out once again.

"That was exceptionally entertaining," Francesca commented, fixing her hairstyle as she slipped out. "I am so glad I came back and didn't miss the show. But Clarence," she added, hopping gracefully toward the window and turning toward him, "don't you even dream about sharing a sleeping nook with me. You are too rowdy."

Clarence sat at the bottom of the wardrobe, silent but displaying an outraged expression.

"Find yourself someone else to share a closet with," Francesca said to him. "Or hopefully, a bed. That shall do you some good."

My cheeks started to burn at her comment, but Clarence didn't even notice, sulking as he was inside the wardrobe and glancing at the place where Carlo had been standing a couple of minutes ago.

"I feel gracious tonight." Francesca sighed. "So, I might ask Alice whether she has a spare, windowless room for me to stay and rest tomorrow. I'm still tired after the long flight. And now I shall take my leave, while the moon is on my side. I have investigations to conduct on my brother and his wife. If I find something useful, I will let you know at once."

Francesca left again, leaving me and Clarence alone. *Finally.*

I glanced at him, twisting my hands. He was still scowling at the air in front of him. Or possibly at Carlo's scent, which even my human nose could detect.

"I barely know that man—" I started to say.

"Fine. I believe you," he answered tensely, interrupting me in a way which made it clear that no more explanations were needed. Or wanted.

I blinked. *That was too easy.* I decided to elaborate, just in case.

"I didn't expect him to kiss me on the boat," I continued, defensively. Clarence reclined his wide back against the empty wardrobe, watching me with intense interest and a slightly prowling stance. "He took me by surprise. I didn't ask him to. It was awful. *Slushy.*"

"I told you," he said very slowly, his eyes on mine. "You needn't explain anything to me. You are a free, grown up woman."

The twitching vein on his forehead didn't seem to agree with his words.

"What?"

Free, like in *I don't want you anymore?*

Or free like in, *I totally understand and everything is truly fine.*

I brought my hands to my head in desperation. I didn't know what to think of his attitude. Was it indifference? Anger? A mixture of both?

"Clarence, please. Can you… I don't know. Can you bring back the old Clarence? The warm, funny one? The one I fell in love with?"

He was about to stand up but froze midway as he heard my last sentence.

"There was a time you loved me?" he said in a choked voice.

He stumbled back into a sitting position and gaped at me. I realized we had never discussed a proper name for whatever existed between us. Perhaps because he had been too busy playing escapism tricks since the day my divorce had become official. But now he was using the past tense and I didn't know whether to laugh at his shocked expression or retreat into a corner and cry.

I wrung my hands and let out a loud, sailor-like curse. For the first time in the whole evening his features softened, and he smiled tenderly in his accustomed way.

"We should be searching for Julia, not arguing like an old married couple," I said, closing my eyes to block the tidal wave of feelings.

"We are not arguing," he pointed out, standing up and finally getting out of the closet. "I'm just agreeing on everything you say."

I growled, because it was true, and that was even more frustrating.

"I'm so confused," I whined. "To be honest, I really wanted you to come. But I didn't expect you to. You said the crossing would be hard, and it would take you a long time," I sat on the bed with my arms around my knees and started to rock back and forth. "Francesca said you weren't coming. And yet, lo and behold, here you are, sitting in my room, four thousand miles away from home."

Clarence pushed my knee lightly to stop my anxious rocking.

"It's all true," he whispered. "But some people are worth crossing a whole ocean for. Once, twice or a hundred times." He sighed. "I just hope I didn't make up my mind a moment too late."

Chapter 17

Clarence

As I sat in that asphyxiating guesthouse chamber, there were two things I could not shake off my mind.

To begin with, my whole body ached with the primal need to kill a certain human. I could still *smell* him on her, and that was beyond maddening. My mind kept presenting me with a variety of efficient approaches to follow the man's trail and drain every single drop of blood in his arteries, until he collapsed at my feet and was safely wiped off the globe for good. Whether I liked it or not, it was in my nature, and it was proving exceptionally hard to fight the instinct.

One simply did not touch a vampire's love interest and walk away unscathed.

Which led me to the second topic, which was about to cause me to lose my senses. I might have been granted a long life, but that did not include the ability to turn back time. Herewith, past mistakes granted me the sheer agony of eternal revisiting and regret. One of those countless mistakes had been leaving Alba's side when she still trusted me. When she still *loved* me, as she had put it. Now I wished I could stop time and kiss her; not just *kiss* her, but also convince myself—or at least, pretend to—that she was completely mine. *Still* mine. If she ever was. For one night, if nothing else. Or one week. Or, ideally, for the entirety of her mortal life.

Regardless, there were a few issues preventing any of that from coming to fruition.

First, that slimeball from the boat. She must find him interesting; at least to an extent—why else would she agree to spend the day with him, alone, and on Christmas day no less?

It wasn't hard to guess she would not be delighted when they found him exsanguinated in the middle of a forest. *By yours truly*. This complicated things greatly and restricted my freedom of movement… and my ability to solve the matter in a vampire-appropriate manner.

My mind was a bloody mess and had been so for the last few months. The memories of Anne still haunted me, together with the awareness that I was doing to Alba the same Anne had done to me—the same I had loathed her for: first as a mortal, later as an immortal. Even if Alba insisted on keeping her head nicely buried in the sand, I was cursed to lure others into my arms and feed off them for the rest of my tormented existence.

The way things were, I just knew I wanted her.

But I wasn't good for her.

I craved her blood.

But I wasn't supposed to.

I wished to keep her forever.

But she was mortal and would remain so.

The Rules were clear on that last issue. And, even if I were to risk everything and break them, her opinion on the matter was clear: I had asked her on the night of the oath, and she had nearly fled The Cloister as a response. There would be no *forever* for us: I was bound to lose her.

Just like I lost Anne.

Just like I was doomed to lose all the lovely, charming, living creatures around me.

Unaware of my musings, Alba stood up and retrieved a few candles from her suitcase, which she lit all over the room right before turning off the other lights.

The electric buzzing stopped, and only then I realized how tense my back had been up to that moment.

She knew me so well.

Alba sat back on the mattress and stared at me: a small, startled bird. Her hair was up in a loose bun, and she radiated such warmth that I could have found her anywhere with my eyes closed, her presence like a blazing, glowing star in a barren desert of empty space.

She reached under the bedspread and picked up the dagger once again.

"Are you telling me why you gave me this?" she asked, dragging her delicate fingers over the decorated sheath.

"So you can defend yourself, what else?" I answered. I stood up and paced around the room, crossing my arms as I thought about the best way to turn the conversation toward the issues which were torturing me.

"Defend myself… *from what*?" She batted her eyelashes with innocence, making me smile.

"From other witches. Assaulters. Ex-husbands. Select the most suitable option for each occasion."

"Because stabbing people is a really smart way to resolve disputes, and I'd probably excel at it anyway." This time it was she who laughed.

I lifted a finger to catch her attention. "Also, vampires. I hear there's at least one stalking you." I nodded intently, observing her reaction.

"Stalking me?" She snorted. "I wish he was!" She shook her head sadly. "That one vampire seems to be always too busy to go to dinner with me, let alone stalk me. As for the rest of them, I'm not afraid; why should I be?"

"You must be the only person on earth capable of asking such a question. Why, Alba? Why should you?"

"Because…" She watched me, open-mouthed, looking truly clueless as she waited for me to finish the sentence for her.

"You are about to fail your *Supernatural Creatures 101* class." I huffed.

"I have no idea what you expect me to say. Vampires don't like my blood." She threw her hands in the air.

"Well, I do."

She was as surprised by my confession as I was myself. I had not planned to declare my little secret out loud. At least not yet.

"You do?" She blinked and pressed the dagger against her chest. "Since when?" She squinted at me with suspicion. "And how do you know?"

"That's a lot of questions at once." I had never found the scent of witches offensive. More an enticing oddity; an interesting disparity worth further… research. "But you should know by now that I have been under your spell for a long time."

"My spell!" She laughed. "There is no spell from my part. But, on the other hand, yesterday I saw Francesca hypnotize a girl. Okay, I'm not sure *what* exactly she did to her, but her voice was very… persuasive. I couldn't stop staring at her while she was speaking. How would you explain that?"

"*Hmm.*" I knew what she was talking about. I had seen Francesca do that before. "I don't know how she does it. It might be a peculiarity of female vampires. Or just one of Francesca's intrinsic talents."

"Are you completely sure?" She pulled at the tie holding her hair, releasing dark waves of lightly tangled hair and allowing them to fall over her shoulders with a soft swishing sound. I fantasized about running my fingers through those locks and working my way through the defying tangles, just to progress down her back and unbutton those dreadful Wild West trousers of hers…

I forced myself back into the present just to find her staring at me with a puzzled expression, unaware of the direction my musings had taken. What was the question, anyway?

"Absolutely," I muttered, hoping the answer made sense. I had lost track of the conversation by then.

"So, are female vampires more dangerous than their male counterparts?" She spoke with that characteristic, charming curiosity of hers, as her invisible defensive walls started to descend once again.

"Just think about praying mantises and lionesses, and you might uncover a pattern," I told her. The thought of *her* as a vampire flashed in my mind, but I shook it off as quickly as it had presented itself. That was a *dreadful* idea. One I should not even contemplate.

"Oh. So that's why Francesca keeps calling you a wimp." She nodded, and her eyes opened wide and round in sudden understanding.

"Pardon me? She calls me a *what*?"

I stopped pacing around the room and stood, affronted, in front of Alba. She started to laugh, holding on to her stomach. I wanted to be angry at Francesca's demeaning remarks, but the only thing I could feel was an excruciating pain in the middle of my chest, which I did my best to ignore.

Alba composed herself and her face became suddenly somber.

"Truth is," she said, as though stricken by a sudden, illuminating thought, "Francesca might be right. You didn't step in to defend me when Elizabeth came up with her ridiculous blood oath. I was so disappointed, Clarence." She threw me a sad glance, and I looked away. She was right. "You were supposed to be my guardian in The Cloister, and I took to considering you my guardian angel, cheesy as it may sound. But I think the days I thought of you in such terms are over. Which is sad, after all we've gone through."

The pressure in my chest became so intense that it left no space whatsoever for any air in my lungs. Fortunately, I didn't need to breathe in order to survive. Otherwise, I might have died—*again*—on the spot.

"It pains me to hear that," I said, slowly. "But I am too indebted to Elizabeth to counter her in public. Also, I'm far from being an angel. You should have known that from the start."

Why was her revelation so distressing? Wasn't that what I had wanted all along, the reason I had tried so hard to stay away from her? I had striven to release her from my influence, to disclose to her the bleak reality: to free both of us. I needed to be absolved from the pain and guilt which loving a mortal entailed. This would also free her from the sorrow I was bound to bring into her life.

"But you were. At least to me." She sighed, swinging her feet back and forth over the edge of the tall bed, like a little girl.

I knelt in front of her and wrapped my arms around her waist, resting my head on her lap. I took a deep breath of her scent as she threaded her fingers through my hair and started to stroke it gently. Her touch was balmy and left faint spurs of chaotic magic all over my neck, making my hairs stand on end.

"Alba." I swallowed before continuing. "You know I'm cursed. You know it's other people's lifeforce that keeps me alive and sane. If you saw that side of me; if you knew where my lips have been after a night outside, would you still want me? Would you still trust me?" She stared at me with dismay, just like I had expected.

"You kiss them, too?" she asked weakly.

"I don't, but does it matter? I lure them, hold them, feed off them. Their blood runs through my veins. Try to fathom the intimacy of it all, just for a second."

"Trust me, I have," she answered. She was on the verge of tears. But I needed to tell her. I could not stand the farce any longer.

I raised my head from her lap so I could look into her eyes. They were dewy but alert. She leaned toward me, expectant.

"I have been trying to set you free, but when I saw you kiss that man by the lake—" I started, but my voice broke. I steadied myself before continuing, "—it was like a stab through the heart. If you were to thrust that silver dagger into my chest, it would not hurt any worse. But, tell me, my Isolde, how would you feel if you saw me holding someone else? How can you live with the facts, with what I do, when even *I* cannot live with it myself?"

"How?" She pulled at my hair distractedly, seemingly searching for an answer. "Because that's how things are. It's not always easy. It's not ideal, either. But it's not your fault, Clarence. I realized very soon this was going to be a *take it or leave it* situation. So, I opted for… taking you as you were." She shrugged. "I thought you knew."

***

Alba's hands slid down my nape and whirled past my hunched shoulders. She pulled me upwards, away from the refuge of her warm embrace until our eyes met.

"It should be my choice to fly away or stay," she whispered, swaying forward to reach my ear. Her living breath, overflowing with the intensity of mortal life, caressed my gelid skin, thawing a small part of my qualms. "Avoiding me won't change the way things are."

I drew her eyebrows with my fingertips, playing her soft cheekbones like piano keys, and rested them on her lips, so plump and rosy and naked of any disguises and artifices. She shivered under my touch.

"Alba…" My voice came out as a yearning growl, giving away my inner turmoil.

In a quick move, she cast away her rough

woolen sweater. Only a sheer, tight camisole covered her upper body, and she lowered the thin straps of the garment slowly, with clear intent; placing emphasis in each of her actions, watching me. My eyes followed her fingers, enthralled by her movements as she exposed her neck.

I knew what she was trying to do and—to my consternation—the anticipation was killing me. Just the thought was enough to daze me. My fangs tingled, her rushed heartbeat deafening me into near unconsciousness.

"You don't have to—" I tried to tell her.

She brushed her dark hair away from her shoulders and tilted her head seductively.

"Yours," she whispered, offering her silken neck.

By then I had already forgotten my name, my origins and my date of birth. *Both of them.*

Our lips clashed.

Cold against hot.

Hard against soft.

"You don't need to…" I repeated without conviction, mumbling against her smooth cheeks.

She nodded, gasping for air, and the rest happened in a blur.

My fangs descended and brushed her skin, and her body squirmed under mine. I paused and she whined softly, pressing me against her in a mute offering. I kept caressing her. Soothing her. Tasting her. I drank, relishing the ecstasy of our union, and she moaned quietly, her eyes and mine rolling back with pleasure. Her blood was surprisingly sweet, brimming with magic sparkles. If this lasted one minute, or one thousand, that I will never know, because time came to a halt while she was in my arms.

I had to gather all my strength to let her go.

That night we loved each other by candlelight, oblivious to the constrictions of time and space, and I held her until there was nothing but silence and quenched thirst.

***

"What are you doing?" Alba asked, a few hours later. The moon was high, and her voice sounded sleepy, lazy. She dragged the syllables adorably.

"*Shh*, you can fall back asleep. I'm just healing these bite marks," I whispered into her ear.

"No." She placed her hand over the two twin dots on her skin, pushing me away from her. "Leave them."

"Someone could see them, my dear."

She shook her head. "Just for tonight."

I nodded and huddled against her like the warmth-seeking parasite I was. The exhaustion of the ocean crossing started to flood me, making my eyes droop. I fell into a deep slumber, and for the first time in years, they were not haunted by memories of devastating fires and gone lovers, but brightened by the company of a lovely, breathing witch instead.

Chapter 18

Alba

I kicked off the covers in my sleep, covered in sweat.

It was scorching hot in the room, which was unusual for this time of year. Particularly, while sharing the bed with a large, cold-blooded creature.

My fingers explored the mattress idly, my eyes still closed: Clarence should have been by my side, but unease started to creep over me as I felt over the sheets, stretching my arm as far as I could and finding nothing.

He wasn't there.

In my lethargic state, I struggled to recall the mystifying events of the previous evening. Had I imagined everything? His arrival? Our conversation? Everything that happened afterwards?

Clarence's absence weighed down the air like an object in the room: I could almost touch it. Placing both hands over my heart, I evoked Alice's words when she had told us about Julia, *"we can sense other witches,"* she had said. *Only witches?* I pondered mindlessly. I had never been able to sense any creatures at all, but suddenly, an unusual, new glow was radiating from my core: it was pleasant, but foreign. I stretched in the bed, letting my skin brush voluptuously against the coarse linen of the sheets.

As I gradually stirred awake, a harsh whiff of smoke invaded my airways. Was it barbecue night in *Foresta Chiara* Inn? I couldn't remember. I was still too dozy after… after everything that ensued when I took off that old woolen sweater.

The acrid-smelling air made me cough and an auburn radiance blinded my half-open eyes. I didn't remember lighting so many candles. Come to think of it, I didn't recall blowing any of them out, either.

My brain finally powered up, and a bout of panic struck me when the situation around me sunk in.

The room was in flames.

I needed to get out, and fast.

Coughing, I yanked the top sheet and draped it around my bare chest, grabbing my purse from the nightstand in a sweeping move.

I jumped over the burning heap of clothes by the closet and tore the door open. The metal of the door handle scalded the palm of my hand, making me scream.

I ran down the corridor, wheezing and yelling, *"Fire! Fire! Wake up! Get out!"*

Room doors started to open, drowsy guests

in pajamas rubbing their eyes in confusion as they stumbled out of them.

"Fire! *Fuoco!*" I shouted in all languages I knew, and people started to follow me to the exit, running around like confused sheep as I barked at them like a herding dog. They pushed each other to get out first, the crackling sounds becoming a loud roar. I grabbed an elderly lady's hand and ushered her out first, struggling to put order in the chaos. I knocked on each door as I passed, desperate to wake everyone up. Whenever I tried to breathe, my lungs filled with dark, bitter smoke, leaving me breathless.

When I finally reached the emergency exit at the end of the corridor, I instructed the rest of guests to run toward the parking lot. As soon as I stepped outside, my legs became wobbly. I was drowning in the smoke I had inhaled, like a wasted pearl diver who had overdone his underwater time. When I tried to breathe in again, my airways let out hissing sounds and I feared I would faint.

People were screaming, children wailing.

Berenice emerged out of a shed behind the house and acknowledged me with a curt nod. She was still in her nightwear, just like everyone else.

"I'll take over from here!" she shouted at me, then turned to the flustered guests. "Follow me!"

She pointed at a clear spot by the road, far enough from the fire and large enough for all the guests to wait in safety. She was oddly calm and steady: a military commander in a rainbow nightgown. People followed her blindly, soothed by her self-assurance.

I stood between the building and the forest behind it, an invisible cord pulling me toward the woods and preventing me from following the others. The blaze soared over the inn, followed by a huge cloud of black smoke which ascended into the night sky like an ominous ghost.

Panic strangled my insides.

Where was Clarence?

And where was Carlo?

Neither of them was visible amongst the small crowd congregated by the other side of the road.

Dragged by an invisible force, I headed to the forest, leaving Berenice and the rest behind.

The night was chilly, and as I delved deeper into the woods, the stench of burnt plastic and smoke was slowly substituted by the fresh scent of pine, fir, and spruce. The brittle grass let out soft crunches under my foot soles, just like treading over tiny shards of glass. I walked in a straight line, allowing my newly found instinct to guide me.

In the distance I spotted a clearing, the space around it draped in Clarence's unmistakable scent. I was still wearing nothing more than a thin linen sheet, my clothes left behind during the escape, and my teeth started to chatter in the cold night. I held the sheet tight, trying not to get tangled in the thorny vegetation.

The screeching of sirens in the distance announced the arrival of firemen to the inn. Their sound came from afar; I must have wandered for longer than I thought through the frosty bushes.

I heard shouts and grunts coming from ahead, and I tiptoed to the last row of trees by the edge of the clearing, leaning against a wide trunk to scan the scene.

Clarence and Carlo were in the middle of a circle of trees, entangled in a fight to death.

Carlo lay on the ground, and even under the shy moonlight I could see the thick, brownish stains covering his closely shaven blond hair. Clarence was over him, pinning him against the ground. His eyes were gleaming red, not unlike the blazing building behind me, and had a demented expression which knocked out the little air I still had in my lungs. I stared in shock as he growled and violently reached for Carlo's neck with a hand which didn't seem to have fingers anymore, but sharp, deadly claws instead.

"No!" I screamed, rushing out of the shrubbery to stop him. "Let him go!"

Clarence swiveled, a dazed expression in his face. There were no signs of recognition in his fiery eyes.

A flame of fury grew inside me.

What was he doing? Just because Carlo had tried to kiss me? How could he be so possessive, so spiteful?

Our eyes met, and then he finally saw me. Stunned, he stood hesitant for a couple of seconds.

This brief falter was enough for Carlo to skip out of his grip and grab a small metallic object which lay beside him on the grass: Clarence's silver dagger.

Carlo lifted the weapon, and Clarence turned around to stop him, only a second too late.

I screamed, or rather I tried to, because breathing suddenly became impossible. I tried to run toward both men, desperate to prevent them from killing each other.

A heavy object hit my head, and I never reached them. I fell half-unconscious onto the frosty mulch and the arms of a stranger dragged me back toward the burning inn and away from the fight.

Chapter 19

Alba

"My little child," a shrill voice said, "how could you be so naïve?"

An old lady was holding my hand and wiping the two tiny wounds on my neck with a damp gauze. I had no idea where I was, but the place reeked of sanitizers and herbs, and whatever she was putting on my skin stung like hell.

Green-haired Alice was kneeling beside me, in the middle of a circle of several women, young and old. Their faces hovered over mine as they sat cross-legged on the floor. I lay naked on a hard mat in the middle of an ample room, surrounded by candles and covered by a lavender-perfumed comforter.

A wrinkled, saintly-looking lady propped me up and forced me to drink a bitter concoction. It was disgusting, and I tried to spit it out, but she pulled my hair and tilted my head backwards. Ignoring my protests, she poured the liquid straight into my throat. I coughed so hard that I thought I was about to spit out my lungs in the next fit.

One of the women started to chant, or possibly pray, and her voice lulled me back to sleep, exhausted and breathless.

When I came to again, I didn't know how long I had slept: it could have been five minutes or five days.

"Where am I?" I mumbled, stirring on the floor. Sunrays leaked through basement windows on the upper half of the walls. My lungs felt shallow, and I struggled to breathe deep enough.

Berenice, the inn owner, was stretching on all fours beside me, and stared at me with her face upside down, her hair resembling an old broom.

"*Sleeping Beauty* woke up," she sang.

"Hi," Alice greeted me, wiggling her fingers shyly.

"Alice?" I asked, searching for Francesca. *Weren't they supposed to be together?* "Where's Francesca?" A strange whistle escaped my lips against my will. "Where is...?" *Clarence*, I wanted to say, but I couldn't decide whether it was wise to ask.

"Don't you worry about the bloodsuckers," Berenice said, stretching her arms and moaning. "We sent them somewhere secure enough. They won't touch you again."

I tried to utter a curse, but the air just wheezed out and tickled my throat, making me cough.

"You can consider yourself lucky that you didn't take one more breath of that nasty smoke, little child." That was the grey-haired lady speaking, the one whose face I had seen first. "You know what they say: *three breaths will maim you; but four breaths will kill you.* Luckily, you must have stopped somewhere around two-and-half."

I propped up on my elbows. The room resembled a yoga studio, with mats on the floor and decorations on the walls featuring goddesses and Catholic saints. Currently the air smelled clean and well ventilated, with a tinge of incense and candles; the stench of sanitizer was gone.

"How did I end up here?" I asked, unable to recognize anyone but Alice and Berenice.

"My name is Valentina Caruso," the elderly woman said, "and we call ourselves The Witches of the Lake. We are the longest-serving coven in Lombardy-Venetia, and we are glad to welcome you to our humble home. We have been trying to contact you for a few months, but you never seemed inclined to talk to us."

I frowned, remembering the times I had been approached by other witches in the past. None of those experiences had been too pleasant.

"So, it was you, all this time?" I asked cautiously. "When I was attacked in the street this summer? Stalked by all sorts of strangers?"

Valentina winced. "Of course not. We would never harm you. We just sent some friends to talk sense into you, because it's imprudent to allow young, capable witches to walk around wielding magic in public places. We were worried people would start asking questions. We also heard you had fallen captive, and I doubt you would have survived much longer in such bad company."

Her eyes fixed meaningfully on the bite marks on my neck.

"This is not what it looks like," I said, covering the marks with one hand. The words didn't come out very convincing, and the women—the *witches*—watched me silently, ostensibly assessing my sanity. Memories of the previous night started to weave once again in my mind, in a complex, confusing tapestry of feelings and images. First the excitement, the fear of the unknown. Then the exhilarating, almost unexpected pleasure. The fire and horror which ensued. The recollections were so bewildering that my head literally started to spin.

"I think it's never too early to learn the basics," Valentina said sternly. "Lesson one: a witch never trusts a vampire." Her tone was harsh, but erudite. "They will fool you. They will trick you. They will make you believe they are capable of love, that they will never harm you, because you are *sooo* special." She dragged the syllables mockingly. "Wrong!" She slapped the floor abruptly, making me jolt. "They are murderous, ruthless creatures. They covet our blood. They have no soul. Why do you think they never stand in front of mirrors? Because they fear us! Because they know witches can see their true nature in the glass. And do you know what we see?"

I frowned my lips and waited for the impending expletive.

"Bloodthirsty beasts," Berenice finished the sentence for her, like the nerdy girl in a high school class. She was doing a headstand and shook her legs in the air for emphasis.

I wanted to contradict her; defend Elizabeth and the rest of inhabitants of The Cloister. But the image of Clarence trying to kill Carlo flickered in my mind like a lethal flash of lightning.

So, I did the next best thing.

I started to weep inconsolably.

Valentina started to chant again, with her eyes closed. Meanwhile, Alice helped me to another revolting drink from a brown clay mug.

"There, there, sister. You drink this. You are safe now. Say thanks to Berenice, she found you and brought you here. Otherwise, you would have died in that forest. The fire spread to the woods. Even if you had managed to escape the fire, the area was infested with vampires yesternight."

I lay back down on the mat and closed my eyes, concentrating in maintaining my lungs as full of air as possible while keeping the rumbling and coughing at bay. It wasn't as easy as it sounded, and the lack of oxygen made me awfully light-headed.

The witches turned their attention away from me. They must have thought I had fallen asleep once again, because they started to talk among themselves.

"So the other one ran away… but did you see what he did to that man?" Alice said to Berenice. It sounded like they were resuming a previous conversation.

"His name is Carlo, I know him," Berenice whispered, just loud enough for me to hear her. "He's my old friend, and he's so brave, and… oh, Alice! I hope he'll survive!" Berenice's voice trembled, and I heard her legs flop on the floor with a low thump.

"He will," Valentina said, ending her chant with the strike of a tuning fork. "We'll cast a healing spell for him tonight. He deserves our blessings: his findings will make us look good in Natasha's eyes, and get us some most needed funding to keep the coven afloat for a while longer."

"Who is Natasha?" I asked weakly, opening an eye.

The women gasped, and I thought for a second Valentina was going to stab me with her tuning fork.

"Didn't you put her to sleep?" Berenice asked dryly.

"Oh, well. I should have sung a little longer. Give her some more tea. That should knock her out."

***

I drifted in and out of consciousness for one night, maybe two, until Valentina kicked me softly with the tip of her bare foot and fully woke me up.

"Do you intend to lie on that mat forever?" she asked in a stern voice.

The gray-haired witch stared at me with her arms crossed. She hunched over me, her twisted, arthritic toes on the jute mat, just an inch from my nose.

"Time to start with your education." She licked her finger and rubbed it over the marks on my neck. "These marks won't go away; seems you will have them forever. The scoundrel didn't even bother to erase them." Valentina shook her head. "Ah! They just get more wicked with the centuries. To mark a witch like a head of cattle! What will be next?"

I might be insane, but the idea of keeping Clarence's marks for the rest of my life lifted my spirits. At least, in this crazy rollercoaster of a life I had been cursed with, *something* would remain a constant. Something *of his.*

The memory of Carlo holding a knife over Clarence's head hit me like a tsunami, and I felt sick. Sick because of what Clarence had done, but also sick with worry for what might have happened to him afterwards. Everything felt so wrong, so surreal. Valentina recognized my unease and handed me a small bowl. I threw up, and once I was done, she took the basin away in silence.

I considered once again asking about Clarence but decided against it. I vaguely remembered hearing the witches say that *the other one* had run away after attacking Carlo. I prayed both of them had survived: I *needed* them to. I might not like Carlo but didn't wish him to die, especially at Clarence's hands. The very thought was unbearable.

Valentina combed her white mane with her fingers, making the golden chain of her glasses tinkle.

"Okay, okay, stand up. Breathe a little. Let's see how you are doing today."

The air rattled in my lungs, but there was some improvement.

"Do you think you could eat?" she asked me.

"Maybe."

"That's a good sign." She nodded with satisfaction. "Follow me upstairs. The coven is assembled, and there's food. Lots of it."

We climbed the stairs which, in my state, was analogous to hiking on Mount Everest under a blizzard. I had to stop to pant at least five times, because the frogs in my throat were seemingly having a house party.

A group of ten witches or so greeted us as we reached the living room. They were a wildly kaleidoscopic collective of women of assorted ages and backgrounds. The space itself perfectly matched Valentina's granny look: lacy curtains, doilies and dozens of houseplants in diverse stages of decay.

Valentina made me sit on the couch: a patterned velour monstrosity covered by a crochet throw. Berenice meditated nearby, crossed-legged in the middle of the musty carpet.

"Look who's here!" Alice said, standing up to greet me with a delighted expression in her dark eyes. "Valentina's teas are short of miraculous. No wonder she's the best herbalist in the whole of Lombardy!"

I eyed her with mistrust. They had mentioned sending Francesca *to a secure place*, and I doubted by that they meant The Cloister. Alice must have been involved which, in my eyes, made her very suspicious.

"Did you sleep well?" Berenice opened her eyes and studied me from head to toe. I was wearing a white linen sleeping gown down to my ankles, which I didn't remember putting on myself. "Not to be mean, but you snore really loud for someone so small."

I grunted instead of answering, because I had just stuffed my face with a piece of sponge cake and some grapes from a platter.

"So, we finally caught the elusive stray!" a woman said, standing up to shake my hand. "This calls for a celebration! I'm Gianna. We've met already. Do you remember me?"

She looked familiar. Not in a good way.

"Home improvement store? Emberbury? Last summer?" I ventured.

"Aha." She pursed her lips. "You were in the company of those enslavers of yours, if I recall correctly. It's a good thing you've escaped their thrall once and for all."

I slumped on the couch and closed my eyes. "I was with them *voluntarily*."

"Voluntarily!" Gianna gasped. "Look at what they did to you!" She pointed at the bite marks with disgust. I tried to hide them, but the borrowed nightgown was too big for me and kept sliding down my shoulders. "Do you know what would have become of you a couple of centuries ago?"

I shook my head, and all the witches stopped eating in order to gasp collectively.

Gianna continued, "You would have got yourself lynched for carrying the Devil's mark. And in such a visible spot! You are lucky today's doctors are stupid enough to believe this could have been a snake… or a really large mosquito."

A really large mosquito, indeed. Six feet three or so. Dark hair, glimmering maroon eyes. Fairly handsome; oversized fangs.

"But you left, didn't you?" Berenice offered. "That wasn't the right place for you. We witches don't bow to anyone. We may assist others, but we don't prostrate ourselves. I'm glad you realized before it was too late."

"*Uh…*" I raised a hand, willing to correct her, but Gianna interrupted me.

"Yes, you should stay with us," she said. "We are the second most powerful coven in Europe. You won't regret it."

"The second?" I asked, but their belligerent looks told me they weren't happy with that second place they were holding, so I steered the conversation to other, more pressing matters. "Ladies," I said cautiously, "I'm thankful for your hospitality, but what do you mean when you say I should *stay* here? Stay, like, forever? Because that's impossible. I have kids at home, a job, a life." Valentina watched me with disdain, like one would a little child who refuses to go to bed. "I just came on vacation to meet a friend. What day is it, by the way? I have a plane to catch..."

A monstrous coughing fit prevented me from finishing the sentence, and Valentina snorted.

"You're not going anywhere without our prior blessing. You are too troublesome. And currently, you can't even walk up the stairs on your own anyway."

"But my daughters…" I said. I needed to call Minnie and check on them. "Wait, have you seen my phone?"

"Yes," Valentina answered haughtily. "I think it was in that bag you were carrying. Alice, can you go to the foyer and bring it?"

Alice disappeared through a narrow gray door. When she came back, she was holding my phone, which she handed to Valentina.

"Is this yours?" The elderly lady asked me, wiping the screen with a handkerchief. I nodded and tried to seize it, but she hid it behind her back. The notification lights were flashing. They must have charged it: such a nice gesture. "Good to know," she said, "now earn it back."

"Excuse me?" I nearly choked on my words. "Do you think I am twelve years old?"

"Judging by your witch milestones, you're closer to a three-year-old." She smirked. "And not a very clever one."

***

The witches fed me cookies and panettone and kept fluttering around me for the rest of the afternoon, checking my pulse and the whites of my eyes to make sure I wasn't going to faint on them yet again. After a while, the older ladies left the living room to make dinner, appointing Alice to watch over me. She sat down next to me silently and munched on a fistful of crunchy grissini, displaying a preoccupied expression.

"Tell me what happened to Francesca," I demanded in a low voice, hoping to take advantage of her visible unease.

She stared silently at the snacks in her hand, a shadow of doubt in her face.

"Alice?" I repeated. "You must know, she was with you, wasn't she? Would you please tell me? Is she alright? Were there others, too?"

Before she could answer, Valentina burst into the room.

"What's going on here?" she asked, hands on hips.

"She's asking about the pretty vampiress," Alice mumbled, averting her eyes.

Valentina huffed. "She's well-guarded now. Our friend will take care of her and make sure she doesn't bite anyone ever again."

"What friend?" I asked nervously.

"You ask too many questions."

Another elderly lady appeared and shoved a bowl of soup in my direction. She sank into a couch and started to play loud video games on a tablet. "Alice, bring a gag from the basement, will you, dear? I can't hear the music properly," she said without lifting her eyes from the screen.

"It's fine, Agnes," Valentina answered, to my relief. "How is she going to eat if we gag her?"

"We have straws somewhere. The eco-friendly ones?"

I grabbed the bowl and quickly slurped the bland soup they had brought me, just in case. Hopefully they were just teasing me, but their impassive expressions were hard to read.

The door opened and the rest of witches joined us, scattering all over the room with rounded bowls of steamy brew on their laps.

"Why do you care so much about those creatures?" Asked the video game lady. "They are a plague, and prone to overpopulation. What's wrong with pest control?"

A couple of witches snorted in the background.

"I'd just like to know my friend is okay," I said, hoping they would not consider my words offensive enough to gag me. "She came here to help me."

Snide glances ensued.

"To help you!" Berenice sneered. She was hanging upside down from the back of the couch, her soup forgotten somewhere on the carpet. "How could you believe such a blundering lie?"

"I think someone should explain the ABCs to her once and for all," another woman said, standing up and walking towards the bookcase in search of something. "Seems she's still very green."

"Would you like some bread?" Alice offered, hovering around me with a wicker basket covered with a napkin.

I took a piece. The bread was white and spongy, still warm from the oven.

"We are the daughters of the Witches of Old," Valentina's voice raised, deep and majestic, surprising me with her authoritarian tone. I set the bread aside to pay attention to her sudden, dignified speech. "We keep the secrets of our tradition, protect those of our kind and the ones weaker than us, and defend commoners from supernatural threats."

As Valentina hunched in her armchair right next to me, wilted and frail, her words started to resemble the opening lines of an old fairytale, more than a description of her role in the real world. How could that tiny, grey grandma—or any of her friends—protect anyone from a supernatural threat? She seemed like the kind of person who wouldn't even be able to protect herself from a mugger, let alone an ancient vampire. Still, she was looking at me in a way which reminded me of Elizabeth when she issued commands in The Cloister.

"We have carried out this philanthropic, tough work for generations," she finished.

"What supernatural threats are we talking about here?" I asked timidly.

"Your *friend* Francesca, for example," Valentina said, crossing her arms and lifting her chin defiantly.

"It's interesting that you say that," I said, unable to help myself, "because the first time I met Alice," I pointed at the green-haired girl with contained anger, "she seemed to enjoy Francesca's attentions very much."

"Alice was brave enough to risk her own life and help us catch that dangerous creature. We all know they are full of empty promises, and we'll never be safe from their bites, despite our scent. Do you know, by any chance, why they find it so repulsive?"

I shook my head, and she continued.

"Because, in the old times, some vampires believed that drinking witch's blood would reverse their curse. They slaughtered many of our kind in their quest to walk under the sun once again. Out of desperation, one of our ancestors devised a spell which made our scent repulsive to their senses. But beware of a vampire who has tried a sample of your blood… that one will always come back for more. Our blood allows the magic to run through their pestilent veins for a while. For many days, they will be able to sense your presence, no matter where you hide… and once they have tasted you, they won't stop until they drain you."

I must be really desperate, because her explanation sounded almost like good news to me.

"Is that true?" I asked with growing interest. "Does our blood reverse their curse?"

Valentina puffed. "Of course not. And even if it did, would you sacrifice yourself just to save one of them? What good would that do?"

A crazy thought crossed my mind for a second, but I quickly shook it off. "No, of course not," I answered, setting the empty bowl on a side table. "I was just curious."

"You are still in his thrall." Valentina sighed and caressed the back of my head, carefully avoiding the spot where Clarence's bite marks were, like they were contagious. "Poor thing."

"There's no thrall," I protested. "Vampires can't bewitch humans. They told me themselves."

A couple of witches snickered in the background. "Do thieves tell you they are about to rob you?"

"I don't believe you." I crossed my arms. "They wouldn't lie to me."

"Some of our kind were like you in the past," Valentina said. "They all died gruesome deaths. Succumbed to their charms. Some were fooled into joining the ranks of the cursed, but witches are not meant to be immortal. We witches are servants of The Great Mother and as such, we are meant to go back to Her after our service is over." She raised her hands and lowered her head in prayer. "I hope you aren't considering anything as foolish as that, because you would meet a horrid end."

I tilted my head, hoping she would elaborate. I had secretly contemplated that option, since the day Clarence had teased me about turning me into a vampire right before the oath ceremony.

"Do you know how they do it?" she asked

coldly.

"No?"

Clarence never told me anything. He was a master at evading uncomfortable questions.

"Of course." Valentina waved a hand in the air contemptuously. "They never tell you the nasty details, do they? Only the glitzy, resplendent side of their world is to be shown: that's how they draw you in. But *Nonna* Valentina will tell you, don't you worry, my child." She sank a sharp nail into the crook of my neck and lowered her voice. "They drain your veins until your heart stops. Then, you die a horrible, slow, painful death." Valentina pinched my skin, making me flinch. "But that's nothing, trust me! Only the beginning of the agony. Right before you are gone, they force you to drink their blood. That works fine for ordinary humans, but not so much for us witches."

I swallowed and squirmed back and away from her sharp nails. "What happens to witches?"

"In the best of scenarios, they go back to The Mother. That's what happens most of the times, as far as I know. But sometimes things go awry and they turn into hideous monsters, unable to control their powers until their magic consumes them and everyone around them."

She paused and stared at me.

"I see," I mumbled quietly.

"Anyways, you stubborn little stray," she said, shaking her arm as if to dispel the heavy atmosphere created by her revelation. "You are here now, and they won't catch you again. Tell me, daughter. Do you want to learn magic?"

I took a deep breath and nodded.

"There are many things we can teach you, but first of all, we'll need to ascertain your level of ability." Valentina took my hand and inspected it from several angles. "Most stray witches are very weak, but that's okay. That still doesn't mean you won't be able to get better with practice. Even we, who kept our roots, have had to hide for generations, and many of our powers have been lost or forgotten. The books were burned; the secret keepers massacred. We are barely regaining our power. But I trust we will get it back one day. Soon. And you could be here with us to witness it."

Berenice stood up and took a book from a shelf, then laid it carefully on Valentina's lap.

"Magic," said the older woman mysteriously, locking her eyes with mine. Her gaze was intense, but I made an effort to hold it, because it looked like a test. She seemed satisfied with my resilience and, after a pause, she continued, "Magic is probably not what you think."

Chapter 20

Alba

The witches seemed terrified to leave my powers unattended for one second longer and concluded we should start with my lessons right away.

"Let's play ball," Valentina said, kneading an invisible mass between the palms of her hands. "That should be easy enough for her."

After that, they started to throw a ball at each other.

Or, at least, so they said.

In all honesty, I couldn't see any balls, let alone any spheres made of light and energy. To me, they were just a bunch of elderly ladies hopping around a dusty living room. They pretended to catch or miss their imaginary bundle, and the only thing I knew for sure was that they were having loads of fun with their absurd match.

"You said you were an engineer?" Valentina asked, kicking the invisible orb with her elbow and—I deduced—redirecting it toward Berenice.

"*Uh-huh*," I answered. Soon I would get used to strangers knowing more about my own life than myself.

"Then you must be familiar with Lavoisier's Law, am I right?" Valentina pretended to throw the ball over her shoulder, and Alice skipped like a goat to grab it with both hands before it—allegedly—touched the ground.

"I am." I nodded. At last, something I excelled at: trusty, real-world Physics. "*Energy can't be created nor destroyed; only transformed*," I recited proudly.

"Watch out!" Gianna said, swatting at my head as if to help me dodge the ball. She slapped me hard and left me feeling sore and giddy. I eyed her angrily. "*Ouch*! Was that necessary?" I shouted.

"Sorry, it was about to fly straight into your eye!" She apologized with a shrug and pretended to lift an imaginary object from the floor.

"That's right, energy can only be transformed." Valentina seemed pleased with my knowledge of Physics. "You can't create it out of nothingness. Which means you only have two options when working with magic: you either use your own life force or source it from somewhere else. The first option is easier, but it can drain you… or even kill you. The second is much harder, but if you learn to do it well, it could make you virtually indestructible."

"Sounds good," I admitted.

"You could blow up a whole city all by yourself!" Berenice clapped excitedly, like blowing up whole cities was something everyone should aspire to.

"Catch!" Alice squealed and gestured toward me.

I stood on the carpet and scowled at her. "There's no ball to catch," I grunted.

"Of course there is," Valentina reprimanded me, squatting to pick up the ball which wasn't there. "It's an *energy* ball. That's what I'm trying to teach you, but you are stubborn. And cork-brained."

I puffed at the insult and the air whistled as it came out of my lungs. "Whatever. I'm sorry. I can't see anything."

"Can't you at least feel it?" Valentina pretended to rub something against my chest, and I stared at her blankly.

"No. Nothing at all."

I stepped away from her, increasingly frustrated by the witches' stupid game.

"Valentina, she's a stray, what did you expect?" That was yet another elderly lady. Was it Agnes? Or Elda? They all looked so similar. "The hardest spells will never be at her reach. Why don't we let her try one of the easiest ones, so we see what she can do?"

Valentina nodded pensively and walked over to a bookcase. She picked up a leather-bound book and thumbed through it for a while. In the end, she flapped it closed, making it clear that there was nothing in there easy enough for me.

"The easiest spells are the ones which

include divination and scrying," she stated, setting the book aside. "Searching and finding. You could start with that. Alice is good at divination. She can teach you." Then she turned toward a teenage girl I hadn't seen before. "Lana," she commanded her, "bring us a scrying bowl, please."

The girl left and came back shortly thereafter, carrying a big silver platter with a matching antique bowl. It contained a black, shiny liquid: ink, I guessed. She placed it carefully onto a coffee table and made a curtsy before retiring to the background.

Valentina gestured towards Alice, who threw the inexistent energy ball into a knitting basket and joined us without much enthusiasm.

"We were having so much fun," she complained, kicking the basket surreptitiously.

"Incense?" Berenice asked, picking a few wooden sticks from a box and lighting them with a match. "To get into the right mood." She winked.

Valentina took my hand and made me kneel between her and Alice over the bowl, facing the coffee table. She raised her arms and sang one powerful, low note which seemed to originate at the very bottom of her gut. The other women started to chant on cue. Together they offered a phantasmagorical chorus, a mixture of low and high-pitched voices intoning a wordless hymn.

"What is…?" I wanted to ask what the chanting was for, but Berenice silenced me with an intimidating warning look.

I squirmed uncomfortably on the floor as

the smell of frankincense started to fill the room. My mistreated lungs weren't enjoying the smoke. And my brain wasn't keen on the chanting, either. A coughing fit shook me like an internal earthquake, and a downpour of memories of the fire sent me straight into panic mode, sweaty hands and trembling limbs included.

"Yes, this is good," Valentina said, misinterpreting my discomfort for some sort of esoteric trance.

"No… I'm…" I tried to explain the problem, but I drowned in yet another wave of coughs and the only thing I managed to utter was a gurgle. She nodded with satisfaction, maybe thinking I was trying to join them in their chanting.

Alice, on the other hand, tapped on my back with a preoccupied glance and offered me a sip of her own tea. I drank it and inhaled deeply, letting out a deep gasp. Grabbing the edge of the table with both hands, I tried to concentrate on the warm, smooth wooden surface in order to escape the haunting memories of my last night at the inn.

"Tell me, Alba," Valentina whispered, pointing at the silver bowl, "what can you see in the water?"

I bent over the liquid but only saw my own face in it, horribly pale and hollow-eyed. "Nothing. Just my own reflection."

"No. Look *inside*." Valentina pressed her index finger between my shoulder blades and started to draw spirals on my back.

I scrutinized the bowl once again.

Nothing.

My reflection informed me that I desperately needed a haircut. And possibly some makeup.

"Shall I add some candles?" Berenice suggested, setting candlesticks around us. Someone turned off the lights, and Berenice lit the candles ceremoniously, speaking in a foreign tongue as she went along. Once she was done, she blew lightly over the flames, making them shake and dance. The shifting flames drew abstract images on the surface of the water, and Valentina drew number-eight shapes with her hand over the bowl, glancing sideways at me.

"See. See inside," she commanded in a deep, almost hypnotic voice which reminded me of a dragon. Not that I had ever seen one. The thought was so ridiculous that it nearly made me laugh, but I restrained myself.

"Still nothing," I groaned, dropping my arms along my body like two saggy wings.

"Look closer," Valentina forced me to place my hands around the bowl once again. She was growing impatient, and I was increasingly exhausted. A headache was looming, and it was clear that this bowl had no intention of talking to me in the near future.

I decided to make up a story and get rid of those unrelenting witches. I really needed a break. And soon.

"Oh, yes, I see something." I squinted, pretending to focus a vision at the bottom of the bowl. They all held their breath, making me feel like the Oracle of Delphi.

"Way to go, sister!" Alice encouraged me. "Tell me, what do you see?"

"Something… rectangular," I ventured.

"Rectangular?" Valentina sprung back. She didn't seem too pleased. Maybe I should have said it was round. She clearly liked spheres better. "Okay," she said with mistrust, "big or small?"

"*Hmm…*" I gave it some thought. "I'd say it's about… sixty inches long?" She stared at me, unconvinced. "Sixty-three?"

"Well, that's unusually accurate." Valentina cocked an eyebrow. "But do tell us more about that rectangle. What is it doing?"

In my imagination, the bowl turned into a cup of ice-cream. A silver cup full of blood-red, slowly melting Italian *gelato*. "It's a chest freezer!" I shouted triumphantly. "The rectangle is a rusty freezer full of ice-cream!"

None of them seemed too impressed.

"Raspberry ice-cream," I added triumphantly.

Valentina sighed and stood up, clapping her hands to end my misery.

"Okay, okay, I think it's enough for the first time. This might be the worst scrying session I have witnessed in my life."

The witches turned on the lights, and soft snickers came from the sitting area.

"You know, Alba," Valentina said, "divination is not about making up stories, but about allowing them to flow through you."

I would have sworn I caught the word *dumbhead* coming from the other side of the room, but it was quickly drowned by the clinking sounds of teaspoons and teapots.

"Take her to her room," Valentina said to Alice. "And don't forget to lock the door." The last sentence sounded gloomy, and her eyes were disturbingly dark when she turned to me and said, "Little child… I think you should have remained an engineer, instead of trying to become a witch. It would have made things so much easier for everyone involved."

Chapter 21

Alba

"You must be tired," Alice motioned toward the jute mat on the floor, fluffing the pillows for me. "Energy work is exhausting, isn't it?"

I yawned and glanced lazily towards the small lavatory located in a corner of the basement room. I couldn't tell whether she meant that seriously or she was making fun of my poor scrying performance.

"So, you don't think I'm a fake, like Valentina? You believed what I saw?"

"*Hmm.*" She poured some more tea from a thermos and forced the cup against my lips, making me drink that foul beverage yet again. At this rate, I'd be soon growing tadpoles in my stomach. "It's hard to say. I have never heard of witches giving such accurate measurements in their visions, but… who knows? Maybe it's normal for you, given your professional background. Anyhow, what you did was energy work, and the first times it leaves you depleted, no matter the outcome. You need to rest."

"Thank you." I closed my eyes. I didn't care what she called it: I was certainly drained. "Tell me, Alice, am I a prisoner here?"

"I think Valentina called you an intern during our last meeting."

"So, can I leave whenever I want?"

"I don't think so."

"That sounds like a prisoner to me."

Alice shrugged. "Sorry. You are a little bit dangerous. To yourself, too."

She headed to the door and started to fiddle with a bunch of keys, trying them one by one in the lock.

"If I was so dangerous, do you think I would lie here in a half-coma and watch while you jail me in a basement?"

She lowered her eyes, her cheeks becoming a deep shade of crimson.

"I wish you would tell me what really happened to Francesca. She never meant you any harm. I'm worried about her."

"I should go," she muttered nervously. "I'm not allowed to talk to you about certain topics."

"Sure," I said, holding my head in the hopes it would stop pounding. It didn't, so I lay down and waited for Alice to leave.

Five minutes later, she was still there, biting her lips and staring at me like a featherless owl.

"Still here?" I snapped. The migraine was in full blow now. It was so bad that I caved in and drank a few sips of the witches' beverage.

"I know you are upset about the pretty vampiress," she whispered.

How perceptive of you, Miss Spinach Hair.

"First of all, I want to say I'm sorry." Alice closed the door, checking there was nobody outside, and came to squat next to my mat, a contrite look on her face. "I didn't know Valentina was going to do what she did. And I didn't know about Natasha."

"What did she do? And who is Natasha?"

Alice stood up once again and started to pace nervously around the room, checking behind the tapestries and altar decorations. She locked the door and came back to my side, still avoiding my gaze.

"What? Is the house bugged?" I laughed at the improbability of a bunch of grandmas hiding microphones behind their spell books and crystals, but stopped abruptly when Alice frowned and brought a finger to her lips.

"You never know." She served some tea for herself and sat cross-legged on the mat. "Was she really your friend?"

Was?

That was a tricky question. I wouldn't have considered Francesca a *friend*. She never really engaged too deeply with anyone at The Cloister, let alone *me*.

"I trust her, if that counts." I sat up and extended my arms over my knees. "I don't know what she did to you, and sure she can be eccentric at times. Reserved… constantly; and yes, plain weird, too, depending on her moods. But even a lousy witch like me can see there's no evil in her. Sadness—maybe; indifference, sure… but she's far from a monster, whatever Valentina thinks."

"I know what you mean. She's quite okay compared to the vampires we were warned about. Like that bloodthirsty monster who attacked Lombardi, did you see him? *Those* are the real enemy."

I rather omitted how that same *bloodthirsty monster* had shared my bed short before the fire. He had seemed more human than monster to me that night. Thinking about Clarence was as painful as holding a rose by the thorniest part of the stem: a beautiful torture; a highly masochistic one.

"When I first saw you and Francesca in the museum garden," Alice said, "I knew what she was right away, even though I had never seen a vampire before. It wasn't hard to guess that you were a stray, either. I thought she was there to kill me, but I didn't care: I was too depressed and… I sort of wanted her to."

"She did look at you in a strange way," I admitted, remembering the hungry glances Francesca had shot at Alice while sitting next to her at the gazebo.

When Alice spoke again, her eyes were surprisingly glassy. "But she was so… gentle. Patient. It might have been an illusion but, for a while, she made me believe that she truly cared for me."

It was dark, and the sound of steps outside the basement windows startled both of us: there must be someone strolling down the sidewalk, at street level. It was drafty and my nightgown was thin, so I stood up and closed the window. Alice waited for me to return to the mat, her silence punctuated by soft, veiled sobs.

"So, why are you crying, if you hate vampires? Didn't you say her sympathy was fake?" I asked her, trying not to sound too snarky. Surprisingly, my head felt slightly better after drinking the witches' brew.

"Because I'm not sure anymore what to think, and I suspect something terrible has happened to her because of me. When I told Valentina I had found a vampire, she was ecstatic. She devised a plan to capture her, using me as bait. I didn't want to collaborate, but what was I supposed to do?" I raised an eyebrow at her, ready to give her at least three better alternatives; but she shook her head and continued, "You don't understand. We are real witches, unlike you. I could tell you enough vampire horror stories to give you nightmares for the rest of your life."

"So, where is she now?" I interrupted her, although I was intrigued by those horror stories and hoped I would get to ask about them some other day.

Alice twisted her fingers. "Francesca wanted to know about that witch I had seen in Turanna's mirror, so I invited her to my house. It was a trap, of course. I don't know anything apart from what I already told you. The coven cast a joint spell on her so we could restrain her."

"What kind of spell?"

"A paralyzing spell. You need to be able to move things with your mind in order to cast it. If you can move them, you can hold them in place, too. It's not easy, but Valentina is strong. And together with the rest of the coven, she can do pretty amazing things."

"I can't believe that a grandma defeated a centuries-old vampire."

"Not just *a grandma:* she's the most powerful witch in Lombardy."

"She definitely doesn't look it."

"Beware of saintly-looking creatures. Those are usually the most wicked ones."

In that, we agreed. And similarly, the opposite was often true.

"What happened next?" I asked.

"They chained her. We have special chains vampires can't break. Then they took her away, to this woman called Natasha. I don't know where she lives, but I heard she's our best donator. Berenice told me this house was about to get foreclosed on when she appeared out of thin air and offered to fund our coven in exchange for bringing her any supernatural creatures we found. I have no idea what she needs them for, nor where she keeps them."

Ah, so that was it: all those stories about goodhearted witches devoting their lives to helping others... in the end, it all added up to the same old adage: witches, just like everyone else, needed money to subsist, and their actions were conditioned by that need. Nothing new here.

The following question was hard to formulate, but I needed to ask it. “Do you think Francesca…” I swallowed for courage. “Do you think she’s still alive?”

“I’m not sure.” Alice let out a soft whimper. “I hope she is. I feel terrible about everything that happened.”

“You should. I’m sure she never meant you any harm.”

“I know.” She was bawling now. “She chose to spare my life at the expense of her own. She was right next to me and could have killed me when the other witches arrived. Valentina, on the other hand, didn’t bother to protect me from Francesca: she used me to lure her, and was willing to sacrifice me as long as she got her prize.” Alice smashed her porcelain cup against the floor and only the handle remained, dangling from her fingers like a broken ring.

I helped her pick up the shards and carry them to a nearby trash can.

“Ok, Alice,” I said firmly, “you need to find out where they took her, do you hear me? You owe it to Francesca. She’s a good person… vampire… whatever, you know what I mean. I need you to help me. We must find her.”

“But… that’s crazy. The coven would expel me if they found out I’m helping you,” she complained. “She’s not even human. I can’t do that."

I puffed. "Why not? You just admitted she spared your life. Human or not, that makes her worthy of your mercy, doesn't it? Or is your compassion reserved only for those who are just like you?"

Alice narrowed her eyes. "You're telling me that because you have been brainwashed by vampires."

I gaped at her, offended. "Excuse me?"

"Everyone here knows you sleep with them, so your opinions are biased. I heard the others talk about it over breakfast."

Wasn't it awesome, having a dozen grandmas discuss my sex life over freshly-baked panettone?

"So what if I do? That's nobody's business."

"You're not going to deny it?" She seemed shocked.

Alice peeked at me from above the thick frame of her black glasses, a sudden gleam of interest illuminating her gaze.

"What is it like?" She asked with curiosity.

"What is *what* like?" I crossed my arms.

"You know…" She let out a girly laugh.

I rolled my eyes. "Why do you want to know?"

"*Er*… well… I'm intrigued, that's it. In case I ever come across the chance, so I know what to expect... or how to defend myself… is it as bad as they say?"

"I have no idea of what they say but no, in my experience, it's not *that* bad," I said, squinting at her.

Nope. Not at all, I added in my mind.

"Yes, but they must be so… cold? Isn't that a bit uncomfortable?"

She giggled. *How old was this girl anyway?*

"No…" I half-smiled at her sudden coyness. "Have you ever hugged someone when they come home after being outside in the cold?"

Alice nodded eagerly.

"Well, that's exactly how it feels." A dreamy sigh left my lips against my will, and a wave of nostalgia stirred inside me. "Imagine kissing someone's nose after they were outside in the snow. It warms up after a while, doesn't it? They don't *generate* cold, they just have no warmth of their own. But they can share yours."

"Cute," she said, seemingly satisfied with my description.

"Yeah."

Alice stared at the ceiling with a dreamy expression, and I wondered whether she could be thinking about Francesca.

"I should be going." She shook her head and checked her watch. "I need to get something from the store before it closes, but I'll be back again tomorrow after work to teach you divination. Be good until then."

She unlocked the door and slipped out silently. Once she left, I tried the door handle, but it was locked. I let out a stifled curse and went back to my mat to nurse the leftovers of my headache as I thought about Clarence, Francesca and my daughters, and all the possible ways to stop being a glorified prisoner of the Witches of the Lake and start helping the friends who needed me… and myself.

***

When Alice came back the next evening, she found me drowning in self-pity while fiddling with the locks and trying to escape my makeshift prison. She was carrying a wooden box and sat down on the floor, waving for me to join her.

"Do you know what this is?" she asked me, handing me a deck of cards with gilded edges.

"Yes!" I exclaimed proudly, remembering a long day spent with Jean-Pierre back in The Cloister. "That's the *Tarot of Marseilles*!"

She frowned. "No. This is the *Visconti-Sforza* deck. But you were close enough. You get two points."

"Oh," I whimpered. "Only two? Out of how many?"

"Out of ten," she said sternly. "You are a Queen of Cups, aren't you?" She shuffled the cards and I watched her, mesmerized, as they flew back and forth like fluttering hummingbirds between her fingers. "It shows."

"No, I'm the Queen of Water, as far as I know." At least, that was what Julia had told me.

"Yeah, that's the same," Alice explained. "It means you are weepy, disorganized… have a victim mentality… cheesy tendencies… isn't that you?"

I cleared my throat, appalled at her awfully accurate report.

"No!" I shouted. "I'm not weepy! Where did you get that from?" I hid behind my back the handkerchief I had been wiping off my tears with right before she had made her appearance.

Alice shrugged and set the cards on the mat, in three ordered piles. "Years of practice reading people, I suppose."

"Why do I have to be the worst of all queens?" I complained, violently crumpling the tissue into a tight ball.

"Who said she's the worst? There are no better or worse archetypes. They all serve a purpose. A balanced Queen of Cups can be great. But that's not your case."

"*Huh*," I grunted. "But I read it in that spell… *Fulminatio*… that I was the least talented of all queens."

"*Fulminatio*?" Alice lifted an eyebrow. "How did you get your hands on it? That's sensitive material which shouldn't be handled by young witches, let alone strays like you. Even I don't have permission to access such manuscripts. I thought they were kept in a secret vault in France."

I remained silent, unwilling to expose Jean-Pierre. "I don't know. I just… found it."

"Anyways," she continued, "that's probably a fire spell. As a Queen of Water you are not well-suited to cast it, unless surrounded by your element. You know… *water extinguishes fire* and all that jazz. That doesn't mean you are worse. It's just not the best match for you."

"And *what* is the best match for me?"

"I can't tell you that. Something more… watery, I suppose. But I don't have access to the Great Spells. I'm just a reader."

"Oh. And what do readers do?"

"We see things. Do you want me to tell you your fortunes?"

I considered her offer for a second. *Did I?* Not really, but maybe she would tell me something useful about Clarence or Francesca.

"Okay. But if I'm going to die soon, just lie to me, will you?"

"Deal," she said, and started to shuffle the deck once again.

Alice asked me to pick a few cards and spread them on my bedsheet in an orderly cross pattern.

"What are you doing now?" I asked.

"*There's one for your past, one for your present, and one for what shall come to pass*," she chanted, pointing at each card separately. "These are the people who'll help you, and these are the obstacles you'll encounter."

"And that one?"

"That one is the most likely end for your story."

"And how does it end?" I asked nervously.

"That depends on you. But I see a couple of meaningful men in your life…" she said pensively, readjusting her glasses.

"I don't need a witch to tell me that. That's

one of those vague statements which would work for anyone. Except for a hermit, maybe."

Alice scowled and continued. "Shut up. This is serious. I see three men. Men you will love or be loved by."

"What? *Three*?" I rubbed my temples. "I hope you're joking. I wouldn't want to become the new Catherine the Great."

"Catherine who?"

"Never mind."

"Anyways. That's not the point." She twirled a card in her fingers, doubtful. "Thing is, the three of them are going to try to kill you at some point."

"Awesome."

"But there's one good thing…"

"*Yees*?"

"Only one will succeed."

***

I stood up in a rage and turned my back to Alice.

"No shit," I growled. "Because you can kill someone more than once, right? *Of course* only one will succeed, if I'm supposed to be murdered. What kind of psychic are you?"

I was pissed at Alice because she had promised not to predict my death and still, there she was, doing exactly—and only—that.

"Don't be so finicky," she persisted, unfazed, "I see three stories here, all interwoven…

it's all very exciting, in my opinion. I rarely see a narrative like this. The problem is, you will have to make the right choice, and there's only one. And it's not the easiest one, I'm afraid."

"And which is that, if I may ask?"

"Let me see…" She picked another card and studied it carefully. "Trust," she rolled the middle *r* the way most Italians did and nodded with satisfaction. "You have to choose trust over fear if you want to succeed."

"That doesn't answer my question," I roared. "I want to know who these people are and how to pick the right one, so I don't end up murdered in the process."

"Don't we all?" She laughed. "But I never said making the right choice would save you from your destiny. I can't give you such detailed information; the only thing I can do is lend you my deck so you can slip it under your pillow tonight. Sometimes a clearer message comes through, or you get to dream of a person who might be able to help you."

"I could try that," I said, as an idea started to form in my mind.

"Okay, because it's getting late, and I still have to drive back home. I hate driving through the forest in the dark. Is there anything else you need before I leave? Water? Food? *More tissues*?"

I ignored her last snide comment and took the cards from her hands.

"Actually, I'd love to have Valentina's divination bowl and some candles," I said slowly.

"I'd love to practice some more after you go. If you don't mind."

Chapter 22

Clarence

The rusty box reeked of burned flesh and singed hair.

My hair, to be accurate.

A thin but deadly slither of sunlight seeped through a crack at the top of the metal chest, leaving scarlet marks wherever it stroked my skin. I cowered in a corner, trying in vain to escape the deadly rays. But the box was small, and daylight relentless.

It was a thrilling way to pass the time.

I had spent two days hiding in a crumbling chest freezer salvaged from the kitchen of the inn; waiting for nightfall as I fought the deadly slivers of light and waited for my injuries to heal. The burns didn't bother me; but the silver dagger wounds had impaired my ability to move and shift properly, leaving me at the mercy of sunshine. That dagger, a present from Anne, had been forged to keep both vampires and hunters at bay: both a much more troubling nuisance in 1834 than nowadays. A stab through the heart with such a weapon would have sealed my fate; but the scoundrel had missed his target by a couple of inches.

At sunset, I dragged my wretched self through the surrounding woods and valleys, trying to find wild beasts to feed from. I would have preferred a human, whose blood would have sped up the healing process; but I was too weak to stalk humans properly, and there were not many treading the surroundings. As I crawled over the frosty mulch, I strove to detect Alba's scent, but the cloud of smoke had blurred any leftover traces of her.

The sound of paws in the treetops alerted me of the presence of a small, warm-blooded creature nearby. I stood still, sniffing the air, and detected a rodent. It stank, and the very thought of drinking animal blood nauseated me; but it would have to do.

I crouched down, very slowly, careful not to crack a single twig. The animal was chewing its food, unaware of my presence at the foot of the tree. It would take just one leap to catch it, but it would have to be quick and clean. A disgusting morsel, but I needed blood to heal: otherwise it would take too long, and I needed to take flight as soon as possible if I wanted to find Alba.

The beast went silent and jerked its head: first left, then right. It stared at me without seeing me: it had smelled me. I wasn't the only one in the forest able to sense other creatures' scent. Stalking humans was so much easier from that point of view: they were so deliciously oblivious, always so trusting and overconfident. A kind word and a smile away from becoming easy prey. Beasts, on the other hand, were much more astute.

I tilted back for a running start, and then I jumped. I tripped clumsily over a broken branch, doubled over by the pain of my wounds.

The squirrel squeaked and scurried away.

I lay on the ground for a long while, scoffing at myself: a couple hundred years ago I had nearly razed a whole city, and the only person able to stop me had been the mighty Elizabeth. Alas, today, what had I become? A weakling unable to catch a hideous, pathetic rodent. Too weak to take flight and find the woman I had come to assist in the first place.

I found nothing to eat that night. Not that I tried again. Ultimately, the looming sunrise forced me to creep back into my hiding place, and I cringed at the prospect of spending yet another day locked in a box.

Caskets always conjured my most miserable memories. Memories of Anne's death, and my mother's shortly thereafter; and how my father, consumed by panic and rage, had locked me in a leaden coffin. He had hoped that would keep me—and the dirty secret of my turning—hidden away from the world for the rest of eternity; or at least, for the remainder of his own life. When Elizabeth had found me, starved and crazed, I had already lost any semblance of humanity I might have ever had. Everyone I held dear was dead. I had exerted my revenge on my father before

Elizabeth had succeeded to restrain me. And, in hindsight, now I fervently wished I had not.

All these recollections made coffins—and somehow, chest freezers, too—a daunting resting place. But this time, at least, I had a reason to endure this claustrophobic torment.

A reason whose blood rushed through my veins like a meteor shower, her magic sparkling and fizzling inside me with a silent melody I had never listened to before.

I had never drunk from a witch before: ordinary humans were easier to catch and much more plentiful. Yet now I couldn't but wonder whether the bitter scent of witches was a cunningly devised self-defense mechanism, meant to conceal the magic their blood carried. A magic strong enough to convey that she was alive and well; albeit out of reach. Even though its effects were becoming gradually feebler, I could sense her heartbeat, fierce and gushing, almost as if she were right next to me.

I curled up at the bottom of the box, sticky with syrup and rotten berries. It was the safest hideout I could find after waking up with my feet peeping out of a foxhole ten minutes before sunrise, with burns all over my body and a few kisses of my own dagger, inflicted by Alba's new Romeo.

That night I had aroused in her warm arms, drunk with her essence. Slumbering in her embrace, I had not only slept, but also dreamt. Of her. *Of us.* Elated under the rising sun. In my dream, I was the man I never became in my mortal life. The man my mother would have been proud of.

I fell asleep so rarely that I had forgotten to blow out the candles. It was the scent of another human in the room that had stolen my fantasy and put me on guard. *Romeo* had a key, and he had tiptoed into the room. He knew I was there.

I had jumped out of bed and pounced on him, but he was fast, and surprisingly well prepared to fight a vampire. He had stolen my dagger and fled into the forest.

I had followed him, blinded by my fury.

Fool.

That was exactly what he had wanted me to do.

In my recklessness, I hadn't paid attention to the overturned candles, nor the first flames rising from the sleeping inn. It wasn't until we were entangled in a fight to the death in the middle of the forest that I had seen the fire engulfing the inn and everything inside it.

Everyone inside it.

Just like another fire, a long time ago, had devoured Anne.

Panic had seized me at the sight. I had tried to rush back to Alba, but my attacker had turned out to be relentless, and extremely hard to kill.

After extricating myself from him, badly wounded and weakened, I had sieved the smoking embers of the building for hours. By then, everybody was gone and the building ruined. Eventually, I had gathered just enough strength to crawl into a fox's burrow and wait for nightfall.

And here I was as yet, bleeding over raspberry ice-cream leftovers; locked in a rusty, half-burnt freezer chest, at the darkest end of a crumbling mountain inn in Northern Italy.

Mulling over a witch.

My witch.

A witch who was still alive; that much I knew.

A witch whose life force coursed through my arteries, creating a bond stronger than any other tie, human or supernatural.

I would find her.

Chapter 23

Alba

I was still wearing a decades-old nightgown reminiscent of a shroud when, after at least ten days of miserable captivity, punctuated only by Alice's brief visits and the young witchling who brought me food, the witches let me out of the basement once again for a morning meditation.

Seemingly, most witches led boring, ordinary lives. They had families, jobs, and mortgages, just like everyone else, which didn't allow them to spend their whole days reading spell books or holding coven gatherings as I had first imagined. The only permanent residents of the house were three retired, widowed ladies: High Priestess Valentina and two other elderly women by the names Agnes and Elda. Berenice was also living with them at the moment, even though she was under seventy; but only temporarily, since her home at the inn had burned down to the ground. When I asked Alice about Berenice's oddly cheerful behavior despite her bad luck, she just brushed it off and said that it was her particular way of coping with difficult stuff.

The night before, after Alice had left, I had tried to contact Julia, using the scrying bowl as a mirror and the words I could remember from Julia's summoning spell.

It didn't come as much of a surprise when the spell didn't work out. I had tried to wield magic a couple of times after my first success and most of them had been a failure: my sorcery seemed to have a mind of its own and do whatever it wanted, only whenever it decided. At any rate, now I was faced with the dreadful thought of never reaching Julia again. In my current situation, with Clarence missing and Francesca held captive, she might have been the only person able to help me.

The only bright side of my forced captivity was that my health had improved very quickly under the care of the witches. My lungs were starting to cooperate, slowly forgiving me for inhaling too much smoke during the fire. Those witches were good healers: at least I'd give them that.

Now, with my own survival cleared up, there were a few pressing matters haunting my thoughts that morning, in no particular order of importance:

I needed to find out where Francesca was and get her out of there.

I missed my daughters, and I needed to call them and confirm they were well.

And I missed Clarence.

I was worried about him, and I missed him so much. I missed that vengeful, truant vampire who had assaulted a man just for kissing me. That vampire who had ghosted me more times than I could count with the fingers of one hand. I should be furious at him. Actually, I was. But still, his memory had populated my thoughts for the best part of my waking—and even more so, non-waking—hours.

And then there was this baffling issue with the bite. Sure, I had never been bitten by a vampire, at least to my knowledge; but something told me that whatever was going on with me was not entirely normal.

The tiny wounds had already healed, but the scar was pulsating… *radiating.* Not a warm radiance, but ice-cold sparkles instead: unlike the fiery itch of a bee sting, these scars were like carrying a kiss from his lips permanently attached to the side of my neck. They had grown invisible roots and even a life of their own. Now they took pleasure in stealthily liquefying my legs and distracting me from anything else around me with thoughts of the culprit, as my fingers kept seeking them out of their own accord and pursuing *him* through *them.* It was confusing and frustrating and oddly sensual all at once.

When Valentina woke me that morning, the tiny scars were already buzzing.

"Still breathing?" she asked me, yanking my lacy sleeve and dragging me up the narrow stairs to the attic. She scrutinized my face, spat on her fingertips and rubbed the dark circles under my eyes, as if trying to erase them. "You look dreadful. And those marks on your neck give off strange vibrations." She turned to Berenice, who was standing on one leg like a flamingo, wearing a t-shirt with the slogan '*Go witch yourself,*' and asked, "Ever read anything about venomous vampires, Berenice? Do you think they might exist?"

"Never heard such a thing," she answered, carefully lifting her leg in an inverted L shape. "But she does look terrible. We could try bone broth; it might help. Did Agnes kill anything last weekend?"

"I doubt it, in this cold, but I'll ask her after the ritual," Valentina said. "Otherwise, I think we still have a couple of Leonardo's bones somewhere in the basement."

I stared at them alternately.

"Ah… I'm okay already," I mumbled, reluctant to have anything brewed out of *someone… something…* named Leonardo. "Just wheezy. But I'd really like to have my phone back. I need to check on my daughters."

Valentina raised an eyebrow. "Pay attention to what we are about to do, and we'll see about that. Don't you want to learn witchcraft? Well, sorry to tell you, but that's not the way it works. You don't just read a spell, spew out a few sparks and magically become a witch. This is about practice, and hard work, and sacrifices."

"What kind of sacrifices?" My voice trembled a little as I speculated about *Leonardo* and how his bones had ended up in a witches' basement.

They plainly ignored my question.

We reached the third floor and entered an attic room with a sloping ceiling.

"We call this the mirror room," Berenice said, leaping through the door like a wild goat.

I didn't need to ask why the name, because all vertical surfaces were covered in mirrors, like in a dance studio or a huge elevator. There was even a long ballet *barre* bolted to the widest wall, and Berenice perched on it upside down just like a bat would have, letting her t-shirt slide down to her chin and show the best part of her bra and her extensively tattooed belly area.

"Berenice, will you please stop monkeying around and bring us old women some pillows?"

The feeble early morning sun shone over us through the dusty window panes, bouncing off the silver surfaces and giving the whole space a pinkish tint. Our reflections multiplied to infinity, creating the illusion of thousands of Albas and Valentinas taking turns to scowl at each other.

Berenice dropped half-heartedly to the floor and grabbed a few cushions from a small pile in the corner. She set them in a flower shape and sat down in the middle, silent and cross-legged. Agnes and Elda created a circle of—*surprise*—candles and one of them started to bang a brass bowl with a tiny wooden mallet.

"Sunrise meditation," Valentina announced, elbowing my ribs. "Close your eyes and let the energy gather inside your core."

"Do you meditate just for fun, or does this serve any magical purposes?" I asked, sitting down and squinting into the increasing morning light.

"Mainly demon summoning," Berenice answered with a smirk.

"Or message channeling," Elda clarified, clasping a crystal pendant around her neck.

"*Shh,*" Agnes admonished them, and a few droplets of spit landed on my cheek.

We remained in that posture for an eternity, until my legs were overcome by pins and needles which fought to overpower the icy roots growing out of Clarence's bites.

After an hour of failed meditation, the only things filling my *core* were unease due to my current situation and a growing sense of hunger. My stomach let out a roaring howl, which in turn forced the witches to open their eyes, my empty guts prematurely rousing them from their trance.

Berenice hit the singing bowl three times, signaling the end of the ritual.

So far, I had summoned exactly zero demons and channeled as many messages. But I had plotted a few nifty ways to get my phone back, most of them including some sort of pleading or guilt-shaming directed to Alice. A phone would allow me to call Minnie and contact someone in The Cloister willing to send help. Elizabeth was mostly illiterate as far as technology concerned, but who knew? There was a possibility she had learned to check her email while she was alone and bored in her chambers.

"I had such an inspiring vision," Agnes said in her shaky, elderly lady voice. "There was a bat trying to get into the house, and we caught it just before it nested on the roof."

"This attic is full of bats. Doesn't sound very prophetic to me," Elda commented.

"Yes, but that one was huge. And rabid."

"Maybe it's a sign that you should add a bat to your Minecraft cross-stitch tapestry," Elda said to Agnes, "it has too much green. A bit of black would add variety."

"Oh, yes! Green smoothie, anyone?" Berenice clapped her hands and started to hop down the stairs, followed by the others.

"Did you hear anything during your meditation?" Valentina asked me as we snailed our way down toward the kitchen on the ground floor.

Did hearing two motorbikes and the garbage truck count?

"*Um*... no, not really," I answered, holding onto the handrail. My legs were still a bit wobbly, and I was glad to reach the last step.

The witches' kitchen was, at first sight, a vast Mason jar warehouse. Pickled things swamped the place, and most of them were *not* cucumbers—I recognized a couple of lizards and two white, soft balls floating in a clear liquid. They were alarmingly similar to animal eyes. Or even human ones.

A vintage pasta maker reigned in the middle of the counter, surrounded by blenders, threatening knife blocks and rusty tins with hand-written labels. Fruits and vegetables, most of them still covered in dirt, filled a fraying basket to the rim. Valentina took a couple of apples and wiped them on her cardigan before sinking her dentures in one of them. She offered me one, and I accepted it meekly: I had expected a stronger breakfast.

"So, you got no visions?" Berenice said pensively. "Ah, never mind. It can be normal for a first-timer." She threw a bunch of green leaves into the blender and started to squeeze a lemon over them. "The only message I channeled today was that I must call my insurance agent about the fire coverage. But I saw my light. Did you at least manage to see yours?"

"What light?" I asked wearily, chewing the apple, which had an unusually thick peel.

"You know, your glow, your power, your witch aura…" She said dreamily.

"No, I don't think so. Maybe I just suck as a witch."

"*Hmm*," Berenice hovered her finger over the power button of the blender, but didn't deny my statement. "Have you ever done anything special? Anything… *witchy*?"

"She cast the *Fulminatio* in a public restroom once," Valentina said through gritted teeth.

"You did *what*?" Agnes shrieked, letting her apple roll onto the floor.

"How do you know that?" I asked Valentina, stiffening.

"Two of our sisters were there, have you forgotten, Alba? And, anyways, it's not like news doesn't spread fast from coven to coven. They even wrote about it in the *Warty Toad Newsletter*. It was a true scandal."

"They cornered me in a bathroom stall," I protested. "I was scared."

"Wow, that's incredible!" Berenice said in awe. "So, do you remember the color of your light when you cast it?" She leaned against the kitchen table, her eyes scanning me like she saw me for the first time.

"I think it was white?" I tried to remember. "No, wait. It started off as a white glow, but it turned purple in the end." I recalled the exhilarating sensation of magic fire coursing through my fingers, and a soft tingling extended down my forearms.

Valentina nodded knowingly and left her half-eaten apple on the counter. She took one of my hands and started to study each finger separately, seemingly searching for tiny flamethrowers under my nails.

"Interesting," she said. "But you must be mistaken. I doubt your light was purple. That's the highest energy one can invoke. Nobody has reached above green in the last five hundred years."

"That's what happens when you spend years singing *Colors of the Rainbow* with toddlers," I said, in a vain attempt to sound funny.

Nobody laughed.

They just looked at me blankly, their eyes stating silently that they now found me even more stupid than the first day.

"What color is yours?" I asked, directing my

question to all of them in general.

"Golden," Berenice sang whimsically, munching on a celery stalk.

"Berenice, stop fantasizing. Yours is just plain yellow, like a ripe lemon." Elda laughed. "But Valentina's is the most beautiful emerald green you'll ever witness."

"Oh, I wish you could show me. I'd love to see that." I turned to the high priestess, but she just frowned.

"Come on, Valentina, show the stray a glimpse of your power. Otherwise she'll think all we can do is chant and blend smoothies." Berenice brandished the celery stalk like a racing flag.

"I don't care what the stray thinks of me." Valentina put her hands on her hips, stubbornly.

"Come on. She needs someone to look up to," Berenice teased her.

Stealthily, Berenice grabbed an apple from the bowl and threw it straight at Valentina's face.

Valentina blocked the flying object with both hands: her reflexes were striking for a lady her age. A greenish glow held the apple in the air for a second, where it hovered, frozen, until she snatched it and put it back on the counter.

I gaped at the scene in awe. It reminded me of my little adventure with the teacup at the dressmaker's, back in Emberbury.

"You always have to get your way, don't you, Berenice?" Valentina said, smashing the apple back into the bowl.

The younger witch flung her a devilish

smirk. "And that's how you catch a flying apple," the innkeeper declared smugly, handing me a glass full to the rim of a disgusting grog, then she added naughtily, "Or a bloodthirsty vampire."

***

We spent the rest of the day baking sweet bread loaves with hidden trinkets inside and singing creepy songs about people with horns. For a while, I forgot about the existence of vampires and about the fact that I was a captive in a witches' home. I fantasized about big families with dozens of loving aunts and grannies; the kind of family I never got to know during my childhood, as we traveled from country to country following my father's nomadic career.

But in the evening, the witches' camaraderie ended abruptly as they locked me back into the basement room.

"Sorry, stray," Berenice said, peeking through the crack of the door before retiring upstairs, "Alice is coming to continue your divination lessons after the museum closes. Try to do something useful in the meanwhile." She ran her eyes over my neglected self and wiggled her nose. "Like washing your hair. You still reek of smoke."

I took a shower, but nobody had bothered to supply me with any fresh clothes. I had no other choice but to put on the same shabby nightgown again, which was starting to get filthy. Half the decorative lace, now yellowed and holey, was torn around the hem, and I observed with apathy how it followed me around me like a quiet snake.

Once showered and relatively refreshed, I searched the room for usable magical items and possible ways to escape the building. Sadly, I found no secret spell books, no incriminating documents, and no unlocked doors. The basement windows were too high for me to jump through, and they were barred anyway.

I grunted, and the exhalation sent me into such a bad coughing fit that I had to lean against the wall until it passed. Just when I thought I was about to die of suffocation, alone in that run-down basement, the door opened and Alice made her appearance. The eyeliner was smeared around her eyes, and she held her glasses in one hand. She patted my back patiently, until the coughing fit stopped.

"Do you have a cold?" I asked, referring to her exaggerated sniffling.

Alice shook her head and handed me a little black, shiny object.

"My cell phone!" I squealed, and hugged her out of impulse.

"I thought you might want to have a look. But do it fast, because if—*when* Valentina finds out, she's going to skin me alive." She snuffled loudly.

I plucked the phone off her hands and unlocked it. To be accurate, I didn't even have to, because someone had removed the password prompt.

"What the hell?" I mumbled, clearing a few breadcrumbs off the screen.

"Yeah, Agnes is our best hacker. She did that."

"Are we talking about flower-aproned, doily crocheting Agnes?" I blinked.

"*Yup.*"

"Why would she do that?"

"So we could read aloud all your messages every night at dinnertime."

I stared at her with horror, but she nudged me impatiently.

"Hurry up. They will notice soon and come for me. Valentina keeps your phone in the cookie tin, and trust me: that tin gets more visitors per day than the Sistine Chapel in August."

I reclined against the small altar in a corner of my room and started to browse heftily through hundreds of unread emails.

There were a few messages from Minnie. The girls were fine, and she had sent me a few photos of them eating lunch and unwrapping Christmas presents together with Minnie's parents in their lavish Boston mansion.

They looked like a freaking happy family without me. My girls even had the same hair color as Minnie, thanks to Mark's blond genes.

I felt sick to my stomach.

"Pretty girls. Your nieces?" Alice commented, pointing at a portrait of Iris and Katie wearing Santa hats and kissing Minnie, one from each side.

"My *daughters*," I growled.

"Ah." She shrugged. "And who's the boyfriend?"

"What boyfriend?" I pressed the phone against my chest so she couldn't read over my shoulder. There were no pictures of Mark, let alone Clarence—whose image couldn't be captured on camera—so I had no idea where she had got the idea of a boyfriend.

"The one who writes SMS's like he's Lord Byron's long-lost brother," she said. "You know, '*My dearest beloved blah, blah*.'"

"They read those, too?" I gasped. A wave of heat rushed to my cheeks. Not that Clarence's messages were exactly X-rated, florid and old-fashioned as they were, but still: they were *personal.* And mine. For my eyes only.

"Okay, give it back." Alice took the phone from my hands.

I tried to keep it a little longer, reluctant to obey. "But I need to write a couple of messages first."

"No way. I can't allow you to call anyone or write anything: Agnes would notice. Sorry. I already risked a lot bringing this here. If they found out what I've done they might kick me out of the coven, or worse."

I sighed, contemplating the possibility of punching Alice and reducing her to the floor for the time necessary to type an email to Elizabeth. The plan was a bit far-fetched, as Alice was larger than I. Also, I didn't think she deserved such rough treatment. She was the only person around trying to be of assistance, after all.

"Okay," I said, handing her my phone with an eye-roll. "Thank you. How come you decided to help me?"

She slipped it in her pocket and collapsed on the mat, sprawling her arms and legs like a black, leather-clad spider.

"They cut off her fingers," she whined.

"What? Whose fingers?"

"Francesca's." Alice started to wail and I couldn't make out her words properly. "They found out she's a musician, and they cut off her fingers to make her talk."

I collapsed on the mat right next to her, covering my mouth in horror.

"Why? Who?" I stammered.

"Valentina was joking about it in the kitchen. The torturers even took a fast-forward video showing how the fingers grew back. They have special infrared cameras just for that purpose. It was hideous. But Valentina found it funny."

"That's sick," I said, bile rising up my throat. "Why would anyone do that?"

"To pry information out of someone, of course."

"What information?"

"I don't know. What secrets could a wandering vampire keep?"

Too many.

I rubbed my temples. "That's why you brought me my phone?"

Alice frowned. "You were right. We must find her. I'm sorry I gave her away to Valentina. I made a mistake, but I'm going to fix it. Once I find out where they took her, we'll think of something, okay?"

I nodded, my mouth too dry to speak. "Yes. Yes. Okay."

"Good. I'm leaving you now. I have no energy for Tarot readings tonight."

"Neither do I," I agreed grimly.

She stood up and lugged herself to the exit.

"Alice," I called her. "If I had a mirror, I might be able to summon a friend. A powerful one. But there are none in this basement, and the water bowl doesn't work."

Alice bit her lips, pensive; then put her glasses back on.

"Yeah, Valentina removed all mirrors from the basement because she doesn't want to risk you making astral calls. Weird, as she considers you a total incompetent. She's been making fun of you since you came up with the freezer story. I think that was when she lost all hope to make a witch out of you." She scanned me with sudden interest. "Don't tell me you can actually use mirrors as portals, like they used to do in the Middle Ages."

"*Um*… I'm not sure I can do it at will, but once I summoned a witch. Although I think it was her doing most of the work from the other side."

"Well, you are a box of surprises, *Mrs. 63-Inch-Chest-Freezer*. I have no mirrors to give you, but there are lots of them in the attic. And, lucky you,

Valentina and her cronies are terribly hard of hearing. Once they take off their hearing aids for the day, there's no way in hell they'll notice your comings and goings around the house," she said, pointing toward the upper floor. "As long as you tiptoe past Berenice's room, that is. She's sleeping in the lab."

"Oh, that's awesome. The only problem is, I'm trapped here…"

Alice winked.

"Are you?" She cooed with impish carelessness. "What if I forgot to lock the door? Just for tonight…"

"Oh," I said, watching the keys dangle from her fingers.

Once she was gone, I stood up and tried the doorknob.

The door was unlocked.

I smiled.

Perhaps Alice wasn't so bad after all.

Chapter 24

Alba

I waited anxiously for everyone to fall asleep. Once the house became absolutely silent, I stuck a few white candles and matches into the pocket of my nightgown and left the basement. I tiptoed past the witches' bedrooms on the first floor, furtive as a thief, making my way straight to the attic.

Upstairs, the moon was shining through the skylights, dyeing everything in shades of azure and silver, with gold and orange specks here and there.

I sat on a cushion in front of the largest mirror and lit three candles. I didn't remember the whole text of Julia's spell, but I would put all my heart into this summoning. I needed it to work because, otherwise, many people would suffer, and I couldn't allow that to happen.

"Here I am," I whispered.

My voice dissolved into the air, thin and quiet as a morning mist. Then the sound reappeared and reverberated in the enclosed space.

It came back to me, shaped into delicate drops of light. I cupped my hands and gathered them, then started to braid the drops into beads of energy, just like the witches had done while playing ball in the living room, the day I had silently made fun of them.

Was this a fantasy? The skeptic inside me wanted to laugh at the absurdity of the situation, but I silenced her and kept braiding.

"I am listening," I murmured into the empty room, opening my arms in a welcoming gesture.

A weak rumble shook the air, and a voice emerged from the center of the mirror.

"It's good to see you again," she said.

Julia's voice didn't startle me; but her image did. For the first time, she didn't manifest as a black cat: on the other side of the looking glass there was a beautiful, ageless woman in a polka dot swing dress, sitting gracefully on a tree stump. She had dark blond, wavy hair with elegant pin curls, and the revealing pallor of the dead. *Or the undead.*

"You look so young… this can't be." I gasped and touched the mirror between us. The tip of my finger created concentric waves on the surface, just like a drop falling into a pool of water. "What are you, Julia? A witch, a vampire… a ghost?"

"Yes," Julia answered beatifically, with an absentminded, muddled expression which oddly reminded me of my own grandma.

"Yes… *what?*" I encouraged her, mesmerized by the circles undulating on the glass.

"Yes, I'm… the three of them, somehow." She sounded confused, but strangely cheerful. "Depends on how you look at it."

I tapped on the mirror with my bare toes, and, to my surprise, I stumbled *inside it*. I fell face-first on the palms of my hands, directly on a damp, grassy surface at Julia's feet.

Julia smiled and tried to help me stand up. Her hand was cold, much colder than Clarence's ever was. It went through my fingers like a specter, unable to attach to anything material.

"Oh, I always forget," she said, knocking on her forehead. "Can't touch you, because you're not really here, and neither am I."

I wiped my hand discreetly on the long linen nightgown. It was gooey where her ghostly skin had brushed against mine. I examined the space around us but saw only fog. We were sitting in the middle of a shadowy forest clearing, surrounded by darkness and thick, grey clouds.

"Julia, do you have an idea what's going on?" I said, my head starting to spin. "I came to Italy because of you, because of that message in your diary. But since I landed in this country everything has been a mess. Also, according to what the witches told me, you should be dead. Possibly twice or thrice."

"*Hmm.*" Julia smiled softly. "Oh, where to start." She stood up, and I tried to ascertain how old she was. To my knowledge, she had died in her fifties of a heart failure. How could she possibly be standing here, looking barely my age?

"First of all," she continued, "I'm so sorry I missed our appointment, but I was faced with a case of *force majeure*. I wanted to show you the Museum of Witchcraft, especially Turanna's Mirror… but then my plans were thwarted. I also tried to warn you not to tell Carlo who you really are, because I saw him talking to the head of the witches… I hope you got my message?"

"More or less," I said, nodding. "But what happened? Why weren't you there on Christmas Eve?"

"My husband, Ludovic, is dying, and all my energy is going toward keeping him alive from a distance. That made it hard to answer your previous calls. He was having a better day today, so I managed to come. But this truce won't last long, especially now I also have Francesca to take care of."

"Francesca! So, you know where she is? Who is behind all this?" A twin, vacant log materialized right next to her, and I took a seat. The wood felt gooey and icy through my clothes, just like Julia.

"Vampire hunters is my guess, although these ones are peculiar. I don't know who is sending them. They've been after us since the dawn of mankind, but these ones… they are different."

Vampire hunters. I remembered the leaflet those Salem witches had given me on the street. Back then, I had laughed it off and made fun of Clarence for taking their anti-vampire propaganda so personally.

In retrospect, I had been an absolute idiot.

"Hunters, you say…" Still, something didn't add up. "But why would hunters keep vampires alive? Why not kill them immediately? Isn't that the point of hunting them down? Combating the *plague*?" She frowned at me, shooting me an eerie, fanged grin. So, she was a vampire, too. Interesting. "Sorry, I didn't mean..."

"That's what I don't understand, either." Julia coiled a lock of hair around her finger. "Anyways, this plays in our favor right now: each day they survive is a day we can get them out of there alive. But I can't do all of this on my own: I'm going to need help. Just keeping them afloat despite the torture is using up most of my magic. I'm nearly drained, and I need you. Can I count on you?"

"Of course," I said, without thinking. "But how could I be of any use? I'm completely inept. Ask High Priestess Valentina if you don't believe me."

Julia dismissed my words with a wave of her hand. "Ah, Valentina. I know her better than you think. I lived right next door to her for a while, and she thinks so highly of herself. But what does she know? In her whole life, she has barely mastered telekinesis. A bit sad for the self-proclaimed most powerful high priestess in Italy, don't you think? And according to her, I should be dead now, didn't you just say that? I've heard their old wives' tales, too. Well, look at me." She stood up and curtsied, showing off her flared vintage dress. According to my calculations she must have been about a hundred years old, but her stance was more than spectacular, with her abundant curves filling the dress so nicely that I felt a pang of envy.

"You look amazing," I admitted. "But how did you become… whatever you are now?"

"Mostly, I have to thank Francesca for everything," she said. "She helped me escape Elizabeth's rule. She would have never approved of me becoming… this." She pointed at her stylish dress. "That's the reason I wrote that message, for you to find it one day. I wanted to warn you against following my path, and back then I thought Elizabeth's rules were my worst problem. I can't believe how wrong I was! We planned for me to reunite with Ludovic in secret, but the hunters kept following him, and he never managed to come for me when promised. When it was finally safe for me to join him, I was almost too old to travel. Francesca helped me feign my death: she took care of everything, even arranged for a proper funeral. She fooled everyone, even those of her own kind. Nobody in The Cloister knows—nobody but you. And neither should they, for Francesca's sake."

"But you must have been older than now back then?" I blinked in confusion. The math didn't add up.

"Ludovic turned me into a vampire, but it's tricky with us, witches… I retained my magic, although I nearly destroyed both of us in the process. Then I learned shapeshifting spells and settled for my forties. I think this age suits me well, don't you agree? Old enough to be taken seriously, but not too decrepit to be shunned due to superficial beauty standards." She rearranged her hairpins, which flashed in the moonlight. "One has to keep up the appearances when dealing with the outside world. Humans are so shallow." She exhaled, plopping back onto the tree stump.

I gaped at her, wordless.

"Wow," I said. "I can't believe you didn't die. Valentina said that was impossible."

"Well, of course I died! I was terminally ill when I arrived here. I barely made it to Rome in 1981." She set a hand over her heart. "Then I talked Ludovic into trying… I knew I might never wake up again, yes; but you know what they say: fortune favors the bold… and nothing ventured, nothing gained! So, we did it anyway. I was so sick that I didn't have much to lose at any rate. And, against all odds, it worked." She sighed wistfully. "It took me a while to adjust, but then we were happy. So happy! Only it lasted so little time…"

"Unbelievable," I said, rubbing my upper arms to warm them up and trying to reconcile Julia's tale with Valentina's warnings. "I'm glad you survived. So, you are a vampire now?"

"I still like to consider myself a witch, given how much effort I had to put into becoming—and staying—one."

"Sounds fair."

We sat in silence for a while, Julia playing with her gorgeous hairdo and waiting for me to process all the new information.

"It's a lot to take in," I said.

"I know. But we should get to work. The stories from the past can wait. Time is scarce, and we need to deal with the present first. Are you willing to help me? To help Francesca and her brother?"

"Of course. Just tell me what I have to do."

"For a start, I want you to remember an address. It's a secret prison in Venice. Listen carefully." Julia rubbed my forehead, and tiny invisible tentacles hugged my brain from several angles. "Sorry, I know this is not very pleasant, but it will help you retain the name. It's the fifth pink house by the canals, in Stella Alley in Venice. That's where they took them. That's where we must go. If anything happens to me, promise you'll go there and find a way to free them."

"I'll try to… I hope I'll remember everything," I said, regretful not to have pen and paper with me.

"Oh, you *will* remember," she simpered just a little. "And now, as I promised you on our first encounter, I'm going to teach you something useful. Because it happens to be valuable for both of us, and you are going to need this expertise."

I stared at her, expectant.

"I know I owe you an apology, so consider this my gift to you." She stood up and a wooden stick, akin to a magic wand, appeared in her right hand. "Tonight, I'm going to pose as your Fairy Godmother, and you get to make a wish."

"A wish?" I said with excitement, dozens of

ideas bubbling in my mind. "What kind of wish?"

"This evening, you're going to learn the real reason why most vampires hate mirrors. Why do you think it is?"

"They can't see themselves?" I ventured.

"Wrong." She touched my shoulder with the tip of her wand, but it just went through my flesh like a snowy breeze. "They are afraid of getting unwanted visitors. Like us. Mirrors are portals. Faster than planes, and much more discreet. With the right training, you can travel just about anywhere using one."

"So, you are sending me to that pink house in Venice, to bring back Francesca and your husband?"

"Of course not. You're not ready yet, you need to practice first. I'll teach you a useful incantation so you can travel on your own, without having to call me. You also get to choose where to send your ghostly self and you can stay there for a little while. Pick somewhere pretty, but not too far. Isn't that exciting?"

It was.

"Can I visit my daughters?" I asked with excitement.

"I said not too far. The further you go, the more energy you are going to need, and you don't have it yet. Try to think about someone or someplace a bit closer so we don't deplete ourselves during the experiment, okay?"

"It's not like I know anyone in this country. Apart from the witches, but I'm already their prisoner."

"No? Nobody?" She threw me a meaningful, expectant glance.

The scar on my neck started to tingle furiously, wiggling its tiny roots down to my heart and growing long, spiral branches which flew toward the forests around Lake Como, pointing vaguely at the creature I had missed the most during these cold winter nights of captivity.

"What if I don't know exactly *where*, but I know *with whom*?"

"As long as you hold strong feelings toward this person, the spell should be able to take you to them," she said patiently.

"Does it matter whether it's love or resentment?"

"Well… resentment is fine; but love works better. Love is the strongest energy in this world, as you must have learned by now." She nodded, holding my gaze. "If there's enough, it will take you anywhere. But for a beginner like you, having something of his—because I'm guessing *who* this could be—will make the ride a bit smoother. Do you happen to have anything from him?"

"No," I answered quietly, feeling suddenly sad about it.

"Are you sure? Nothing?"

The tiny, invisibly spider legs growing from my neck seemed to tie around my wrist and a tubular bracelet of white light appeared on my forearm.

"That should be enough," Julia said. She

pinched the bracelet with two translucent fingers and made it spin. Platinum sparkles flew around it, and I tried to imitate her; but when I touched the bangle, my fingers found nothing.

"That's a glittery bond you have there," she commented. "Although a bit weak, in my opinion. You two should water it a bit more often."

"*Water* it?" I frowned. Was that an old-fashioned euphemism I wasn't aware of?

She half-smiled. "Never mind. You are still so young. And he never grew up to his real age. Probably not the best combination, but we must work with what we have."

"What are you talking about, Julia?"

She flapped her hands around her, looking embarrassed. "I'm sorry. I was trying to get into the fairy role. Aren't Fairy Godmothers supposed to meddle in young ladies' affairs?" She sighed, and I gave her a blank stare. I wasn't sure I could still be categorized as a young lady. "Good, let's begin."

She started to wave her wand and murmur unintelligible words, but a sudden sense of worry pervaded me. I had no idea what had happened to Clarence after the fire. He could be just about anywhere, as far as I knew.

"Wait, Julia," I ventured. "What if he is somewhere dangerous? What if they are holding him captive, too? The last time I saw him he was fighting a man because he tried to kiss me…"

Julia stopped in her tracks and chuckled.

"Good old Clarence, that must have been a fun sight! I wish I hadn't missed it. You should know dueling was considered a sport in Georgian times, and he was quite passionate about it back then…"

"No, you don't understand!" I shrieked. "That was *definitely not* fun, and I don't know where he went afterward. What if your spell throws me straight into a trap? What if someone attacks me?"

"Don't you think you would know it, if he was somewhere dangerous?" She caressed my light bracelet meaningfully and her fingers tiptoed to the glowing bite marks on my neck. "You know more than you think, little girl. If only you wanted to listen to your inner voice."

I sighed. My inner voice was chatty indeed, but I didn't really trust it.

"But just in case, I'll show you a quick way to get back," Julia continued. "Nobody can harm you, because your body won't travel with you. There is nothing to fear, my child. And now," she said, waving her makeshift wand, "watch with attention, because we don't know what will be of me if the hunters find me. This might be the last time we get to practice together. Do you understand?"

"Yes." I stood up, shaking with excitement.

"Fine." Her lips curved upwards. "And, before we start, there are two important things. Listen up."

"Tell me."

"First: if anything happens to me, you have to promise to help Ludovic and his sister."

"I promise I will try," I agreed. It was the

best I could offer her, given the unstable situation.

"All right." She lay a cold, weightless hand on my arm. "And second, as your Fairy Godmother, I'm bound to remind you to make good use of this journey, because the spell will be automatically reversed at midnight."

Chapter 25

Alba

Julia recited an incantation and asked me to repeat it. As I pronounced the verses, the mirror turned into a gushing, silent glass waterfall.

"Now we wait for the glass to fade away, so you can step in," Julia instructed me. She stood next to me, imposing despite her small size. "And remember: never fear. Nobody can touch you. You will be safe at all times. Until midnight, that is."

"Why can't I stay past midnight and escape the witches for good?"

"Because we are not sending your physical body all the way there. That would take vast amounts of energy and knowledge… energy I can't afford now and expertise you don't possess. Tonight is just for practice." She twirled in her skirt and winked. "This spell will turn you into a wandering spirit for a couple of hours. I bet *he*'s going to be thrilled."

I had no idea what *he* was going to think, and I could only hope I wasn't about to walk into a lion's den, in spirit form or not. But the thought of finding Clarence, of seeing him and finding out what had happened to him, was inspiring enough to compensate for any fears or doubts I might have had against Julia's plan.

The mirror was nearly gone, and I caught a glimpse of a blurry dark forest on the other side.

"Where are we leaving my body?" It felt strange to talk about it like it was a shirt one could let go of. "Will *it* lie unconscious in the attic of the witches' house, or will you take care of it while my spirit, *um… flies around*?"

I imagined what the witches might do to me if they found me knocked out in the mirror room. A memory of the time Katie had drawn cat whiskers on her sleeping sister with permanent markers came to mind, exacerbating my anxiety.

Julia extended her hand and touched the melting mirror, creating rainbow waves on its surface.

"Don't worry," she said, dismissing my words. "Your body will remain somewhere in between worlds, right at the boundary below the veil. Just don't get lost on your way, because that would force your soul to remain forever in another dimension."

"Oh… okay…?" I swallowed. *What was I getting myself into?* "How do I avoid that?"

"Concentrate on the place —the person—you are about to visit." She scanned me with narrowed eyes. "That will keep you anchored, and you won't get lost in time and space."

"So that you know, if I remain a ghost forever because of this, I'm going to haunt you for the rest of your immortal life," I warned her.

Julia let out a brief laugh. "I can live with that. If only you knew about all the entities already haunting me." I arched an eyebrow, but she had already lifted her wand. "The portal is now open. Are you ready?" she asked.

"As ready as I'll ever be," I answered, and closed my eyes.

***

A flash of light engulfed me, then dissipated into a silent vacuum.

I was back at the inn, and Julia was gone.

I sensed Clarence before I saw him. To my shock, he didn't notice my arrival despite his fine hearing.

This was new.

Clarence was sitting on a crumbling wicker chair among the ruins of the burnt inn, concentrated on folding a piece of paper into an intricate swan shape. His long, strong fingers formed the paper swan's neck delicately: he was lost in his thoughts and unaware of my presence.

I studied him attentively, taking advantage of this rare occasion to take in his clean-cut features at leisure. The tailored white shirt hung open, currently sooty and stained, with the tails sticking out of his trousers. It offered an ample—and delightful—view of his torso, now marred by a few dark scars I had never seen before. I wondered what he might have gone through during the past days. His hair had become shorter on one side, slightly charred and sticking out in all directions, unrulier than usual but still framing the angles of his face as nicely as always. It was such an uncommon sight, to find this usually pristine, eternally graceful man in such a state of delicious messiness. He looked so human: so vulnerable.

Before I could decide how to greet him, an involuntary wheeze escaped my lungs, giving away my presence.

The paper swan dropped from his fingers onto the ashy ground, and he gaped at me, quickly jumping into a stalking position. His maroon gaze flared wildly in the darkness, a predatory gleam flickering in his eyes. In less than a second, he appeared by my side, so swift that I didn't even see him coming.

"Alba!" he gasped, and tried to embrace me, but his arms passed right through my ethereal body.

A deranged look flashed in his eyes as he took in my half-presence in the clearing, clad as I was in a hideous, threadbare linen nightgown. Did he turn even paler, or was it just my imagination?

In vain, he tried to touch me once again, becoming more and more agitated when he realized he couldn't.

"Clarence," I whispered quietly, trying to translate the turmoil of feelings inside me into something I could understand. Was it love? Was it spite? Whatever it was, it had brought me to him, and I was awfully relieved to see him. I breathed in his calming scent, trying to decide what to tell him first; but the only thing that came to mind was, "You look as though you've seen a ghost."

"My dear…" he mumbled, his voice unsteady as he sank his claws into his own arms with an expression of sheer horror. "What happened to you?"

Chapter 26

Clarence

Alba had a sickly air about herself.

She was surrounded by a faint purple glimmer and clad in a tattered cream shroud which floated eerily around her, defying the gentle breeze. An inquisitive gaze lit her face, but her skin remained a diluted watercolor of ivory and grey, its ashen hue unnervingly similar to my own.

The ghostly creature facing me was but a vague reflection of the warm-blooded, lively woman I had held in my arms just a few days earlier; an unsettling vision made of air, who was there… but then again wasn't.

Was I dreaming?

I dreamed so rarely.

But I couldn't feel her.

There was no scent. No energy. *Nothing.*

Just a spectral vision.

A *ghost.*

I had thought she was safe.

Had I fooled myself?

Could she be…?

Did she really escape the fire, as I had wanted to believe?

I had sifted through the ashes, combing the area with my heart in my throat, praying to gods I didn't believe in so I would not find her there.

This could not be.

I started to choke.

No.

The word burned in the back of my mind, but I did not want to acknowledge it.

My hands dampened and flapped fruitlessly all through the space she should have occupied.

"Have I startled you?" she asked. The voice, though hers, was but a distant echo.

She gave me a weak smile, which made her appear slightly less specter-like. I had never seen a ghost smile that way. I had never seen *any* ghosts do *anything*, to be frank. This ghost seemed oddly approachable.

"Sorry I was stalking you." Her cheeks were hollower, but that didn't make her any less alluring than before. "It wasn't my intention to frighten you."

Out of instinct, I tried to touch her once again, and my hand passed right through her body. She was so cold. Even colder than I. A pointillist painting made from droplets of winter dew.

"Alba…" I repeated. When I attempted to say her name, my voice broke. "Where were you? I have been hiding, I was injured… I was so concerned about you."

I fell to my knees, at her feet.

She sat beside me, her eyes half-closed as if trying to conjure yet another spirit.

"Don't worry, there's nothing wrong with me," she said, or rather *echoed*. "I was with the witches. They locked me in a basement, but I think I found a way to get out. What about you? Were you here all this time?"

I dismissed the question. "I'm well, thank you. But you…? What is… what is *this*? Is this really you?"

She exhaled a little naughty laugh. "Of course it's me."

"Well, don't be offended, my dear, but you appear fairly washed out."

I regretted the remark as soon as I said it, seeing as it caused her features to turn somber again.

"Clarence, I'm fine, I already told you. I had to use a little trick to come to you," she said. Given her appearance, it was hard to accept she was *fine*. "I'm relieved to see you are okay, too. But before you start with the teasing…" She smoothed her threadbare nightgown, pensively. "Our time tonight is limited. Please know that I'm really confused about you at the moment. I saw what you did to Carlo and…" She looked away. "So many things have happened lately… I'm not sure what to believe, whether to trust you. I know you gave me an explanation, but then you went and attacked him right after that. I'm not sure I know you anymore."

I stared at her, speechless.

That bastard from the boat had tried to steal her from me *twice*. First with a kiss, then outright attempting to kidnap her in her sleep. For all I knew, he could have caused the fire on purpose, in a bout of morbid, jealous retaliation.

As for my trustworthiness, I had to agree. I had been an absolute fool. Thanks to the profusion of idle hours spent evading the sun in a leaky chest freezer I had come to regret most of my past choices immensely.

I propped my elbow on one knee and massaged my forehead in a desperate attempt to summon some lucidity—and a few less ghosts.

"Forgive me, my dear. I can't think clearly, seeing you like this," I confessed. "For the moment, I need you to trust me. I'm not proud of all my actions, and it saddens me you feel like that toward me. Please, know that there was a reason for everything I did. For everything that happened. Can I have your trust for now?"

"Trust, you say," she muttered, pensive, seemingly remembering something important. "Okay." She nodded. "You have my trust. I believe you. But I expect a lengthy explanation as soon as life goes back to normal. Hopefully soon."

"I promise you will have it," I studied her surreptitiously. She did believe me. "But now, Alba, have mercy and tell me why you look so *transparent* tonight."

She raised her eyebrows, watching me with a sudden mixture of endearment and mischief.

"Why do *you* think I do?"

"Are you or are you not a ghost?" I said, *no:* I implored her. "I need to know. Then we can discuss whatever you desire."

"And what if I was one?" she asked quietly, her eyes half-closed.

"Then, I would have to die again and find a way to keep you company in the *after-afterlife*. It was never my wish to wander the earth as a ghost; but I will, if that's what it takes to embrace you once again."

"Ah." She sighed, her lips curling up just slightly. "That must be the most romantic thing I have ever been told." Alba leaned toward me and a minute, ethereal droplet of rain of a kiss found its way to the side of my ear. "Still, I believe it would be very unwise of you to try. I'm not sure you could become a ghost, even if you wished for it so… *fervently*."

I twisted my fingers so hard that I nearly snapped one of them.

"Is this… a consequence of the fire?" I asked, trying to keep the horrid recollections at bay. "Did you…" I took a deep, coerced breath, for courage. "Did you die that night?"

A brief silence ensued, although it might have lasted a century, for all I knew.

She shook her head, and her body started to quiver gently with what turned out to be a soft chuckle. She was so amused by my assumption, that the urge to rip off my thumb receded—at least momentarily.

"Then who did this to you?" I inquired nervously.

So, she had *not* died in the fire. *Fabulous news.* But she had turned into an intangible mist, and such things didn't just happen on their own.

"I did it myself," she declared proudly.

I sprung to my feet. "Are you insane? Please tell me this is not what I think."

Had she…? Would she…?

I knew things had been hard for her, but…

I held my head in my hands, unable to think logically any longer.

"*This is not what you think*," she repeated my words very slowly, brushing her icy fingers over my shoulder.

I shivered under her touch. I had always been the coldest creature of both of us. It was a peculiar sensation, to put it mildly.

"You really believe I'm a ghost?" She raised her eyebrows with fascination. "You *do* look frightened, Clarence. Since when are vampires scared of ghosts? Aren't you supposed to be in the same league? Peers in undeath?" She laughed quietly once more.

"Alba…" I grunted, crouching once again to look directly into her eyes. They were clouded and faded, the green in them almost grey now. I turned aside, unable to stare into them any longer. "Don't taunt me. This is not amusing at all."

"All right," she drawled. "I'll tell you who it was. It was Julia. She was playing the Fairy Godmother, and I got to make a wish."

"And you wished to become a disembodied soul?" I growled, trying not to pull out the remainder of my hair out of sheer exasperation.

She laughed. "I wished to be able to ghost you just like you did to me so very often during the past months."

I tried to exhale, but there was no more air in my lungs, so I pounded the crumbling wall behind us instead. Seeing the remaining bricks collapse into a pile of rumble provided me with some relief, though not even remotely enough to withstand the current conversation.

"I'm going to kill Julia for this," I said.

"Clarence, calm down." Her smile became a lighthouse, beaming in the middle of the ruined inn. "It's just an astral projection, I thought you would recognize that right away. She was teaching me a spell. I'm fine. I'm not dead. I promise."

I stood up and paced around her. Having her so close with no way to touch her was the closest thing to hell I could fathom at that moment.

Fine. She was alive, even though she was more a mirage than a normal human. She claimed to still possess a physical body, so it must be there… somewhere.

We only had to get her back into it.

I would drag Julia back from the Underworld with my bare hands if necessary, and I would make her turn this witch back into her tangible form, even if it was the last thing I did in this atrocious world.

"Listen to me." She cut my train of thought

abruptly. "Francesca is in danger, and her brother, too. They have been captured by hunters, and they are being tortured. I managed to summon Julia, and she helped me get to you. She also gave me the exact address where they are keeping them hostage. I think I've made an ally among the witches, and she could help me escape. I have a plan."

I froze as she spoke of Francesca. My dear Francesca. Being captured by hunters was the worst possible fate for a vampire. And not only her, also Ludovic. None of them deserved such an end.

For some reason, immortality was prone to whole decades of tedium sprinkled with sudden bouts of tragedies, all ensuing in a matter of hours. This seemed just like the beginning of one of those.

"Clarence, are you paying attention to me?" Alba asked, and I nodded, making an effort to look at her colorless face without wincing. "I suggest you meet me tomorrow night at the witches' house, by the Museum of Witchcraft, and help me escape. I can wait for you in the attic. There's an old window you could use to break in. Do you think you could make it? Will you find it on your own?"

I was feeling much better that evening. Slumbering in the chest freezer had helped, and the wound caused by the silver dagger had nearly closed. Yet, I was still starving to death, and so far, I hadn't been able to shift, which limited my ability to go outside during the day. Silver daggers were vicious weapons, and they caused all sorts of trouble. But perhaps, in a day or two, I would be able to fly again and make it to Como. It was hard to be certain.

"Definitely," I said, trying to sound convincing.

"Okay. That was the urgent part," she said. "Now come here." She sat back on the grass and tapped on the ground for me to join her. "We still have a while to talk before the spell sends me back to the place I came from. I can only stay until midnight."

"Midnight?" I sneered. "*Centuries shall pass away; secret things be known*; but witches will keep making a fuss about bloody midnight forevermore." I held my forehead, paraphrasing Poe. It was too much witchcraft nonsense for one single evening. "And then *we* vampires are supposed to be stuck in time."

"This has nothing to do with being stuck in time, Clarence," she said, in her *mother* voice. "Midnight is the magical moment when today becomes tomorrow. Don't you think that's kind of special?"

"At least you seem to be benefitting from the forceful mingling with witches," I groaned. "Probably more beneficial than cowering in a freezer chest while sitting on a puddle of rotten raspberry ice-cream."

She gaped at me. "Did you just say a freezer chest?" She blinked. "Was it, by any chance, a 63-inch-long freezer chest?"

I snorted. "Do you think I walk around with a measuring tape?"

She rubbed her neck, her mouth still wide

open. "Incredible," she said.

"What is so incredible?" I asked, confused.

"Never mind. It's too long to explain."

We remained silent, sitting next to each other.

"I guess it wasn't too much fun," she said, "being there for so long."

"Boredom was the least of my concerns. The only thing I wanted was to fly again and find you. You were the only thing in my mind all these days."

"Trust me, you have been living in my thoughts, too." She stirred, and the air carried a cold sigh my way. "Not only in my thoughts. I can't explain it, but… I could feel you, Clarence. Normally, I would have worried sick about you, but somehow I sensed you were safe."

"I know. I felt the same, too." I paused. "That is, until you turned up looking like The Canterville Ghost, minus the chains."

"I thought he was a really silly, clumsy ghost who didn't manage to scare anyone?" She raised her eyebrows with suspicion.

"Well, yes, that's right," I said, trying not to smile at her accurate—and fitting—description of Sir Simon de Canterville. "Anyhow, your new appearance was… a little bit distracting."

She lowered her hand, uncovering the two small scars on the crook of her neck.

"Bloody hell!" I shouted, leaning forward to take a closer look. It was a good thing I couldn't touch her, because just the sight of those two little lumps caused such an intense reaction inside me that I had to pause and close my eyes before speaking again. "Why did I listen to you? People will see it! This… this is going to remain forever!"

She danced a little, sitting with her arms around her knees. "I like *forever,* even if you don't. In these turbulent days, and given the uncertainty of everything around me, it sounds so… reassuring."

She stretched her back and the formless, hideous nightgown slid off her perfectly rounded shoulders.

"You are an obstinate, incorporeal witch." I said, shaking my head. "But you will always be my Isolde, translucent or not."

Alba grinned and tried to wrap me in her arms, forgetting she was a mere hologram. She nearly toppled over, unable as she was to prop herself against me, and I loathed not being able to help her stand up.

"And you will always be my ancient, infuriating vampire," she said, regaining her balance on her own.

"That's right," I admitted. "So, what now?"

"Now it's when the spectral entity goes and kisses you," she said mischievously, and winked.

Her lips left a halo of ice on mine: I was a warmblood again compared to her newfound coolness.

They say ghost kisses send whirlwinds rushing in your ears.

It is true.

Weaving the translucent wisps of air around her, I conjured her peculiar witch smell, so distracting now it was absent. I remembered it so well that I could almost bring it back, just with the power of my mind.

For a second, my fingers got tangled in a chestnut, silky mess.

Or didn't they?

No, they did not.

It must have been my imagination.

She may be a ghost, but she was still her, and she was here, and she was alive.

And I was ever so thankful to have my beloved witch back.

Chapter 27

Alba

I had never seen Clarence in such a state of distress.

As far as I knew, he was supposed to be the one startling people, and not the other way around. And yet, on my arrival, he had been terrified of a ridiculous fake ghost… which happened to be *me*.

It was so endearing that, for a second, I forgot about the precarious situation we all found ourselves in.

The only thing I really wished, right there, right then, was to kiss him properly before midnight stole him from me and threw me back into the witches' den.

"Damn it," he said, rubbing his forehead, "you scared me, Isolde."

I heard a low buzz coming out of my chest, and a ball of light started to form between us.

At first, it was tiny, not larger than a pebble; but then, it started to grow and became fluffy and round.

"Another new trick?" Clarence took the sphere in his hands and turned it around.

"You can see it?" I gasped. "No way, you can *hold* it?"

"I certainly can. There's this halo around you all the time, hadn't I told you?" He seemed truly surprised I didn't know. "It used to be grey and frayed, but it's definitely improving! This bundle must have detached from the loose fringes around your head. You are shedding those ugly chunks of stale energy, at last."

He had been seeing that all this time? What else were vampires able to see? What wonders did he just take for granted, not even considering them mention-worthy?

"You'll never cease to amaze me," I confessed with a head shake.

"Well, what can I say… my prowess is rather splendid." Clarence smirked, gradually returning to his normal self. He kneaded the light ball, twisting it into an infinity shape before leaping back far enough to throw it at me. The orb spun in the air, in a boomerang-like pattern. I jumped to catch it mid-flight but missed. He laughed at me and allowed the orb to land on the ground, bouncing into the nearby shrubbery.

"The Witches of the Lake pretended to play ball with energy spheres." I was perplexed. "Maybe they weren't pretending, after all?"

Clarence smiled and leapt into the shrubbery, reappearing with the shining object in his hand. "Catch!" he shouted with glee.

I stepped back to seize it, but the impulse made me stumble backwards.

"This is so cool!" I giggled. The ball squirmed against my ethereal fingers like a living being. It reminded me of a warm—but oddly weightless—little bunny.

We played fetch for a while, nestled in our magic bubble in between time and space, and tacitly agreed to set aside the worries while the Fairy Godmother's spell lasted. Clarence kept leaping cheerfully in the air, following the light ball with predatory skill: I stared at him with astonishment, as I had rarely been privy to that feral side of him. He could virtually fly, his movements so swift and effortless that I could have watched his little performance for days on end and never got tired of it. Obviously, there was no way for me to best him: if he ever missed the ball, it was mostly because he was rolling on the floor, laughing too hard at my clumsiness to pay attention to the game. It was too easy for him, but he seemed to enjoy himself as much as I did.

As for me, I relished in my temporary ability to hover over the ground; but even as a ghost, I soon became tired and breathless. It didn't take me long to end up slumping with exhaustion, my hands raised in surrender.

"Okay, vampire, you win," I grunted, and he bowed in a gentlemanly gesture of appreciation, a satisfied grin illuminating his face.

I lay on the ground, or at least I tried to: being insubstantial made things harder than they seemed. I kept floating an inch over the frosty grass, blissfully ignored by the law of gravitation.

"Why hadn't we done this before?" Clarence asked, beaming as he lay next to me and crossed his arms nonchalantly behind his head.

It occurred to me that, currently, he appeared much more human than I did. For a start, he wasn't transparent, nor levitating over the ground.

He looked dazzling, relaxed, and *so* happy.

Right then and there, I realized I was irrevocably in love with that vampire—with that man. For the first time ever, I secretly admitted the truth to myself—*with the proper words*. No matter what life threw at us, be it bundles of light or darkness, I didn't wish to stay away from someone, dead or undead, who was able to make me smile and forget my sorrows even in the bleakest of times.

"Clarence…" I muttered, suddenly overwhelmed by all the emotions dashing inside me. I caressed the air above his cheek, taking care not to let my spectral fingers disappear into his skin. Things were weird enough already, without the added perk of untouchability.

"That tickles," he complained, contorting his face in a funny grimace.

I turned my hand in the air and studied the beautiful curve of his dark eyebrows through it. I leaned over him with fascination and tried again.

"Does it, really?" I asked. "I can't feel anything."

"*Uh-huh.* But keep doing it." He closed his eyes, and a simper found its way to his lips. "Mind you, in two centuries I have had it much worse."

I tried to slap his leg, unsuccessfully.

"Clarence! You ungrateful vampire! I'm doing my best, given the circumstances."

"What about this?" He propped himself up on an elbow and drew a very slight line, wiggling his fingertips from the crown of my head to my hip.

This time, I shuddered.

"Still nothing?" He was clearly growing intrigued by our fun supernatural experiment.

"No—I actually felt something. It was like… tiny creepy snakes… or fleas," I reflected aloud.

He snorted, which made the snakes crawl even faster and pinch the sensitive spot right under my armpit. I tried to shake them off, but they didn't want to go away.

"*Snakes?*" He shook his head. "*Fleas?* Isolde, can you at least *make an effort* to be faintly romantic? Just for once? Please?"

"Okay…" I sighed. "It's like… frozen satin ribbons… growing out of your fingertips; so thin and light that it's a torment. But they are pleasant too, and binding, and… relentless."

Clarence tilted his head. Sheer delight radiated out of him as he struggled to hide his admiration. "That was so much better, my dear! Mary Shelley would have been proud of you."

He bent to face me, his maroon eyes gleaming in the chilly night as he kissed me, very slowly. His hair was ruffled, and his pale skin shone under the moonlight like polished selenite. He was, and would always be, a bedazzling sight.

"How am I doing?" he asked, raising a hesitant glance.

"*Um*… not to be harsh, but… more than a kiss, that was a bunch of spiders tap-dancing below my nose."

"I'm taking back the Mary Shelley analogy, just so you know. At least until you stop comparing my efforts to insects and reptiles," he grunted, arching an eyebrow. "Was this better or worse than the fleas?"

"No, slightly better. But…" I bit my lip. "Maybe a bit too soft? I guess I've grown used to vampire nibbles," I teased him.

He became so still that I thought he had literally turned to stone.

"Clarence, are you alright?" I waved my hand through his chest until he finally blinked.

He scratched the back of his head and looked away.

"About that…" he said ruefully, fixing his gaze on the marks on my neck. "I'm aware we still haven't had time to discuss the subject properly after…"

"Wait a minute," I interrupted him, "are you blushing?" Of course, he wasn't; but the way he rubbed his neck he might have, if he could. "You're *vampire-blushing*, Clarence! In all shades of white!"

"I'm most definitely not blushing," he declared. "That is virtually impossible."

"So I thought, but look at you! You are so cute when you do that!"

"Excuse me, but vampires are not supposed to be cute," he admonished me in all seriousness. "And besides, you should try harder if you want me to *vampire-blush*, as you name it."

He stared at me with lustful defiance in his eyes.

"Be careful what you wish for," I said softly. "I'm an entity now. I'm sure I could be really dangerous if I wanted to."

I closed my eyes and inched closer to him, allowing my weightless body to float gently. I circled around him with my arms open and he watched me, absolutely enthralled. The air rushed around us in whirlwinds, and before I knew, I felt a slight resistance, a vague pressure under my palms.

"What…?" I murmured, my hand over his shoulders, now clearly feeling the firmness of his muscles under my fingertips.

I didn't know how I had done it, but I was there.

Whole.

I materialized beside him and my feet touched the ground with a quiet thump, right on the ashes of the burned inn. He burrowed in my arms, as astounded as I was to find out that my hands were warm and consistent again.

"Very well, witch," he whispered in a ragged voice, "this time, you win."

We got rid of the sooty shirt and the tattered nightgown, hurrying and well aware of the invisible magic clock ticking against us.

The simple ability to sense each other's skin suddenly became the most precious treasure. A simple thing, but so essential: as always in life, losing something turned to be the only way to start valuing it.

I caressed every tiny nook of him with fervor, realizing what a gift it was: just being able to touch each other.

To be there, all of me.

Nude and lost in each other.

We blended, mist and earth rising and falling in a mystical ballet. I let his solid chest shelter me, forgetting to breathe as his lips found mine, and we both came to life a minute before midnight.

Chapter 28

Alba

There was no bell to strike the hour in the wrecked inn, but the moon flickered twelve times in the sky to signal the end of our sweet truce.

"I'm coming for you tomorrow. At midnight, as proper magical customs dictate," Clarence said solemnly. "Find your way to that attic, and I will take care of the rest."

My hands started to fade and became faintly transparent again.

"I'll be there," I whispered, my voice swept away by a ghostly wind current.

The large mirror from the witches' house emerged behind us: a daunting, spectral presence threatening to suck me in like a black hole.

"Look at me now, Alba, for this is important." He placed one hand on his unbeating heart and the other over mine. "On this night, I vow to never leave your side again, unless it's you who sends me away. For I love you, my Isolde, and trying to deny that was the most foolish mistake of both my lives. And I hope one day you shall forgive me for all the grief I caused you and find it in you to love me back in the same manner."

I gaped at him as my body dissolved like salt into water and my fingertips blurred into the surrounding space.

His mesmerizing maroon eyes flashed, fixed on mine as he added with a significant nod, "And I mean this. Forever."

Forever, I tried to repeat, but my voice was gone before I could answer and tell him how I felt. My eyes filled with tears, drawn away by the inevitable pull of the mirror.

I extended my misty arms toward Clarence, hoping for one more second to kiss him goodbye; but the mirror's energy sucked me in with the force of a tornado and pulled us apart.

A flash followed, and Clarence and the inn were gone.

***

After the burst of light, I found myself lying on the floor, back in the attic of the witches' house. I was exhausted. Just like Alice had warned me, the extensive use of magic had left me depleted. When I tried to stand up, I found my limbs heavy and virtually unable to move.

Crawling, I started to drag my sluggish, alien body toward the door, when a soft cackle startled me.

"Julia?" I asked weakly, striving to lift my

head off the hardwood floor.

It wasn't Julia waiting for me by the door.

"Sorry, the traitor left early," Valentina said. "I wouldn't have expected less from that vixen. She reeked of death to high heaven. I had to air the whole house after she escaped."

I exhaled and flopped back on the floor. My real-world body had become too cumbersome to handle.

"Aren't you going to tell me where you went?" Valentina asked, nudging me with her foot.

"I fell asleep," I lied. It sounded plausible enough.

"Of course you did. Did you have sweet dreams?" Valentina crossed her arms. She was standing under the door lintel in her sleeping gown, her white hair gleaming under the moon. "Such an endearing love story. *The Beauty and the Beast*, wasn't it? Or was it rather *Little Red Riding Hood*… and the wolf?"

"No, it's the one called *The Wicked Old Witch Who Should Have Minded Her Own Business*," I growled, feeling for the buttons of my nightgown and realizing with dismay that the garment wasn't there at all. Oh, shit. I was stark naked in front of Valentina, sprawled on the floor like a dead starfish.

"Sometimes, when mice are hiding in their hole, they forget their tail is out," she said with a smirk. "Did you think us so stupid not to notice your little escapade?"

I didn't answer. I had trusted Julia to keep

me safe. There must have been a good reason for her to leave me in the lurch like that.

"So, we should expect our guest tomorrow at midnight, is that right?" Valentina sneered. "You know, my witchling, that lady friend of yours is not the only one who can put mirrors to good use. I peeked into the other side and let me tell you: it was distressing to watch one of our kind involved in such improper behavior with an undead… but you know I'd do anything for the highest good of my sisters."

I swallowed, mortified at the thought of what Valentina might have seen and heard. This must be one of the most humiliating moments in my whole life.

"Rest assured," she continued, "I'll take care personally that you get hold of no more mirrors. Intruding in another witch's home like that old rockabilly did tonight is considered very bad manners in our world. Although I doubt you could repeat the feat on your own. Or would you, little witchling?"

I clenched my teeth, helpless. She was probably right.

"Don't worry about your vampire lover," she said, as she started to descend the stairs, dragging me by the hair like the witches in fairy tales. "He won't be disappointed. There will be a witch waiting for him tomorrow… though it might not be the one he's expecting."

***

The witches locked me back into the basement. I yelled and kicked, throwing all objects at my reach against the doors and windows. I even attempted to cast the *Fulminatio* spell to bust the door lock, but I encountered two obstacles: first, I was absolutely drained after my mirror travel adventure; and second, as soon as I blurted the first verse of the spell, Valentina barged into the room carrying an imposing staff. Either she had uncanny ways to detect magic in the bud, or she wasn't as deaf as Alice had suggested.

"Would you like me to chain you to the wall and muzzle you? Because I think you are begging me to," she cautioned me. "Just knowing the text of one Great Spell doesn't automatically turn you into a match for a veteran high priestess."

She strolled around the room, a true earthquake scene after my destructive bout of frustration.

"If you behave properly, we're sending you back home as soon as we catch the bloodsucker. Until then, be a good girl, will you? Don't make me chastise you."

She raised her staff and all the objects in the room flew to the ceiling and hovered right over my head. I recoiled, but the floating altar table and all the shiny—and sharp—crystals on it followed my steps like an ominous cloud.

"Do anything stupid again and those rocks will hail on your head, *capisci*?"

***

That day the witches didn't bring me any food, nor did I receive Alice's customary visit. I was dizzy and still very weak due to hunger and exhaustion when Elda finally brought me some watery soup toward the evening. She delivered it to my doorstep with a silent, accusatory glance. It tasted off, bitter and spicy, but I had got used to their bizarre cookery and ate it up without a question.

The soft winter daylight faded slowly, until the golden glare of the streetlights started to filter through the high barred windows of my prison.

The clock on the stairs struck each hour unhurriedly, oblivious to my fear and sorrow.

Clarence had promised to come for me. My original plan had been to convince Alice to leave my door open so I could sneak silently into the attic, taking advantage of the witches' deafness. He had promised to come, and he always kept his promises.

You must choose trust over fear, Alice had told me after reading my fortune in the cards. Well, trust I had. But we hadn't planned a fight. And the fear was threatening to overpower me.

I started to feel queasy. The soup had left a strange aftertaste in my mouth, and my head was starting to spin.

Would Clarence be foolhardy enough to try to face a whole coven of witches on his own, once he realized what he had walked into?

Would he put himself at risk just to get me out of there?

I prayed he wouldn't.

I knew he would.

Chapter 29

Clarence

The lake shone like an Y-shaped mirror of onyx as I hovered above it, headed to the scenic city of Como. The silhouette of its blue shores reminded me of the dowsing rods used by diviners to find water, and I laughed at the irony: I had spent days wondering about Alba's whereabouts, while overlooking a thirty-mile long arrow pointing directly at her location. It was unsettling to think of the many times I had been blind to the answers glaring right at me.

Unsurprisingly, the smell of witches pervaded the streets surrounding the Museum of Witchcraft. It was practically a miracle I hadn't detected it in all the hours I spent hiding in the devastated inn. I blamed it on the wind, which had been blowing south and away from the lake for many days.

I had been lucky enough to come across a wandering human right before sunrise. He was an early hunter, unlikely to kill anything with that nasty cigar giving away his presence to all forest creatures in a hundred-mile radius. Smoker blood was not my favorite, but the chances of finding a better catch in such dark and wintry weather were very slim. So, I hunted the hunter and drank enough from him to recover my strength—more than expected, which had rendered him unconscious. I left him in a sheltered spot near a human settlement with his memories—and my bite marks—suitably erased. Not my proudest moment, but necessary for that vicious silver wound to finally vanish and allow me to fly again.

Following Alba's directions, I headed to the roof of the neighboring townhouse. I perched patiently on the orange clay tiles and listened to the sounds inside through the windowpane.

Her breathing sounded close, but oddly irregular. Almost sickly. She definitely hadn't been poorly last night. Ghostly, yes; but not unwell, like she appeared to be now, judging by the ragged, paused breaths leaking out of the house.

Slow and labored, the sounds were coming from a nearby spot right below the roof. I could hear and smell other people, too: the other witches, perhaps sleeping in the lower floors.

I waited for Alba's sign for me to come in, as agreed.

I waited some more, but the sign never came.

Life as a vampire had taught me the value of patience. As the long-lived predator I was, I had become a master of calm perseverance. But all the tribulations of the past weeks had caused my patience to start running awfully thin.

I grew tired of waiting.

Shifting discreetly into a human form, I broke the window lock and slipped into the dark attic.

I found Alba curled up in the corner of a nearly empty room, rocking herself like a madwoman. Most of the walls were covered in mirrors, and I frowned at the vast glass surfaces, which taunted me in return and denied me a reflection.

Swiftly, I leaped to her side and tried to help her on her feet. But she resisted, striving to pull me downwards with all her weight. She was never too heavy but, for some unexpected reason, that petite little witch had turned from weightless ghost to human boulder in the roughly twenty-four hours we had been apart.

"What are you doing?" I whispered, lifting her off the floor against her will. "We need to go."

She struggled against my grip with erratic, uncoordinated movements.

"Are you… drunk?" I asked.

Go away, she mouthed silently, her eyes glancing sideways just slightly, alternating from the door to the roof window. *Fast. Now. Leave!*

I released her, blinking in confusion.

What was all this about? Had she changed her mind about me?

Why did she suddenly want to stay with the witches?

Why on earth had she chosen the night of our escape to be half seas over, like a bloody buccaneer?

"The witches," she hissed in a slurry tone, as if reading my mind, "It's a trap. Leave me, Clarence! Go!"

"I fear no witches but you," I mumbled, draping an arm around her waist and taking a swift leap to the roof. I held onto a ceiling beam, holding Alba like a sack of grain with my free arm. The door to the room opened, and an elderly lady in a frilly nightgown entered the room, holding a young girl's hand. The girl must be barely fifteen, practically a child.

"So, what do we have here?" the lady said. "Looking for your long-lost reflection, sir? Come down, I will hand it back to you: I hear bonedust has no trouble with mirrors."

Several thoughts crossed my mind at the same time. Would it be too reckless to take off without erasing those women's memories? Oblivion required touching them, but how safe could it be, touching that old witch's hands? Not quite, I decided.

I kicked the ceiling window wide open with my knee: we would deal with these witches some other day. I passed one leg through the frame, which left us hanging from it upside down like bats. I struggled to reach the roof and get out without dropping sluggish Alba in the process.

Just when I was about to succeed, the window slammed closed of its own accord, stabbing my legs with shattered glass shards and forcing me to let go of the wooden frame.

We dropped to the floor, at the witches' feet. They were still holding hands, and the eldest one snapped her fingers. Three more witches appeared and surrounded us, forming a small, eerie circle.

I deposited somnolent Alba gently on the floor and studied the witches as I got up on my knees. There were five of them. I could probably kill them all relatively fast: just jump at their throats and slaughter them one by one. A bit messy, but effective. Nevertheless, attacking a group of elderly women and teenagers felt ridiculously wrong. I needed to find a better way out. And fast.

Alba had fallen asleep. I held her tight and stood up, turning to look at each of the witches, assessing their weaknesses. They must know I was hesitating.

"Surrender now, and she lives," the white-haired lady said, pointing at Alba.

"Would you murder your own sister?" I asked with a mixture of fascination and disbelief.

"That one is not our sister," she spat. "She's too far gone to help her. She will never be one of us."

No, that she would not.

Fortunately.

"I have a better proposal," I said slowly, flexing my knees to gather momentum. "I'm going to leap out of this room, and you all are going to stay put where you are. And then, I shall spare your lives *and* your memories."

I jumped up, ready to break the window glass with the crown of my head if necessary; but we never reached the ceiling.

An invisible wall appeared mid-air, and my arms and legs turned to stone.

I could not move.

Invisible ties restrained me, immobilizing each part of my body.

The witches had closed their eyes: all but the eldest one, who was muttering an incantation under her teeth with her gaze fixed on us.

"You seem to be a properly educated gentleman," she said. "I'm sure you are familiar with Medusa's legend."

I squinted at her, my eyelids stalled half-closed and unwilling to open any further. Alba was about to slip off my arm, which was numb and had ceased to obey me. We were floating over the witches' circle, and they were staring at us triumphantly.

"You should have never entered Medusa's home, vampire," the lady continued, "for a man your age should already know what happens to those who stare upon a powerful witch's face when she's cross."

Alba fell off my useless arms and crashed to the floor below us, hitting the middle of the witches circle with a soft thud.

I fell right after her, trapped in a body which had turned into a prison. Another witch came and took Alba away, while another one chained me and dragged me down a flight of stairs.

Stiff like a corpse, I watched the events unfold with horrified detachment.

Medusa had turned me into stone, and stone I would remain until she released me.

Chapter 30

Alba

"Why is she petrified?" Agnes said, pricking my ribs with a sharp, red nail. "I thought you only cast the spell on the vampire."

"So I did," Valentina answered, pursing her lips. "This is odd. It has nothing to do with my spell. I released it half an hour ago, anyway. I may be gifted, but even I can't hold an immobilizing spell for hours on end."

I was back in the basement of the witches' house.

Clarence wasn't there.

They had taken him away.

Chained.

In a *hearse.*

The witches had drugged me and used me as bait to lure him into their trap. They must have spiked that awfully bitter soup with a powerful sedative. By the time they had guided me upstairs to await him, I could barely speak, let alone use any spells.

Slowly, long after Clarence was gone, the effects of the narcotic herbs had begun to dissipate, and the events of the night started to replay in my mind.

I felt nauseous—again—and I arched to throw up all over the sleeping mat. It was colder than usual in the basement room, and I started to shiver uncontrollably. The witches covered me with sheets and blankets, and I vomited all over them. One of them rushed to hold a bowl under my chin.

"Side effects of valerian root," Valentina said casually. "It will wear off."

"How much did you give her?" another one asked.

"I don't know, five grams or so? I didn't want to risk it, so I put some in the tea, and some more in the soup… who knows how much she took in the end? I didn't expect her to eat everything up!"

"Are you insane?" Berenice whisper-shouted. "That's twenty times more than she should have taken! Enough to knock out a mammoth. What if she dies on us? She's already undernourished!"

I didn't know much about valerian root, but I doubted the sheer devastation which consumed me could be solely caused by the side effects of that herb. I had just lured the love of my life to a mortal trap. Worst of all: I had done it approximately two seconds after realizing he *was* the love of my life. A piece of information I hadn't had the time to share with him, and now I never might.

I threw up again.

Berenice joined the small group hovering around me. There was a deep frown on her forehead, and she put a warm cup to my lips.

"This girl is in shock, can't you see that?" she chided the others, making her way among them and sitting next to me on the floormat.

"What, are you on their side now?" Valentina fanned herself with a piece of parchment. Seemingly I was the only one about to freeze.

The taste of bile still filled my mouth, so I downed the beverage Berenice was offering in one noisy gulp, not caring anymore whether they outright poisoned me. To my surprise, the liquid was sweet, thick, and vaguely comforting. I drank the whole cup and closed my eyes.

I wanted to cry. Shriek. But the tears had dried up and there was nothing left. Just a profound, devastating emptiness.

"Of course I'm not on their side," Berenice answered with a huff. "But you could show a bit more empathy for the witchling. It might be the first time she saw such potent magic. No wonder she's in shock."

I was too weak to roll my eyes, otherwise I would have. When Valentina bent over to check my pulse, I made sure to be sick all over her. And that was the only highlight of that bleak and utterly gruesome night.

***

I woke up the next morning and found the door to my room hanging wide open for the first time since my arrival. Nobody stood watch next to it.

Was I free to go?

The memories of the last hours trickled in irregular—and increasingly painful—ripples, but I pushed them back, at least temporarily. A deep void was growing inside my chest, and if I allowed it to, it might have ended up devouring me.

I stood up and got out of the lavender-smelling basement, following the laughs of the witches coming from the kitchen upstairs. They were in the middle of a very animated conversation, admiring some dreadful works of stitchery and slurping their customary green smoothies for breakfast.

"Good morning, little witchling," Berenice said from behind the sink, "glad to see you up so early. Would you like some orange juice?"

I snarled a guttural yes and slumped on one of the empty chairs around the table, with my face in my hands, my head too heavy for my neck to hold it. It must be the herbs the witches had put in my food, combined with the fall from the ceiling to the floor. *Clarence,* I thought, fighting the mind fog, *where are you?*

The sound of the orange juicer put an end to the witches' mindless chatter, and I was thankful for their enforced stillness. Their strident voices were worse than woodpeckers hammering on my brain.

When Berenice turned the appliance off, someone was ringing wildly at the door.

"I'll get it," she said, putting a tall glass in front of me and wiping her hands on a multicolored apron.

She disappeared down the narrow corridor and the main door screeched when she opened it. There was plenty of cooing, and a few low-pitched, dismissive grunts.

"*O Dio mio*, come in, you're freezing!" she squealed, and a few thumps on the floor informed me that she must be skipping like an excited kangaroo.

Berenice trotted back to the kitchen, followed by the newcomer's heavy footsteps, which faded into one of the adjacent rooms.

"You won't guess who came!" she shouted, peeking into the kitchen and ripping off her apron. She smoothed her dress and fixed her lipstick with a fingertip, using a pot lid as a mirror. "He's waiting in the living room," she muttered through puckered lips.

The witches put down their breakfasts and marched out of the kitchen, but nobody invited me to join them. I settled in my chair and sipped my orange juice with disinterest, almost wishing there was some sort of drug inside it to numb the corroding grief which was threatening to spread through all my body.

"Come, Alba," Valentina came back in and forced me to stand up. "I don't like it when you remain alone for too long."

***

When the group of witches reached the living room, their lively chatter came to an abrupt halt.

The man standing in the middle of the dusty Persian rug had the look of someone who had just come back from a date with Death herself. Rivers of reddened veins outlined his azure blue eyes, and his otherwise well-tanned complexion had turned a washed out yellow. A startling changeover for the sporty, robust man I had shared a plane ride with not so long ago.

"Carlo, my sweet child!" Valentina exclaimed, hugging him.

She was tiny against the wide-shouldered policeman, but I had seen what she was able to do, and that made her much scarier than him.

The four women swarmed around Carlo, but I remained under the door lintel, silent.

"Shouldn't she go back to the basement?" Agnes whispered. She had forgotten to put on her hearing aids, which meant her whispers were perfectly audible for anyone else in the room.

"No, it's her I came to talk to," he said, dangling his coat over his shoulder.

The women exchanged surprised glances.

"All right, Alba can stay," Valentina said with a frown.

"I'd rather speak to her in private," Carlo

added with a lopsided grin. Berenice nearly choked. "Glad you two made it out of the fire alive," he said, in a tone which was all but glad, referring to me and Berenice. "I don't know about you, but I saw my whole life flash before my eyes that night."

I swallowed and nodded slowly.

Carlo grabbed my arm, his touch inappropriately warm as compared to Clarence's icy hands.

"The woman looks awful, what have you been doing with her?" Carlo asked the witches, taking in the shabby rags I was wearing and my neglected and underfed appearance. They averted their gazes and none answered. "She's pale as a ghost. A walk outside would do her well. What do you think, Valentina?"

"Please. That would be nice," I said weakly. Apart from my spectral visit to Clarence, I hadn't left the house since my arrival.

"Better not," Valentina grunted. She stood in front of the door, blocking the exit.

"Just to the lake and back," Carlo said, rubbing the high priestess' shoulders amiably.

"I'm not sure I trust her." She crossed her arms, eyeing me with suspicion. "She's problematic."

"Don't worry, I'll keep an eye on her. We'll be back before lunch," Carlo said in an appeasing tone.

"You better behave," Valentina warned me.

I let out a ragged breath as my only reply. Even if I had wanted to, there was no way I could pull off anything heroic in my current physical and mental state. I was heartbroken, exhausted, and still suffering the after-effects of whatever drugs they had given me the previous night.

"She'll be a good girl," Carlo answered instead of me, flipping his trench coat in the air. He paused for a second and pinched my nightgown with disgust. "Just put normal clothes on her, okay? I can't take her out wearing this filthy bedsheet."

***

Carlo held my arm as we walked down the narrow street, headed toward the shores of Lake Como. I dragged my feet like a zombie, too defeated to resist.

Stepping outside seemed like a good enough reason to allow him to do whatever he wanted with me.

Want to hold my hand?

Fine.

Want to throw me into the lake to be devoured by the fish?

Please, be my guest.

Berenice had lent me some of her colorful, clown-like clothes, and their cheerfulness was physically painful. Meanwhile, the bite marks on my neck had gone dormant, their roots vanished like they had never been there.

The morning was pleasant, bright and chilly; the air infused with the scent of algae and pine trees and a slight whiff of spring wafting shyly from the south.

The stores were opening, and their metallic roller shutters went up with deafening rumbles. Many locals sat comfortably in the sun, sipping espressos on the narrow terraces which bordered the cobbled streets of Como. Everyone around us was in an enviably delightful, relaxed mood.

Everyone—but me.

When people looked at us, they probably saw just a couple of foreign tourists strolling arm in arm toward the lakeshore.

If only they knew I was crumbling inside.

Carlo pointed at the only empty table in a café nearby. It was next to a window, overlooking the blistering waters.

"Coffee?" he asked.

I grunted, shaking my head. "I've been sitting inside for days. I'd rather keep walking."

"Yes. Me too," he answered curtly. "Although I've spent longer lying than sitting."

I eyed him attentively. Judging by his yellowish face, he must have been discharged from hospital barely a day or two ago.

"So, you are alive," I said, hoping he would finally tell me what he wanted from me. The last time we had met, he had brought me wildflowers and I had kicked him out of my room because of the two vampires hiding in my closet.

Carlo remained silent for a while, which was unlike him. When he finally answered, his eyes were fixed in the reflections of the sun over the minute golden ripples of the lake.

"I need you to be honest with me," he said. "Otherwise, I'll have to resort to harsher persuasion techniques, and I really don't feel like doing that. You look bad enough already."

Was he threatening to torture me? I laughed inwardly: that man really had no idea how little I cared about anything anymore.

"Okay," I said with a tired puff. "Ask away."

"You asked whether I was alive, and the question is not that far-fetched: I could be dead now," he said, his voice hoarse as he looked deeply into my eyes. "But I'm not, and someone is going to pay for this."

He lifted his t-shirt and showed me his torso, toned by thousands of hours spent in a gym. It was covered now in dreadful-looking scars; scars caused by a beast with sharp claws and fangs.

My stomach churned.

"Do you know what happened to him?" I asked. My voice shook. I was so desperate to know about Clarence that I didn't realize what a stupid question that was in the given situation.

Carlo pounded his fist against an old tree beside us, causing dry leaves to rain on us.

"What's wrong with you, woman?" he shouted. "Is this really the only thing you can think of after seeing what that monster did to me? I said I was going to ask the questions, not the other way around. But if you must know, he's on his way to the place where dead things belong."

I stifled a gasp and shook his hand off my

arm.

"So, the witches were right." He huffed with disdain. "When I met you, I wanted to believe he had enthralled you, the way their kind do. But it's obvious there's something else going on here, or you are a lost cause."

"What?" I stopped and leaned against an old house overlooking the lake. My legs refused to hold me any longer.

"Tell me why I found a vampire that night—" he lowered his voice, pulling me so close that I could smell his leather jacket, "tell me you didn't invite him in. Tell me why, when the witches sent me for you, I found him next to you—in your bed."

"What's the point of this conversation?" I asked, eyes closed, as the floor seemed to melt under my feet. "I didn't invite anyone in."

That, at least, was the truth. Those vampires just kept wandering into people's dwellings without anyone's permission. They didn't seem to be aware of proper vampire lore.

Carlo yanked the sides of my body with massive strength, then started to shake me like a ragdoll.

"I want you to tell me everything about him. What's his name? Where did he come from?" There was hardly contained rage in his voice. An elder couple passed by and flung him a condemning look. He released me and waited for them to disappear. Then he pulled me closer, placing his lips over my ear. "Is he related to the vampire girl? How many more are there, and where are they hiding?"

I prayed for the earth to open and swallow me whole so I could escape Carlo's questions. Why hadn't I stayed at the witches' house?

"Answer!" he roared. "Who was he, and what was he doing in your bed?"

"I'm old enough to share my bed with whomever I want," I muttered wearily. "And I know nothing about any vampires. Vampires don't exist, as far as I know."

Carlo sniggered. "Right. You know nothing, huh?" He cornered me against the stone wall. Anyone passing by would have mistaken us for two lovers seeking privacy. "Do you have an idea how long I have been after you? Do you think it was by chance that I found you at the police station in Saint Emery? I needed to have a look at the lady who had been caught doing black magic rites among the tombs, in a cemetery frequented by vampires…"

I remembered that night very well. He had called me a necromancer, and I had barely escaped imprisonment.

"You know, Alba—confession time." He clutched my upper arms. It hurt. "I have always liked playing with fire, and you… you smell like smoldering embers. I liked that about you on the very first day." He started to caress my back and I tried to squirm away from him, but he was too strong, so I gave up. "I have a proposition for you. Barter. How do you feel about bartering?"

I stood back, as far away from him as I could. "I prefer paying for things normally, to be honest."

"How much are your friends worth to you? What would you give to keep them safe?"

"I have no friends," I replied. It wasn't entirely false.

"I hear the hot blondie bloodsucker is tough as nails," he said pensively, twisting my hair around his finger. "They say she doesn't even scream when they torture her. There's no way to pry information out of that tiny devil." He made a tsking sound. "Then there's the first guy we caught, but Natasha overdid it with him, and now he's useless. And then there's the new arrival…" His eyes hardened. "We both know him well, don't we? The problem is, he won't tell us anything. But Natasha says he seems weak. She thinks he will break much faster than the others, although she's worried she might kill him by accident. And you? What do you think?"

I wriggled to get away from Carlo's clutch, but he seemed to enjoy the resistance and smirked with pleasure, sticking his nose into my hair.

"What do you want from me?" I roared.

"What do *you* want, Alba?"

"Would you help me if I told you?"

He made a show of sniffing the air around me. "Obviously not. By the way, about that smell of smoke you have…" he commented, "I like it. But do they still burn witches nowadays?"

"Some try to," I hissed. "But we usually escape riding our brooms, don't we?"

"So, you don't want to cooperate," he said, and I wasn't sure whether the sad tinge in his voice was true or feigned.

"I have nothing else to say."

"Okay: your loss. Let's go back to the house. But you are going to regret this."

He nudged me behind the ear with the tip of his nose, then stopped to stare with disgust at the bite marks on my skin.

"I can't believe I kissed you." He stepped back and studied me from head to toe. "Now that I know the places your mouth has been to, it makes me want to barf." His lips curled in a grimace of revulsion… or was it jealousy? "Tell me, *amore*, did the beast kiss you better than I?"

Oh, he did, and how.

I remained silent, but I let him read the answer in my eyes. He kicked every kickable object he found on our way back to the house.

That day the witches invited me to join them for lunch, but I declined and ran to my room. I slammed the door closed like a grounded teenager and cried myself to sleep, my mind still jumbled with the side effects of the witch's herbs and distressing thoughts of Clarence, Francesca, and my children, and all the people who were currently suffering because of all my terrible choices.

Chapter 31

Alba

When Alice came to visit me in the evening, she found me sitting in the same position I had fallen into four hours earlier: hugging my knees and gazing blindly at the eclectic objects which adorned the witches' altar, still in shock because they had taken Clarence away. I had learned that, if I stared at the items on the altar for long enough, they would come to life and start to dance. I was almost sure that one of the Catholic prayer cards had talked to me a while ago. It was the one with *Sant'Antonio* written on it and some sort of love prayer engraved in gold lettering. I could have sworn that, mid-dance, he had said "*Get off your ass and wash your face already,*" which was absurd and probably not the way a real saint would address a person. Therefore, I ignored it and kept staring into the void.

"Hey," Alice said with awkwardness. She took a seat on the mat, then stood up again when she realized how badly it stank of old vomit. "How are you doing?"

I raised an eyebrow and grunted. "Are you seriously asking me that?"

She studied her feet, then picked up a bottle of rose water and started to spray the room with it. "Yeah, sorry. Bad conversation starter."

"Can't think of a worse one. I'm sick. I'm heartbroken. And I think I'm going crazy, too, because Saint Anthony's prayer card just talked to me."

"Did he?" She walked over to the altar and straightened the old cardboard *immaginetta*. "And what did he say?"

"He told me to go wash my face."

She nodded, her expression grave. "Yeah, sounds like him. He has a sense of humor, and he's usually spot on, too. Always take notice of whatever he tells you, even if it sounds absurd. There's usually a reason."

"Okay. I'll go have a shower." I stood up and headed to the bathroom, but Alice stopped me. A great thing, because my legs were numb after hours of sitting cross-legged and I nearly collapsed.

"Wait, I can't stay long. You can shower later. They sent me to tell you the good news." She hesitated before adding, "You are going home."

I straightened my back, wondering whether I had heard that wrong. "Really?" I asked without much enthusiasm. "Home, *home?*"

"Yes, Valentina told us during lunch. She has given up on teaching you, and she's sending you back to Emberbury. Her words, not mine."

"Nice." I exhaled.

It was *not nice*. Francesca and her brother, and now also Clarence, were being held hostage in Venice; if not already dead, then close to being it.

On the other hand, my kids had been opening Christmas presents with a bunch of strangers, possibly thinking I had abandoned them. That was, if they still remembered me after my days-long silence. For all I knew, they might have started to consider Minnie their new mother, just like Mark had been dreaming of.

"Aren't you happy, or what?" Alice asked, blinking. "You are finally free to go."

"As much as I miss my daughters, I can't go home now," I said, considering my options. "Not yet. Not until I make sure the people I love are safe."

Alice nodded and continued, "Agnes got you plane tickets, and Carlo is driving you to the airport tomorrow morning, and..."

"I said I'm not going anywhere!" I shouted. "I don't care whether they bought me plane tickets or a camel ride!"

Alice stared at me, offended.

"I'm just passing on the message," she said raising her hands. "No need to kill the messenger, sister."

"What about Francesca? What about…?" I didn't finish the sentence. Even saying his name was hurtful. "I can't just go and leave them: those are the people who helped me when I reached rock bottom. If it wasn't for them, I might be dead by a curbside now. And now that they are in trouble, I'm not going to fly home and leave them here. Especially when all of this happened because of me."

"I'm sorry," Alice said, glancing left and right. She lowered her voice. "If you stop fretting and allow me to finish, I'll explain my plan to you."

"You have a plan?"

I was perplexed. Even though Alice had shown me some kindness, and she had admitted being sorry about Francesca, it was hard to trust her after seeing what those witches had done to Clarence. True, Alice hadn't been there that night, but she was one of them. Then again, I wasn't in a position to refuse anyone's help.

"Carlo won't be flying back with you. Which means that nobody is going to find out if you never board that plane. You can go through security check and hide in the airport bathrooms for a while. Miss the plane *by accident*, then wait for me outside. I could meet you at the terminal in the evening, when the museum closes."

"And then what?"

"Then we'll see. You can hide in my house for a while. I live in the mountains; if we're careful, Valentina won't find out. I have a few friends who could help, witches from other covens in the south. I could convince them to come up here. I'm not sure how I'll get them onboard, given their opinion on vampires, but it's worth a try. Meanwhile, we can research a spell to cast together. Even if none of us is very strong, we can accomplish larger things if we join our forces."

I nodded. I had seen that.

"So, what do you say?" she asked, extending her hand for me to take it. "Are you in?"

Her words seemed to breathe new life into my wretched self, and a rush of adrenaline flooded me. I stood up and started to pace around the room, suddenly realizing how hungry I was. I hadn't eaten real food for days.

"Okay," I said, "it's not like I have a better plan anyway, so we'll stick to yours for now."

***

That night I had strange dreams, starring Julia and Saint Anthony of Padua. They were arguing heatedly over me.

"She needs to clip those grimy nails and get a proper haircut. The woman is more neglected than a hermit's beard. I can't do much for her if she keeps walking around in such a state," Saint Anthony complained, waving a bunch of white lilies in my direction as if to banish a ghost or possibly dispel a horrible stench. "Have you had a look at yourself lately, young lady?"

He turned toward me, and I staggered in shock. I hadn't expected him to see me—he was a saint, not a normal person; and he was part of a dream my brain had made up.

For some reason I wasn't lying on the mat any longer but standing between Julia and Saint Anthony in my awful nightgown as two pairs of eyes watched me, expectant.

"*Hhhh…*" I tried to speak, but my vocal cords were on strike. Only a weak, useless hiss left my lips.

"Well, you really should see yourself," he said, clicking his tongue. "You look a sight."

I refrained from pointing out that he was wearing an ancient, mud-colored habit and wasn't exactly the epitome of elegance, either.

"How is the poor girl to know?" Julia twirled in her polka dot dress. Tonight she was posing as a cute, blonde twenty-year-old pin-up girl in high-heeled silver shoes. "She needs a mirror. She can't see herself properly as it is. Can you, sweetheart?" She kissed my cheek with a loud noise. "You must get hold of Turanna's Mirror, Alba. Promise?"

Turanna's Mirror? The one from the museum? Yes, of course, and I could also steal the Monna Lisa from The Louvre right after that.

I inspected my hands: Saint Anthony was right, and my nails were black and grubby: worse than a gravedigger's. Who knew what my face might look like… his criticism was probably founded.

"Don't fret, love, just ask Alice and everything will be fine," Julia was saying. "But don't you dare leave Como without it, do you hear me?"

I nodded hesitantly, in a vain attempt to say, *Okay*.

"Good girl," she said with satisfaction.

"You must, because I'm in the middle of a murky situation here keeping all those vampires and myself alive with all sorts of spells. They caught me snooping and now I'm trapped here, too. I won't be able to mentor you for a while."

They had caught Julia, too? I would have asked, but I couldn't.

"Just remember the verses I taught you," she said, "and if you can't find yourself in the mirror, you should be looking deeper."

After that, Julia started to dissolve. Her skin turned into a greyish, see-through mass, melting into a disgusting, brain-like form which started to get dry at the edges until it collapsed in a heap of dust. It was so horrifying that I wanted to scream, but my throat was blocked.

"Ah, these cursed creatures and their unholy habits." Saint Anthony fanned himself and smudged the space previously occupied by Julia with his white lilies. "They are all the same: can't they muster a proper *adieu*? Surely, you aren't thinking of becoming one of them, are you? I think you would make a great nun, with a few minor adjustments. That would be a marvelous career for a bright woman like you."

He crossed himself prudishly and that was when my throat decided to become functional again. I woke up screaming in the dark basement room, with Valentina standing by the door in a sleeping cap, a dog-print pajamas and a deep, menacing frown. She muttered a few foreign words and waved her hand in a figure-eight shape.

Everything turned to black, and I had no more dreams.

***

"Breakfast!" I opened my eyes to find Berenice tugging at my sleeve. It must be early morning, judging by the faint light filtering through the basement windows. "Did you sleep well?" She forced me on my feet and I wobbled like a penguin. My stomach growled. I was starving. "I hear Carlo is picking you up at ten. Have you packed your things already?"

I rubbed my eyes, slowly processing all the new information and drudging after her to the kitchen.

Carlo? Packing? Things?

"What things?"

As far as I knew, only my purse had survived the fire, containing just my passport and phone. Alice had mentioned the phone was hidden in a cookie tin. As for the rest of items, I had no clue about their whereabouts.

"Is Alice here?" I asked with a yawn, grabbing an apple with silent acceptance. It was too sour, and my empty stomach complained after the very first bite.

Berenice pursed her lips and started to chop cucumbers for one of her milkshakes from hell.

"Alice? No, why? What do you need from her? She's probably working today. The museum doesn't open until half past nine."

I waved my hand. "Never mind. I…" I looked around, a dozen stupid excuses flooding my mind. I couldn't tell her about my dream. First of all, it would sound like I was crazy; and second, I doubted she would approve of me stealing Turanna's mirror. "I wanted her to look at my future in the cards one last time."

She nearly choked on a piece of cucumber.

"Oh, no, no. You don't need a fortune teller now. Everything is going to be fine." She drawled the word *fine* for so long that all my danger radars turned on. "What could go wrong? You are going home to your children, isn't that beautiful?"

I raised an eyebrow instead of answering. Yes, *what* could go wrong? Apart from everything, that was.

Breakfast was as bland and depressing as usual. Apart from the apple, the only remotely edible thing they offered me was a bunch of blended raw spinach with lemon juice. It was disgusting, but I drank as much as I could, in the hopes of getting some of my strength back and surviving the day. Over the course of two weeks, I had been starved, poisoned, and drained of all my energy—physical and metaphysical. I needed to regain my health if I was to escape Carlo's watch and find my way to Venice to help Clarence, Francesca and the others.

At the thought of Clarence, my fingers traveled to my neck. The little bumps were still there, but I could barely feel their tiny, elongated roots the way I used to.

I shuddered, pushing aside the resulting gloomy thoughts. Delving too deep into grim speculations wasn't going to help me out of this. Clarence's shadow was still crawling under my skin: but the pulse of our invisible connection had become worryingly feeble and distant. It was a mute cry of help; one only I could hear.

I needed to get to him as soon as possible.

I prayed silently for Alice to keep her promise and help me.

"Tea?" Berenice asked, unaware of my copious concerns.

"Yes, please," I answered weakly.

"Pick the one you want," she said.

Meanwhile, Elda and Agnes joined us in the kitchen with baskets full of mushrooms and started to clean them under running water and slice them for soup.

I rummaged through the glass jars on the counter. One of them contained a pink mass with… limbs? The thing *waved* at me from a pool of transparent liquid. Only then I noticed it had dots which vaguely resembled a pair of eyes.

I gasped and nearly dropped the jar, and the witches burst into laughter at my reaction.

"What on earth was that?" I shrieked, wiping my hands on my clothes.

"Just one of Elda's experiments," Valentina clarified, stepping in to check the label. She handed it to Elda. "If you don't intend to finish that hex, you could at least put it in your bedroom, dear," she said. "You promised to take care of Paolo in

1993."

Elda sighed and took the jar, disappearing with it grudgingly into the corridor.

Valentina gave me an enigmatic smile. "It was nice having you here, and I'm sorry things didn't work out as expected. Still, I hope you are happy with our decision to send you home. It's what you wanted, isn't it?"

I looked at her blankly. How could she talk to me so casually, after all she had done to me and the people I loved? Did she realize the extent of her actions at all?

"I'm very happy. Thank you."

That was the best I could muster without hitting her. I needed to keep calm. Just a couple of hours, and I would be on my way to finally doing something about the horrible mess my seemingly innocent Italian vacation had caused. I might alert the police, too, but not before making sure Clarence was safe and well hidden from the authorities' prying eyes.

"Godspeed, Alba," Valentina said, sipping her sage tea with half-closed eyes. "I doubt our paths will cross again in this world, but it was nice meeting you. Or, at least, productive."

Chapter 32

Alba

At engineering school they never mentioned how fast *Godspeed* was supposed to be, but seemingly quite quick, because Carlo made his appearance minutes after Valentina said her unsettling goodbyes. Berenice gifted me an old pair of boots, one of her crazy patchwork dresses and even a warm parka. All the witches hugged me in an uncomfortably friendly fashion, somehow oblivious to the fact that they had kept me prisoner in that house for days and sent my vampire lover to a very likely demise.

Carlo arrived in his shiny red cabriolet and honked from the other side of the cobbled street.

The witches ushered me out the door in their mother-hen way; I nearly had to hold myself to a streetlamp so they didn't shove me straight into Carlo's car.

"I'll need my passport, please," I said, holding the lamp post with both hands. "And my phone!"

"Oh yes!" Agnes came out running and threw me my purse. I caught it in the air, shocked by the strong smoke stench coming from it. "The plane ticket is inside, but sorry about the phone," Agnes said, glancing away coyly. "You must have dropped your bag during the fire."

Yeah sure. *During the fire.*

The phone—or rather, its remains—could have well been trampled by a wildebeest stampede. The witches had thrown all the crushed pieces together into a Ziplock bag, so at least I didn't have to fish out the odd chips and glass shards from the bottom of my purse.

Of course, that same phone had been working perfectly when Alice had shown it to me a couple of days ago. No doubt, those women must be direct descendants of Snow White's wicked stepmother.

On the plus side, my passport was still there, and so was Clarence's vintage copy of Robin Hood. Thankfully, the black feather was still inside, untouched, and I caressed it secretly as Carlo turned on the engine and sped out of the small city of Como.

"I see you like to travel light," Carlo commented, adjusting the rear-view mirror. The rosiness was slowly returning to his cheeks, and he was in a better mood than the previous day.

I grunted and checked the car clock. Ten fifteen. The museum must be open already.

"I need you to turn around," I said to Carlo, not really expecting him to comply.

"Forgot anything?"

"Yes. I must return something to Alice. She's at the museum, working."

"What museum? The Murano Glass Museum?"

"No. The Museum of Witchcraft. It won't take me long, but it's important, because I'm not sure I'll see her again. Can you please turn back? *Please?*"

I flashed him what I considered my sweetest smile, hoping it didn't make me resemble a hyena in my current state of neglect. He studied me with unaccustomed depth, almost like he pitied me.

"Okay." He hesitated and exhaled loudly. "But be quick, or you might…" He paused and made a dangerous U-turn in the middle of the road that sent my stomach up my throat. "Miss your flight."

He parked in front of the glass door, settling himself right under the big round sign which read *divieto di sosta*—no parking.

I jumped out of the car as fast as I could, praying the witches didn't notice we were back, as they lived in the same street: that would unleash many unpleasant questions I didn't have answers for.

"I don't like waiting," Carlo warned me, as he turned on the radio and started to browse on his phone.

***

I raced through the main door and barged into the museum reception. Alice was standing behind the counter wearing military attire and a jaded expression.

"What the hell are you doing here? Aren't we supposed to meet at the airport this evening?" She flung me a confused look, covering her mouth like she expected someone to read her lips.

"You said I should pay attention to Saint Anthony, didn't you?" I said, pulling at her sleeve to get her out of the reception nook. "Take me to the mirror room. I don't have much time, the witches could see me, and Carlo is waiting outside."

The museum had been invaded by dozens of primary school children, who raced through the corridors under the despairing watch of two worn-out teachers. A little girl with golden locks smiled at me. She reminded me of Iris, and my heart constricted a little. *Soon*, I told myself, *mommy will be home soon.*

"He visited me in a dream last night," I muttered, ushering Alice down the halls and trying to avoid the tiny museum visitors who were virtually everywhere.

"Who?" Alice threw a deadly glance to a wild seven-year-old who was trying to climb an iron torture device.

"Saint Anthony, who else?" I puffed with impatience.

"Saint Anthony doesn't do that." She shook her head, like she was Saint Anthony's best friend and knew what he enjoyed doing and what not.

"Anyways, whoever it was looked just like that picture of him: tonsure, lilies and habit. There was someone else in the dream: a witch friend. She urged me to take the mirror with me," I whispered into Alice's ear.

She blanched. "I hope you don't mean Turanna's Mirror."

At that point, her face resembled a live reproduction of *The Scream* by Edvard Munch.

"I'll give it back, okay? But she said under no circumstances should I leave Como without it. I know there must be a reason." I grinned. "Please, Alice? I'm sure you can find a way. I'll take good care of it."

"The museum is crowded," she moaned. "Visitors will notice!"

As we passed the toilets, a crazy idea formed in my mind.

"Give me a second," I said, and stepped swiftly into the small lavatory.

It didn't take me much effort to unhang the bathroom mirror. It was a simple rectangle with a wooden frame, full of soap splatters and a bit rusty at the corners.

I carried the heavy piece of glass out of the bathrooms, tucked under my arm, while Alice stared at me in shock. She had probably guessed what I was about to do... and she clearly didn't like it.

"You are insane," she shouted, trying to make herself heard above the voices of the screaming children.

"Get rid of the kids," I commanded. In the middle of the schoolchildren chaos, nobody had even glanced at me. "Tell them there are mice… tarantulas… whatever you want."

She rolled her eyes but did as I asked her. Somehow, she managed to dislodge a bunch of kids to the potions section, and we remained alone.

"Cameras?" I pointed at the offending black devices on the ceiling.

"They are all fake," she reassured me.

I took the smaller Etruscan mirror with one hand and placed it gently on the floor, then clutched the cheap bathroom mirror with the other one and gestured toward Alice. "Help me lift this."

"I'm going to lose my job," she grumbled, her face pale as a sheet.

"It's a lousy job anyway." I elbowed her a little so she would stop complaining. "You deserve something better. Come on, *heave-ho*!"

We hung the bathroom mirror on the wall, and Alice stuck the antique one in a paper bag with the museum logo. Her hands were shaking violently when she handed it to me.

"Guard it with your life, do you hear me? You have no idea how much this is worth."

I nodded. "I will! Bye, Alice, see you at the airport." I placed a tiny kiss on her cheek and rushed out of the museum.

Carlo was tapping on the steering wheel with impatience when I got back into the car.

"What the hell are you carrying there?" he asked, squinting at the bulk under my arm.

"Souvenirs for the kids," I answered, repressing a sneer.

"Want me to open the trunk?" He glanced at the bag sideways, trying to see what was inside.

I shook my head and slid the bag into my purse. "Better not. Fragile goods."

Carlo shrugged, and we left the lake city behind, as the sun shone bright on the road to Venice and set his aviator glasses on fire.

Chapter 33

Clarence

A crimson halo framed Anne's deceitfully angelic face as she bent over me, her irises casting golden sparkles in the darkness which surrounded us.

I didn't know where I was, nor where she had come from. But she moved with magnificent self-assurance as she caressed me and carved magical symbols into my cheek with the tips of her sharp claws. I was shaking, lying on an ivory marble slab reminiscent of a medieval knight's tombstone. I hadn't felt that cold for centuries.

I tried to move, but found my limbs merged with the stone bed. She noticed my struggle and laughed softly.

I observed with bitterness how much I had missed that laugh, even though it never preceded anything good.

"You died in the fire," I muttered. My lips were sealed, but she understood me, nonetheless.

Anne nodded and caressed my forehead.

"I *burned* in that fire," she corrected me. "Burned to ashes. But did I ever die for you, my beloved Clarence?" Her hands wandered idly under my torn shirt. Her fingertips were scorching hot, like painful flames licking my skin. I shuddered. "I don't think so," she said with a fiery squint.

"Why are you here, after all this time?" I asked her.

"I missed you," she said quietly. "I heard your call from the other side, and I came to assist your crossing. You are at the edge of afterlife and eternal death."

"I did not summon you, Anne. I'm not going anywhere yet."

"We can finally be together, Clarence. For all eternity, just like you wished. You are my only legacy, my best creation. True, it was purely your appearance that drew me to you first, and your lingering humanity that deterred me. But all these years of loneliness have taught me that, perhaps, you were not the worst option…" She smirked and kissed me. I contorted under the pressure of her burning lips, which scorched my skin and made me want to scream. "Take my hand, Clarence. Take it. Come with me."

"Go away, Anne," I grumbled in my thoughts. "You and I were never meant to be together. You told me yourself, a long time ago, and I was a fool not to listen."

She pouted. "I can't believe you are sending me away, after all I had to risk to reach you here. We are the same, my dear. We share the same blood. You are mine, and I am willing to be yours now. We belong together. Come."

"No," I tried to say, but she placed a sweltering finger over my lips, causing them to dissolve into smoldering blisters.

"It's the witch, isn't it?" She shook her luscious mane of black hair. "Do you believe she would still want you if she knew everything about you? If she knew about all the things we did together? If she knew about… me?"

I closed my eyes, her words sharp as darts in their truthfulness. She kissed me once again, a burning, painful caress over my already aching skin.

"Do not worry, my dear. Those are lowly, mortal creatures. Our kind must hold together. You belong with me. You always have."

"No," I answered, this time firmly.

Anne stepped back, and the flames which surrounded her turned wild and started to consume her, melting her hands and face into a horrible red and black mass of charred flesh.

"Clarence. You will never be good enough," she screamed, her face reduced to a monstrous amalgam of bones and blackened tendons.

"Neither will you," I whispered, as I watched the flames consume her once again—but this time, unlike the first time, all I felt was peace.

"You shall die, and sleep the sleep of the dead all alone…" she shrieked the beginning of a curse, but her last words were lost forever, for she had already turned to ashes.

"Farewell, Anne," I repeated, sensing the pull of slumber. "I must let you go now."

Chapter 34

Alba

"You just missed the airport exit," I said, pointing at the green sign right behind us from the passenger seat of Carlo's rented Alfa Romeo.

We had been driving for a couple of hours, and judging by the road signs, Venice airport must be around the corner.

"Ah, didn't I tell you?" Carlo said, turning down the radio. "We are going sightseeing first. There's plenty of time, anyway."

"Sightseeing?" I checked the time. According to the tickets Agnes had printed for me, we did have time to spare; but the last thing I wanted to do was strolling around touristic sites with Carlo Lombardi, all while Clarence and the others might be suffering unthinkable tortures somewhere nearby. "Can't you just leave me at the airport and go alone?" I pleaded.

"No, no. I was just joking about the sightseeing," he said, on a more serious note. "I need to deliver some goods to a business partner. It's just a small detour; it won't take us long."

"Okay." I slumped into the seat, defeated. Carlo's rental car was oddly low, so much so that I could peek at the underskirts of the truck in front of us.

"Isn't it funny?" Carlo asked. "When we chatted on the plane, you didn't want to go to Venice, but it seems you'll end up going anyway. Aren't you thrilled to see the channels?"

"Dying to," I retorted, taking a deep breath to calm down my nerves.

We were really going to Venice—not to the airport.

What were the odds of me escaping Carlo and finding Stella Alley on my own?

Was that the most stupid idea ever?

Should I just keep to Alice's plan, which might take days, or possibly weeks to come to fruition?

Would Clarence, Francesca and the rest remain alive long enough for us to find them?

Hundreds of variations of those same thoughts crammed in my mind as we cruised along the narrow car-and-railway bridge which crossed the lagoon and connected mainland Venice with the more touristy island half. The bridge was old, long and gray; a concrete abomination which had none of the dreamy connotations one would expect from the city of Casanova. But inspiringly enough, it had been baptized *The Bridge of Freedom*, which I decided to take as a good omen.

My first glimpse of *La Serenissima* was highly unromantic and encompassed a bunch of coaches, loud tour-guides, people dragging suitcases and no gondolas whatsoever.

I pondered bitterly about how often high expectations led us, mortals, to disappointment.

One should not expect Venice to be as stunning in real life as in postcards.

One should not expect a vampire lover to remain loyal forever.

And one should *definitely not* expect to be treated with decency by a coven of witches, when fairy tales kept warning us against them since early childhood.

All those affirmations were universal truths, and my overly optimistic expectations toward them had led me—and many others—to disaster.

Or perhaps I was just nervous and in a terrible mood, and I should stop philosophizing and start devising a smart escape strategy.

A loud screech took me out of my theoretical musings. We had reached a garage and Carlo was struggling to park in a ridiculously narrow spot. He had squeezed in the sleek Alfa Romeo, but he had also scratched the shiny red paint against one of the pillars. A colorful string of curses left his lips as he got out of the car and slammed the door closed with anger.

Even though I didn't like Carlo much, I had to sympathize with him—I had a talent for ruining things in the blink of an eye, too.

He was still muttering to himself when we

left the boring-looking building, crossed a few streets and—finally—got a peek at the famous canals right before jumping on a vaporetto water bus.

"Nice, huh?" Carlo commented, waving toward the picturesque water scene around us.

"Very nice," I agreed, taking in postcard-Venice in all its glory. It wasn't so bad, after all.

"Such a shame you never allowed me to take you sightseeing in Como," he muttered, shaking his head. "I'm a good tour guide."

I nodded absently and thought about the address Julia had told me about. If only my phone wasn't broken, I could have checked the exact location, then try to outsmart Carlo and lose him among the narrow streets. And if only I knew in which direction to flee, I could go and check the place for myself.

"Where are we going?" I inquired, trying to keep my tone as casual as possible.

"You will find out soon enough," he said, turning his back to me, his eyes focused on the green depths of the channels.

***

I stared at the street plaque name in disbelief as I followed Carlo down the narrow sidewalk by the canal.

"*Stella Alley*?" I asked, staring at the name. My voice shook, and not only my voice, as we approached the fifth house of the row, which was—evidently—a washed out shade of salmon pink.

'It's the fifth pink house by the canals, in Stella Alley in Venice. That's where they took them. That's where we must go. If anything happens to me, promise you'll go there and find a way to free them."

Carlo blinked and stared at me with suspicion. He rang the bell and propped himself against the flaky façade with his elbow.

"Stella, yes, like a star," he said casually. I wasn't asking for the meaning of the word, but he couldn't know that.

Clarence was in that house. I could feel him.

I should be happy I just landed there so easily… shouldn't I?

But I wasn't.

This was *wrong.*

There was no way on earth walking through the main entrance of that building, in plain daylight, would help me get him out.

There was something dreadful about Carlo bringing me—just by chance—to the undercover prison I should be sneaking into with Alice's help.

My feet were glued to the ground as the key turned on the other side of the heavy wooden door. Right then I noticed Carlo's hands were empty. No bags. No files. Just the car keys, dancing merrily around his index finger.

"What exactly are you supposed to deliver at

this address?" I asked, my fear growing into an out-of-control beast thumping against my chest.

Carlo grinned before he answered.

"Why, didn't I tell you?" he said smugly, as the door swiveled open and a middle-aged lady dragged me into a pastel-colored lobby. "You, of course."

Chapter 35

Alba

If it wasn't for the horrible sensation in the pit of my stomach which suggested my life was about to spiral out of control, I would have appreciated how the inside of Stella Alley's house was a tourist's dream come true. Overlooking one of the minor waterways, the coral pink three story construction had arched windows and pine needle green shutters. Stepping inside immersed us in a sea of Baroque decadence and lavishly splurged funds, complete with paintings of chubby angels and azure Murano glass chandeliers.

This was a true Venetian Duke's palace, and bore no resemblance whatsoever to the prison I had been told it concealed.

"Coffee or tea? Or do you witches drink just repugnant herb concoctions?" The lady of the house asked, taking a seat on a sapphire blue divan.

"I'll drink anything but herb concoctions," I answered, clutching my purse as a shield. I had been poisoned enough times already, thank you.

The lady snapped her fingers. Out of a nook framed in plaster reliefs appeared an overly well-built man in uniform, who resembled a bodyguard more than a butler. He took our orders with a notebook and a golden pen, pretending that was the most normal thing to do.

"Alba, let me introduce you to our business partner, Mrs. Grabnar," Carlo said, while we waited for our refreshments. I was amazed to find out he was actually capable of polite conversation.

"Natasha?" I asked without a trace of surprise.

"You seem to be quite knowledgeable about me," the lady observed. She must be in her fifties, with a perfect blond bob reminiscent of a wig. Her head-to-toe beige business casual attire matched the stucco on the ceilings perfectly, and several rows of fake ethnic necklaces tinkled as she drew closer and studied me with a critical eye. "That's interesting, given how hard I work to keep a low profile."

The wardrobe-sized butler came back with a tray containing a solid silver teapot and thin porcelain cups. I immediately made up my mind not to drink a single sip of whatever that teapot contained. It had taken me a while, but I had finally learned my lesson about accepting poisoned apples from strangers.

Natasha dropped at least four sugar cubes into her beverage and started to sip it with abandonment. "I hear you are a powerful witch," she said slowly, staring at me from behind the golden rim of her cup.

"Excuse me?" I blinked.

"Mrs. Valentina told me. That's why she sent you, isn't it?"

"She said that?" I was baffled. She must have heard that wrong.

I watched for Carlo's reaction, but he sat stoically, picking his teeth like he was alone in the room. He must have noticed my inquisitive stares because he took his finger out of his mouth and glanced at the clock on the opposite wall.

"Natasha, it's better if you start with the interview as soon as possible, otherwise we'll be late," he said, inspecting the food leftovers under his nails. They were full of orange and green speckles and absolutely disgusting. I repressed my gag reflex, not sure whether it had been triggered by Carlo's tooth picking or the idea of Clarence agonizing somewhere in the bowels of that very house.

"Actually, Carlo..." Natasha looked away from him and his dubious etiquette. "If you are in a hurry, you can leave us. She will be well taken care of here with me."

"No, Natasha, you don't understand, the witches booked her a flight and hired me to drive her. She lives abroad. We have twenty minutes at most, or she'll miss it."

"No, dear Carlo, it's you who doesn't understand. She's staying here." She nodded meaningfully. "For a while."

I gaped at them. I wanted to join their peculiar verbal ping-pong match, but I couldn't decide whether I should take Natasha's side or Carlo's. All in all, I had a mission to accomplish, and it might be easier to do so from the inside, wouldn't it?

For goodness sake, this situation was getting surreal.

"What do you mean? The plane tickets are paid." Carlo sounded sincerely shocked. "Valentina was clear about my duties."

"Did you really believe those plane tickets were real? Haven't you heard about Agnes and her hacking talents yet? Why would they buy a plane ticket if they promised to hand me those pretty, magic-wielding hands for my research?"

Okay. *Definitely retreat and abort mission.* Leaving that place had started to sound like the best option, at least until I could get back with Alice and her witch friends. That woman sounded dangerous. And very much insane. She wanted my pretty, magic-wielding hands? In marriage, to chop them off…?

I raised my hand—while I still had it. "Excuse me," I said, trying to sound calm. "I don't know who promised you my… hands… or well, whatever body part you need for your doubtful purposes, but I'm not interested in participating." I stood up slowly. "Strange as it sounds, I agree with Carlo. We need to go."

"You're not going anywhere," Natasha said, pressing a button on the wall next to her. "Carlo, conversely, has become a bit of a hassle." She pointed at the exit. "*Arrivederci*, sweetheart. Thanks for the present."

"Natasha, no," Carlo said firmly. "You can't keep her here. This is not what the witches wanted. You are going to get me into trouble. I should have driven her straight to the airport."

I thought of using their distraction to my advantage and looked around for a route of escape. The door was close enough, so I started to tiptoe in its direction while they merrily discussed what to do with me next.

"First of all, the witches are aware of my plans. And second, since when do you care about stray witches?" Natasha said. "Have you forgotten what brought you here in the first place?"

"It wasn't the witches who took Eleanor's life. True, I don't like them, but I thought we were on the same side in this fight."

"You and I have one thing in common, Carlo. We both are always on the same side: the side of the money. Aren't we?"

Carlo didn't answer. Instead, he scowled at Natasha and edged towards me, walking backwards to keep her under his watch. When he reached my side, I had almost made it to the plastered archway which led to the lavish foyer.

What the hell was going on here?

"I'm not leaving her here," he said. "This is not what we agreed. My hands might not be the cleanest, but this is totally wrong."

"You didn't seem to mind when you

brought me her coldblooded colleagues."

"She's not one of them."

"Isn't she?"

Wasn't I?

In any case, I wasn't staying around to discuss whether I should be granted a spot in a vampire family tree or not. I sneaked one foot out of the tearoom.

"Don't make me use my gun, Natasha," Carlo said, sticking a hand in his back pocket.

"Even as a policeman, I doubt you are allowed to shoot whoever you want just to settle personal grievances," Natasha pointed out, playing with her jangly necklaces. "The chief of Emberbury police department won't be pleased to find out what you did on that doomed August night, don't you think?"

"Natasha, are you trying to blackmail me?"

"The long answer is I'm not interested in returning paid goods. The short one is… yes, I am."

Carlo wrapped his arm around my waist and pulled me against him. From my position behind him I could see his back pocket was empty: no guns in sight; he had been bluffing. "This is wrong, Natasha. We are leaving. *Arrivederci.*"

"Carlo, Carlo." Natasha oozed arrogance from her perfectly botoxed pores. "Is it me, or do you have a thing for this little witch?"

"Go fuck yourself, Natasha."

She produced a silver cell phone from the pocket of her blazer and dialed a number.

"Security?" She spoke into the handset, "I need help showing a guest to the door."

I stood in the middle of the two, still holding my purse—heavy due to the mirror inside it—and wondering what the hell to do.

"Okay," Carlo said, "You don't need your minions, spare them the trip. I will show myself out."

Natasha nodded with satisfaction, typing a brief message into her phone. "Good," she said, "consider yourself fired, by the way. But thanks for the little mouse. You'll get a reward with your last paycheck. To compensate you for the inconveniences."

The butler came in, only this time he was carrying a gun instead of a silver tray. A real one, not like Carlo's imaginary weapon.

"Domingo, Mr. Lombardi was leaving," Natasha said softly. The butler pointed the gun at Carlo's skull with the same calm expression he had while serving our tea. "Have fun outside, boys, but don't overdo it."

Carlo nudged me and dragged his hand down my back, pretending to hug me good-bye. He pulled at the handle of my purse, which was right behind us and out of Natasha's sight. Then, he slipped something cold and sharp into the bag, right before detaching himself from my side and raising his hands in surrender.

"Okay," he said, walking away from me. "But she's not a vampire. You can't just kidnap a normal person and expect not to get caught. It's illegal, you know? Nobody will notice a missing bloodsucker, but people with papers and families are a very different thing."

Good that they didn't know the truth about the family part. Nobody in Emberbury would miss me if I never turned up again. At least nobody with a constant heartbeat or old enough to call a police station.

"I appreciate your input," Natasha answered calmly. "But she's mine now, and forget about alerting the authorities. Because, in that case, I might remember a thing or two about you, too." She gestured toward the giant butler-turned-bouncer, who pushed Carlo toward the exit, possibly to bid him a proper farewell. "Bye Carlo. It was nice working with you."

***

As soon as I remained alone with Natasha, the house became empty and incredibly crowded at the same time. In the newly found quiet, the aura of suffering coming from the depths of the house was overwhelming. There was dread and misery exuding from the underground, but not only that: there were presences I knew, and their agony started to leak into my soul, turning my knees into jelly.

But what could I do for them, if I had just become Natasha's newest prisoner?

I felt into my bag, searching for the object

Carlo had tucked secretively inside.

My fingers stroked the hilt of a knife: a decently-sized, ornate knife in a soft, leather sheath. The blade had delicate engravings along the hilt, and as soon as I touched them I recognized it: Clarence's dagger. Carlo must have carried it hidden in the waist of his pants. But what did he expect me to do with it? Kill Natasha? Not very likely for someone who wasn't even able to chop carrots properly.

"Ah, men," Natasha said with an exhale, "always thinking with their lower… brains. It makes them terrible associates. Especially when you are trying to make a living off science."

I didn't answer. You didn't need to be Einstein to realize the woman had a well-developed reptilian brain, too.

"You look pretty harmless for a witch," Natasha commented, brushing her thumb along my jawbone and making me feel like a newly bought stallion meeting its owner.

"What's going on in this place?" I asked her, my back still glued to the wall and my fingers around the hidden dagger.

"Just research," she answered sweetly. "I'm a pathologist on a quest, and I'd appreciate your participation in a study. I used to be a coroner when I met our dear Carlo a long while ago, but those patients were quite boring. I needed something more motivating."

"I thought coroners worked with dead people." My voice broke as the possible ramifications of that statement started to sink in.

"And what do you think I'm doing?" She winked and clutched my wrist. "Follow me. I'll show you to your accommodations and ask you a couple of questions. Do you prefer blue or red?"

I raked my mind for a way to fix the mess I had fallen into. Apparently, I had no other choice but to stab her if I wanted to get out. How and where did you stab a person for the best results? Why hadn't Clarence nor Carlo explained to me the actually useful details?

"We just sent off two specimens to the better equipped laboratory in France, but we still have here Blondie and the one we call *DDH*: *Dead, Dark and Handsome.* I still haven't been able to solve the mystery of his identity or his origins. Do you think you could help me out?"

"No," I grunted. "I don't think so. I don't know anyone by that description."

"No? Because I'm willing to reward your cooperation. Not necessarily with money… mercy is a legitimate form of currency, too."

"I'm quite sure I don't know him."

Natasha snapped her fingers for me to follow her.

"This way, darling." Natasha pointed at a glass elevator which opened into the wide hallway. "You know, it's funny that you don't know each other," she said, "because he keeps mumbling your name in his dreams."

Chapter 36

Clarence

Drifting to and fro by the shores of lucidity, memories of the witches from my past shuffled incessantly in my mind's eye.

Witches. I had long known them; I had mostly avoided them. I had even loved one, or so I believed.

"Alba?" I called her, not sure that was a name or just a foreign word I had made up in my feverish delirium.

My thoughts were jumbled. I recalled witches never caring for us. They were always indifferent to our existence, as long as we left them in peace: which we did. Or, at least, as indifferent as witches could be to the creatures they despised.

I could still remember a time, at the turn of a century—*but which one?*—when we had battled together against a common enemy. But the truce hadn't lasted long, and none of our kinds had expected it to.

Even so, I never anticipated meeting my

ultimate death at the hands of witches. Their vampire hunting propaganda always sounded like a bad taste jest. For decades, I had scoffed at their comical attempts to draw human customers their way by spreading misinformation about us. They thrived on giving us bad press; not that we didn't deserve it.

The last days had painfully taught me how printed words can be blown with the wind, but tungsten chains and coffin nails… not so much.

They could become fairly troublesome after very short periods of use.

But it wasn't just the chains keeping me still and at the edge of death and madness: I had been the victim of a curse, perhaps just a spell; whatever it was, it had turned my limbs to stone; my vision was blurred, and my mind even more so.

For some reason, in my delirium, I kept having visions of Francesca by my side.

Francesca, and the scent of roses.

She was fond of roses, wasn't she?

Roses…

Or was it Rose?

"Mother?" I whispered, feeling her invisible presence for the hundredth time, her kisses on my forehead.

My voice echoed in an empty room: Rose never answered, but I knew she was there with me.

My mind kept wandering into the strangest of places, in a pleasant hallucination which was much more pleasant than the present.

And then, there was Julia.

I had seen her, but she was gone now.

She had been so fair and lovely in my vision. Was it 1961 again? And if not, why wasn't she dead?

Was *I* dead?

Or rather—*how dead was I, precisely?* Perhaps a nine, on a scale from zero to ten?

Now it was just Francesca and I in our respective glass coffins. Francesca, and I, and the scent of roses.

She was the Sleeping Beauty, our lovely Briar Rose.

Only I was asleep, and she was not.

Which left me with… what role exactly?

I always thought I would be the savior prince, armed with the Sword of Truth and the Shield of Virtue: seemingly, I was not.

Steps shook the ground below me and I foresaw the old witch coming back; or possibly Rose… perchance Julia?

However, it wasn't Julia's scent, nor Julia's voice that inundated our glass prison.

Since when did angels assist the damned?

Since never, certainly.

It was Alba instead.

Why was she wielding a dagger?

With my name on it, no less!

But my eyelids were so heavy.

I closed my eyes and gave in to slumber.

Chapter 37

Alba

Natasha shepherded me to an elevator. I had never seen one in a private home before, but then, I had never been to a luxurious Venetian palace before either. She pressed a button, and a gleaming silver door glided aside silently.

"Witches first," she said cynically.

I sighed and entered the cab after her. Natasha stuck a key into a lock to start the elevator. I followed her actions with my eyes as she put the key in a pocket of her trousers. I would need to get hold of it if I ever wanted to get out of that house again.

The elevator started to descend.

"I thought old Venetian houses had no basement," I commented, striving to keep my voice calm. The back wall of the shaft was made of glass, and the stone foundations of the ancient house passed by, followed by—was that even possible?—water. Plenty of murky, greenish water. The elevator started to sink like a submarine into an underground aquarium of sorts. I checked the joints of the cab with unease, hoping they had been properly waterproofed.

Natasha hummed a song and pouted in the elevator mirror, checking her makeup.

"Ordinary Venetian houses are not usually built like this, you are right. But you are not the first witch to step into this house," she explained casually. It was difficult to make out the words because her mouth was stretched in an odd *O* shape. "Even if you don't know it yet, magic can be used to build things, not just destroy them."

Was she insinuating there had been magic involved in the construction of the house? Watching the elevator descend into the dark waters of the canals, it wasn't so hard to believe.

Magic, science, engineering: baffling how, sometimes, they could become absolutely undistinguishable.

"This is one of the deepest canals in Venice, reaching twelve meters or more." She eyed me with contempt. "That's forty feet for you."

"I know. I'm familiar with the metric system, thank you."

I slid the knife silently out of its sheath, without taking it out of the bag just yet. The indentures on the hilt dug at my fingertips, and I traced the rose petals of Clarence's emblem on it.

A silver dagger. There were odd presents, and then there was… *this.* A weapon designed to kill vampires, gifted by a vampire to the most inept fighter in history. Stabbing people in cold blood was far from a talent of mine. I had never done such a thing and wasn't sure I would be able to pull it off at all. I closed my eyes and bit my lip as I waited for the elevator to stop. The butler was still with Carlo, which gave me a few minutes to act.

Please, Clarence, send me the skill and the strength to do what I'm about to do, I pleaded in silence.

The cab shuddered with the characteristic thud of a hydraulic mechanism, and the door opened into a dark corridor.

A corridor full of presences.

The presences of people I knew and loved.

Natasha pressed a button on the wall, and a set of industrial fluorescent lights flashed a couple of times before illuminating the space with a sterile, bluish glow.

We stepped into a state-of-the-art, white and steel square room with a wide counter in the middle, which contrasted sharply against the carefully manicured, pastel and vintage upper floor. She turned toward a row of metallic cabinets and retrieved yet another bunch of keys.

"The red room might be the right one for you, after all," she muttered to herself. "It's full of… fond memories and souvenirs."

She studied the other side of the submerged basement, where several glass cubicles opened into the square space we were standing in. They resembled the glass cages of a terrarium in a zoo. I tried to peek inside them, but they were in complete darkness, all the lamps in them still off.

The presences became so strong that my

throat constricted. A soft moan came from the cage to my right, accompanied by a low lament in Francesca's soprano voice.

"Francesca?" I ran to the source of the sound. A dark, trembling figure sat in the back of a cell, all skin and bones and tufts of lackluster, once golden hair.

"How I love happy reunions!" Natasha clapped her hands with glee. "Let's see if you remember the name of the other one too! Funny that he would risk his life for a woman who doesn't even know him, isn't it? Anyways, follow me."

Natasha pressed a switch and the lights of the cells turned on, offering now a clearer—and even more horrifying—sight.

The middle cubicle was empty, but the floor, otherwise made of light grey cement, was covered in dark crimson stains. To the right, I recognized Francesca, chained to a pillar in the corner of a glass and steel cell. Her locks were stiff and messy, and her eyes seemed lost in a distant spot beyond us. She sat hunched on the floor, and it took her a while to notice my existence. She looked up at me through tired, sleepy eyes, but showed no signs of recognition. When she extended her hands—or rather, the stumps which were left of them—she stared at her fingerless palms with melancholy and started to sing a macabre lullaby.

My stomach clenched.

"Ms. Lumin, come see the other one, I'd really appreciate your insight here," Natasha said, her voice carrying no empathy for any of her prisoners. "I'll let you catch up with Blondie in a minute."

She knocked on the glass door of the other cell to attract my attention. I forced myself to stop staring at what was left of splendid Francesca, and took a deep breath to gather some courage. The pain and horror radiating from those underwater chambers was starting to make me nauseous.

I closed my eyes, then opened them slowly, mindful that, whatever sight awaited me, it wasn't going to be pleasant.

The other cell was devoid of any furniture as well, except for a narrow metallic cot pushed against a grey cement bearing wall. The rest of partitions were transparent, which allowed the prisoners—and their jailers—to see through. The floors were filthy, the cells lacking any sinks or latrines.

The metallic cot held a vague resemblance to an altar, or a dissection table, and my eyes wandered until they found *him* lying on top of it, totally still and chained to vertical pillars on either side. A bloodied white sheet covered him up to the collar bones, revealing a mortally pale countenance.

That was no sheet: it was a shroud.

Clarence's dark hair fell in short waves over the silver rim of the table, his eyes closed; the eyelids blue, purple and disturbingly thin and lifeless like the rest of his body.

But he wasn't dead—yet.

I could feel it, and I knew only one thing:

alive meant *hope.*

As I approached the clear door, the sheet over his chest raised just slightly, and he let out an almost imperceptible breath. I slid, powerless, to the floor, dragging my hands down the glass between us and leaving damp traces of desperation on it.

"So, who is this, and where did he come from?" Natasha smirked. "Maybe if you told me, I could do something to convince the witches to reverse the spell they cast on him. Would you be interested in such a deal?"

"What spell?" My voice seemed to come from a distant place.

"It's not your turn to ask questions yet," Natasha warned me. "Answer mine first."

"I don't know him," I muttered softly. I couldn't tell her about Clarence or The Cloister. That would just sentence even more innocent people to a certain death. "I don't know why he tried to kidnap me from the witches' house."

Natasha burst into laughter. "Sure, you don't. You are virtually melting down in front of his cell. It's obvious you know each other *very well.* Don't you want him to live? Why don't you tell me where all the vampires are hiding, and I'll make sure he wakes up again for a heartfelt goodbye kiss?"

"I don't know any other vampires," I replied, steadying myself against the glass as I tried to make my lie sound convincing. "But please, I beg you, do something if you can. This man is at death's door. He desperately needs help."

"At death's door?" Natasha repeated, still laughing. "This creature is no man, and he has been dancing in Death's parlor for centuries. Your pity is unnecessary."

I closed my eyes and combed my fingers through my greasy, tangled hair. Natasha's butler might appear at any moment, and once he did, my chances of freeing myself and the prisoners would be next to nil. I thought about the *Fulminatio* spell and, in my desperation, I started to recite the words in a soft whisper. Natasha pinched my arm, shaking her index finger in front of my face.

"Naughty, naughty girl," she reprimanded me, seemingly unconcerned, and her words broke my already feeble concentration. "No magic allowed here. I know what you are trying to do, and it's extremely stupid. We are surrounded by water in this basement. Can you imagine what would happen if you blew up the whole place?"

I could imagine it very well. One didn't even need an engineering degree for that.

"Exactly," Natasha continued, "try to picture this: first, the whole house would collapse over our heads. And then, even if we didn't die crushed under the weight of the ceiling, we would drown in the canals before making it to the surface. Is that what you want?"

No, growled my inner voice in frustration.

"Neither do I. So, are you going to tell me what you know about the bloodsuckers, or do I have to stick you in the chill-out cell? The red one is vacant. You can stay in it for as long as you want, and rejoice in the sight of your dying friends until you feel like talking to me. But better hurry up, because I can't promise these fellows will survive the night."

She forced me to stand up, pulling under my arm, then pointed at the cell in the middle. The floor was dark, and disturbingly gooey and shiny.

"This is where our mischievous visitors stay," she explained. "Our previous guest was an undefined creature we caught snooping around the house. She was wicked, bloodthirsty, and quite chameleonic. She took at least three different appearances during her stay. She even tried to impersonate me and fool the guard once, can you imagine? Anyways, I'm not easily deceived by supernatural tricks. I'm an expert at death and strange phenomena, and quick to catch quirky antics. So, please, don't try anything stupid. I'll notice right away and punish everyone for it."

Natasha unlocked the empty cell, and the stench of blood and stale air hit me like a slap in the face.

"In case you were wondering," she said with a cackle, "we ended up relocating Chameleon Lady to a safer place, together with her pretty boyfriend. But don't worry, they left you souvenirs." She studied the brown and red stains on the walls with a frown. "There's some pretty sprinkle art for you to admire while you make up your mind."

In order to throw me into that hole, she would have to kill me first.

The unsheathed dagger tinkled against Turanna's mirror in my bag, expectant.

In one swift, clean move, I pulled the knife out of my purse and pressed its tip against Natasha's back.

Natasha stumbled, recoiling with a shriek, and raised her arms in surrender.

How easy, I thought, pleased with myself.

"Give me the cell keys," I snarled. The dagger was sharper than I thought, and I accidentally tore the back of her elegant shirt with the tip of the blade. She gasped, a drop of blood extending like a cherry spiderweb over the white fabric. Francesca moaned in her compartment and rattled her chains like a soul in pain. The scent of fresh blood must have awoken her from her detached reverie.

Natasha quickly recovered her composure.

"Child, you are going to hurt yourself," she hissed, keeping her back stiff to evade the dagger.

"I don't think so," I retorted without much conviction. "Step into the cell and hand me the keys. No sudden moves, or I'll stab you."

I kicked her behind the knees, just like in the movies, but she didn't even falter. She was taller and larger than me.

"No," she said firmly, not a shred of tension in her voice. She extended a hand slowly in my direction. "Now you give me that knife. Domingo is about to come, and it's obvious you don't even know how to hold a weapon."

She was probably right.

I tightened my grip around the hilt, but Natasha leaped back unexpectedly, swivelled, and attempted to take the dagger from me. Her hand grasped mine, and the dagger slid to her side as we both struggled to get hold of the weapon. I lunged at her with all my weight and sank the dagger into her flesh. My hand slipped down the blade, over the handguard, and the metal sliced my skin as the blade cut right above Natasha's waist. She bent forwards, and we both let out a piercing shriek. Then, she clasped my wrist and pressed between my index and thumb fingers, forcing my hand open.

The dagger clanked as it hit the floor. Natasha pressed one hand against her ribs to stop the blood flow and retrieved the knife with the other one, pointing it at me.

"That was not very polite of you," she grumbled. "But the difference between us is that I do know how to use this properly." She stumbled back and leaned against the cell doors, ignoring her injuries. "Not so different from a scalpel." She pricked me, and I bit my lips to drown a gasp. "Or a skull chisel."

I looked frantically around us in search of a getaway, but she pressed the blade under my chin just a little harder.

"Don't you even think about using an incantation now, unless you want me to chop off your vocal cords and perform an autopsy… on your still breathing body." She kicked me into the middle cell and slammed the door shut, then faced me through the door. "It's toughened glass, by the way," she said, pointing at the transparent surfaces around me. "I'll go upstairs to clean the wound, but I'm sending Domingo to see you in a minute. You better be good."

Blood started to trickle down my injured hand and onto the sticky floor, mixing on the ground with Julia's. Natasha hadn't taken my purse, so I pressed the wound against its fabric in a futile attempt to stop the bleeding.

Natasha went out, and a soft click echoed in the distance. All the lights went off, and we prisoners were left in complete darkness.

Chapter 38

Alba

My eyes gradually got used to the weak glow coming from the sparse emergency lights above the elevator.

I stumbled to an upwards position, feeling the sticky ground under the fingertips of my healthy hand but disregarding the nature of the substances smeared on it.

"Francesca!" I whispered, tapping on the partition between us. It consisted of two thick glass panes with a fine metallic grid embedded in the middle. Francesca was a formless black bundle in a corner, hunched like an old beggar, her dress turned to rags.

She crawled toward me, followed by a rumble of thick metallic chains.

"Alba?" Her voice was hoarse, and I wondered how much screaming would do that to a vampire's throat. "Is that you?"

"Yes," I answered hurriedly. "What did they do to you? Are you okay?"

She grumbled softly and flopped back down languidly on the stone floor before answering, "I'm so thirsty, Alba. So, so thirsty…"

I closed my eyes, unable to stand the sight.

"I'm sorry, Francesca. We'll find you something to eat, but we need to get out of here first. Do you have an idea how?" I winced as the pain in my hand became sharper. I had tried to apply some pressure, but the blood kept dripping down my forearm.

"Are we alone now?" she asked weakly.

"Yes. But we must hurry. The guard is coming."

"There's no way to leave this place," she said. "This is a glass coffin."

"Can't you just smash the glass and get us out?"

"I'm so weak… I can hardly speak. Even if I shatter the glass, these chains are indestructible. Tungsten chains. Vampireproof. You think I didn't try?"

She rattled them, showcasing the wounds made on her wrists and ankles by the constant contact with the spiked metal shackles that restrained her.

"There must be a way. But we need to wake up Clarence first. What's wrong with him?" My fingers clenched as I waited for her slow reaction to my question.

"A spell…" she muttered drowsily, as her eyes glazed over. "The witch cast a spell on him."

"What kind of spell?"

"The Silver Cast…"

"What's a silver cast?"

"What? Everyone knows about it... but I thought it was extinct by now."

"Francesca, *I don't know* about it," I muttered, my patience wearing thin. "Will you tell me, please?" I knelt next to her from my side of the glass, and she approached me from hers. A small pool of fresh blood had started to gather on the floor, and I scooted over to avoid sitting directly on it.

Francesca blinked and swayed left and right like a drunkard, staring at my blood as it merged into a small puddle in the cell. "I can't… think… I'm just so… thirsty…"

"Francesca, please!" I pleaded, wishing to shake her back into her senses. "Please, focus! I need you!"

She bared her fangs and grinned. For the first time ever, I saw the monster in her. Torture had tainted her fair beauty, leaving just a gaunt, demented expression on what once was the most beautiful creature I had ever laid eyes on.

The hydraulic hiss of the elevator caught my attention, and the door opened brusquely into the main space.

Domingo, the butler-bodyguard, burst out of the elevator and approached us with a frown.

"So now we keep witches in here, too," he stated, crossing two muscular arms in front of his chest as he studied me.

He was still carrying a gun and, oddly, my

first thought was, *I hope he didn't shoot Carlo.* Since when did I care so much about Carlo?

"Natasha is turning this place into a freaking paranormal zoo." He rolled his eyes. "What will be next? Elves and pixies? The freaking Tooth Fairy?"

He snorted and turned around to sit at a desk in the main area, overlooking our cells as he twirled the gun like a roulette in his hand.

Francesca had fallen back into her trance, weeping and moaning bitterly about her thirst. I leaned against Clarence's cell, yearning to touch him. My breath created a veil of steam between us, blurring the image of his inert body on the sterile metal table. As I stared at him in tears he flinched in his sleep, as if acknowledging my presence.

"I'm the worst witch ever," I murmured against the glass. It was hard and cold, and it reminded me of his lips. "This is all my fault."

Clarence's eyes flashed open for a second, and his head shook slightly, in what could have been a feeble *"No."*

His head fell down on the hard table once again, this time turned toward me. I could see his whole face now, emaciated and wounded. There were red stains around the corners of his closed eyes, and dry tears mixed with blood over his temples.

He had been crying, and so was I now.

What was I going to do?

Were we all bound to die in this underwater grave, forgotten below the Venetian waterways?

Could this really be the end?

Would my children grow up with Minnie as their mother, believing I had abandoned them? Thinking I didn't love them?

My thoughts slipped to the happy days back in The Cloister. To the day we had kissed on the roof of Saint Magdalene's church. To the afternoon I had watched him play pick up sticks with my daughters, and his wide, heart-melting smile when I had been right and beaten him.

Pick up sticks.

I looked at the pillars holding the ceiling above us, studying the structure of the underwater basement. What would happen if I removed just one single *stick* out of a dozen? What if I removed two?

Francesca's chains rattled again, and I traced them with my eyes. They were coiled around the steel pillars.

She had said those chains were made of tungsten: vampire hunters' chains. I had read about them in the leaflet those Salem witches had given me, what seemed like an eternity ago. That leaflet was still in my purse, wasn't it? I searched for it and Turanna's mirror stared back at me from the inside of the bag, glowing faintly with a dim, purple glimmer. Just like my own.

A crazy idea sparked in my mind.

The guard was scrolling on his phone, oblivious to my scheming. Francesca stopped whining, and for a second her eyes regained a vague degree of sanity.

"I have an idea," I whispered.

She tilted her head, like an expectant doll.

"I know a way…" I started to say.

"*No talkie*," the guard grunted, banging the desk with a heavy paper punch.

Francesca's glimpse caught mine as I allowed the blood from my wounded hand to pool and run under the glass partition between us. A quick glimpse of understanding ignited her eyes, and she prostrated herself on the floor, licking greedily the dark drops I was offering.

Chapter 39

Alba

"He's about to leave for dinner," Francesca murmured, pointing discreetly at the guard.

I nodded slightly, unwilling to attract the gorilla's attention.

Francesca had licked the few drops of my blood which had seeped under the glass. She hadn't complained about the bitter taste, which wasn't so surprising, given her moribund state. The characteristic teal glow was now starting to return to her eyes, and I trusted her sanity would make a speedy reappearance, too.

The guard threw a dismissive glance in our direction before standing up and disappearing into the elevator in search of food.

As soon as the door closed with a thud, I turned back to Francesca.

"This is the plan," I told her hurriedly. "You break the glass. I take care of the pillars."

She nodded slowly. "I can do that."

"Then I get us out of here. I have a magic

mirror, and I think I know how to use it. If I hold your hand, it will take you with me. But I'll need to get hold of Clarence's, too."

"Fine," she said, exhausted. "But once you remove the four pillars we are tied to, the building is going to collapse over our heads. Have you considered that?"

"Leave it to me. I'm the expert here." I took a deep breath, hoping I was right. *I always won at pick up sticks, didn't I?* We just had to remove them in the right order, and clear out as fast as possible. "But I'll need your help. Do you think you could hold the ceiling? Just for two minutes, so I can get to Clarence and cast the spell?"

"I could try." Francesca smacked her lips, then bent down and licked the floor squeaky clean.

"Good. Let's do it."

She stood up, her fingerless hands raised in a magnificent stance despite the days of torture and starvation. She was such a resilient creature, Francesca. Her eyes set on fire, otherworldly and blue, and she gave me a sign with her head, inviting me to proceed.

I cowered in the furthest corner of the cell and took out Turanna's mirror.

"If this goes wrong," Francesca said, her voice back to its deep, melodic hum, "you should know that you and Julia are the only two witches I ever trusted. And I'm glad we met in this life."

My awkward, grateful smile lasted less than a second, because Francesca's colossal blow shattered the safety glass in a million pieces, triggering a deafening alarm. Amidst the roar, she leaped into my cell and smashed the wall to Clarence's side with her naked fist.

Clarence was still unconscious, lying on the metal slab with his hands on his lap and his eyes closed. I ran to him and threw my arms around his ice-cold chest.

"Your turn," Francesca said, tugging at her chains. The whole building shook as she did so, and a wave of panic raised from the pit of my stomach. "I trust you, Alba. Remember."

At least someone did.

"You both need to get closer," I shouted. "I need to touch you both at the same time!"

"I can't reach him while I'm chained!" she yelled over the growing noise. "Find a way!"

A downward arrow of light shone over the elevator door. Someone was coming.

Clarence was heavy, too heavy for me.

"Stand in that corner," I ordered Francesca, pointing at one of the master pillars. "I'll drag Clarence to your side, blow the pillars and take your hand so we can teleport the hell out of here."

She raised an eyebrow, echoing my doubts, but obeyed silently.

I recited the *Fulminatio* spell, imbuing all my hopes in the words as I pronounced them.

Rays of light flew through my arms and out of my fingers, and the pillars blasted one by one.

The explosions were deafening, so much that I didn't even hear the elevator doors opening and the guard rushing toward us, pointing his gun at me.

The ceiling started to crumble, deadly boulders raining on us.

Francesca stood just like Atlas, holding the sky on her shoulders. The veins in her neck bulged, and a feral grunt escaped her throat.

I embraced Clarence, holding his lifeless body against my chest as I tried to drag him closer to Francesca.

The mirror glowed, blinding and purple.

Clouds of grey dust.

The outer walls exploding under the pressure of the water outside.

Dark streams rushing in from all sides.

The guard opening fire.

Francesca twisted herself and intercepted the bullet aimed at my heart. She never let go of the collapsing ceiling.

"Go! Now!" She shouted, as the bullet burned a growing hole in the middle of her chest.

Turanna's mirror was so hot that I could smell my skin sizzling. There was no reflection on its smoldering surface, and I started to panic. Alice had told me, back in the museum, that it should turn reflective when activated. I forced myself to hold both Clarence and the magic tool, despite the horrible pain and burns it was causing me.

The skies crumbled over Atlas, over Francesca, over us. I couldn't reach her anymore.

Just remember the verses I taught you, Julia had said in the dream, smiling in her silver shoes, *and if you can't find yourself in the mirror, you should be looking deeper.*

I squeezed Clarence's hand, and Julia's words echoed in my mind, right before Francesca, and the guard, and the basement, all disappeared into a flash of purple light.

Chapter 40

Alba

Water bubbled in my ears, and I found myself hobbling over the sludgy bottom of the canals in complete darkness. The mirror had fallen from my hand, disappearing forever into the bottom of the Venice lagoon; but I was still holding Clarence, my elbow linked around his shoulder like a twining vine. He was still lifeless, and horribly stiff, which made the task of hauling him to the surface grueling at best.

And, to make things worse, I was drowning.

If I let go of him, I might get out of the water fast enough to save myself. He didn't need to breathe, but I did.

Still, I could not leave him. Not in that state.

I swam upwards, not sure where upwards was. Clarence was lighter underwater, but his dead weight still made me clumsy and kept sinking me back.

I hadn't had time to think where to teleport, so Turanna, or the mirror, must have decided for me. I guessed we were outside Natasha's house, immersed in the water. In one of the deepest canals of the whole city. *Lucky me.*

My lungs hurt, and I longed to take a deep breath. But I knew that, if I did, I would be dead within minutes.

But if I didn't, I would die before long, too.

I flailed my free arm in desperation, trying to spot a glow in the darkness: any signs of dry land. Water gushed in my ears and left a filthy sewage taste on my tightly closed lips.

I hadn't perished tortured by Natasha; nor crushed under the weight of a collapsing building. Yet here I was, about to meet my end drowned in a fetid lagoon.

Unless I let go of Clarence.

The water trembled over my head, and a muffled noise reverberated around me.

A motorboat.

I kicked my legs in desperation, following the sound of the engine, disregarding the possibility of being run over. By then, I didn't really care. I just wanted to breathe.

Breathe…

***

The world was rocking left and right.

Had I had too much to drink?

"Too much water, *signorina,* yes," someone answered. I must have voiced my thoughts aloud. A man was sitting next to me, wearing an orange softshell jacket. He had wrapped me in a coarse grey blanket, and I was aboard an expensive-looking motorboat traveling along one of the canals under a plump full moon.

I looked around frantically, searching for Clarence. There was a clean bandage on my hand, and the wound had stopped bleeding.

I remembered swimming to the surface and clasping a wooden post. A group of tourists had found us and dragged us up to the pier.

But how I had ended up on a leather couch, in the cabin of a luxurious water taxi—seemingly losing Clarence in the process—was beyond my recollection.

Had he fallen back into the water?

Had he been found by humans?

I started to panic.

"Where are we going?" I asked the man in the orange softshell. There were two more people, but the other just kept staring at me in silence, with a mixture of pity and discomfort.

"You fell into the canals, madam. We were passing by on the way to our hotel and volunteered to take you to a hospital. You swallowed a few gallons of sewer water. Not the best after-dinner choice."

As if on cue, something—an eel?—gurgled inside my chest, and I started to cough. He eyed me with sympathy.

"No, no, I don't need a hospital, I'm perfectly fine," I said, once I could finally stop coughing and gurgling, but he raised an eyebrow.

"I'm serious. I just want to see my friend. The one who was with me. Where is he? There was a girl too. Young, blond hair," I added, hoping Francesca had made it out of the crumbling building.

The man lowered his eyes and tilted his head toward the other two people, silently seeking their support.

"We didn't see any girls, but about your other friend…" he started in a compassionate tone, then turned anxiously to an older lady who had been watching us from the other side of the motorboat.

She was draped in a black trench coat and could have been the man's mother, because they shared the same aquiline nose. She sat next to me on the bench and took my hand, the way people usually do right before delivering terrible news.

"I'm sorry, madam," she said softly. "One of the passersby happened to be a nurse. She checked your friend's vitals…" She squeezed my hand and paused to make sure I understood what she was saying. "She advised us to take you to the mainland, to a hospital. She was really kind and stayed behind with him, to wait for the police and the…" she paused, "and the coroners."

My chest tightened as she spoke.

Of course they had taken him for dead.

Clarence *was* dead, for goodness sake.

Had been so for two centuries: nothing wrong with that.

He was cold, rarely had a heartbeat, and breathed just when he felt like it.

What else were they to think?

I forbid myself to consider any other possibilities.

Still, Clarence in the hands of physicians, or the authorities, especially in his ill state, was extremely bad news. Much worse than the fact that he was relatively dead—I had already come to terms with that minor issue short after my arrival at The Cloister.

"Can we go back?" I croaked, trying to sound calm and failing miserably.

The tourists looked at each other, doubt clearly visible in their eyes. "Are you sure, madam? You don't want to see a doctor?"

"Completely sure. Please. I need to see him."

***

When we reached the place where we had emerged from the canals, the moon was high in the sky and cast kaleidoscopic reflections over the tar-colored waters.

Carlo Lombardi was standing by the pier and waved at us.

"I know her," he said to the water taxi driver. "You can leave her with me."

He greeted me with a chin nod from the embankment.

"You know him?" The elder lady didn't seem keen on trusting him. I didn't blame her: he had never seemed very trustworthy to me, either.

"It's okay," I said, swallowing and hoping I wasn't wrong. Carlo offered me a hand to disembark the motorboat, and I took it, leaning to speak in his ear.

"Do you know where… *he* is?" I whispered.

"Yes," he answered curtly. After that, he said goodbye to the helpful tourists, reassuring them I would be fine with him. "You can go home, thank you for your help," he told them. "I'm a cop, we are friends."

"I'm not your friend," I hissed after they left. He might have defended me against Natasha and provided me with a weapon, but it was him who had brought me to her in the first place.

I was still wet and shivering, and Carlo helped me wrap the thick borrowed blanket around my shoulders. It was heavy and a bit damp, and it kept slipping down; but it was better than walking around Venice in my soaked clothes, on a chilly January night.

"I saw the house blow up in the air from afar, and I got a feeling you had something to do with it," he said. "It wasn't hard to find you after that."

"So, where is he?" I asked, scanning Carlo's body language and trying to read his intentions. If he didn't know where Clarence was, I had no reason to stay with him.

"Do you trust me?" he asked with an inscrutable squint.

"Of course not," I retorted.

"Smart girl. But you will have to, if you want

me to help you. I won't be able to keep him there for too long. I might have picked that piece of scum off the sidewalk, but don't expect me to do anything beyond that. I'm doing this for you, not him. He can go to hell, as far as I'm concerned."

I tried hard to control my urge to strangle him.

"You still didn't tell me where he is," I pointed out. Was this a trick to lure me into yet another trap?

"There's this place, not far from here…" he answered, steering us toward a winding alley, away from the main waterways.

"You will have to tie me, drug me and possibly kill me if you intend me to go into that dark alley with you," I roared. "You and the witches sold me to Natasha. Do you think I'm stupid enough to step into yet another ambush?"

He sighed and gave me an exhausted glance.

"Look, I'm sorry. I didn't know they were so crazy. The witches said Natasha wanted a brief interview with you. They didn't mention she would carry it out in a dungeon."

"You are sorry?" I screamed, and a couple of tourists stopped kissing just to stare at us, so I lowered my tone. "A whole house just collapsed over my head. I nearly drowned. My friends are… I don't even know what became of them! They could all be dead, for all I know!" My jaw twitched, and I reminded myself I shouldn't be shouting. "And you played a good part in all this."

"Okay, look, yes, I've been working for

Natasha. I've been finding vampires for her. She pays well, and I don't like the bloodsuckers anyway. I don't really know if she kills them, nor do I care if that's what she wants them for. She probably does, eventually. It doesn't count as murder if they were dead to start with, does it?"

He raised his eyebrows, and I growled as a reply.

"But living people," he continued, "people like you and me… that's a different story. You are not a soulless creature like them, so I didn't expect her to jail you. So, yes, I'm sorry, and I'm trying to make it up to you. Don't make this harder for me than it is already, okay?"

"First of all, they are not soulless," I hissed. "And second, why is she so keen on hunting vampires? What does she need them for?"

He stared at me with half-closed eyes. "She wants to know what keeps them alive after death. Seems someone is willing to pay for the formula."

"Someone, who?" I rubbed my hands together to warm them up.

"Do you think she shares her secrets with me?" He shrugged. "I was just a pawn in her game. Maybe the government, maybe a private investor: I have no idea. I just helped the witches get her the subjects she needed, that's it."

"Why should I believe you? Why should I go with you now? For all I know, Natasha could be waiting for me right now in the place you are taking me to."

"I tried to defend you from her, didn't I? I

lied to the crowd on the pier and pretended I was a policeman to get your friend out of sight before the real cops arrived. I took him to the only safe place I know nearby, but I'm not the only one who has the keys. Sorry, but you'll have to believe me or accept he might not be there tomorrow when you change your mind."

"And why would you do this?" I asked with suspicion. "He tried to kill you."

"Because I'm stupid, I guess." He took out his wallet and extracted a small photograph from it, then handed it to me. "Look. This is Eleanor Lombardi," he said quietly. It was a picture of him with a sweet-looking, curvy, red-haired woman. They were both smiling, and he still didn't have any of the wrinkles which now festooned the corners of his blue eyes. "My wife."

They looked happy together. I remembered what Berenice had told me about his wife's death, and I felt a pang of pity for him.

"I'm… I'm sorry for your loss," I said, handing him back the photo. "Berenice told me about her, back at the inn."

"Did she? But did she tell you *everything*? Do you know how she died?"

"She said it was a violent death."

"A vampire murdered my wife," he murmured, waiting for my reaction. I gasped, not knowing what to answer. "Yes, she was an innocent. I saw the bastard jump off the window of our bedroom when I came home from a night shift. She was lying in bed when I found her, and everything was covered in blood. *Her* blood. There were no bite marks, but I had known about vampires since I was born. My great-grandfather and all the Lombardis before him were hunters. Such things were openly discussed in my family. That bastard must have traced me. He used my wife to settle the score with my long dead relatives." His voice broke, and I felt truly sorry for him. "My wife's case is still open for the police. It will forever be."

I stared at him, paralyzed, Elizabeth's rules echoing in my mind: *"You will not kill gratuitously."* Whoever that vampire had been, it couldn't have been anyone from The Cloister.

Or so I hoped.

"Sure this will be enough for you to understand how I feel about your… *friends.* I will never side with those creatures. They stole the only thing I ever loved. I have only hatred for them, and I wish them all dead. For good."

I steadied myself against a metal fence overlooking the water, listening to the boats and the rumor of conversations around us. It was a busy evening in Venice, despite the cold and humidity.

"I'm so sorry this happened to you. I… I have no words." I said, tugging at the corners of the blanket to keep it from falling to the ground. "But this doesn't sound like a reason for you to help me. More like… the opposite."

"Yes. I told you, I'm stupid." His eyes were glassy, and he sounded so raw, so sincere. Gone was the cocky man from the plane. This was just a wounded, broken man telling me his life story, and I felt a sudden and deep empathy for Carlo Lombardi.

"So… why?"

"Because I'm sorry I dragged you into this mess, and I have a conscience after all. I like you, Alba. If you remember, I took you on a date on that boat. I brought you flowers. That was not part of my contract. You can imagine how I felt when I found you with him," he said sorely. "And yes, I was jealous, and I'm sorry I set the inn on fire. It wasn't on purpose. I didn't expect your interview with Natasha to snowball into this nightmare. So, consider this my apology for everything that happened. Even though I think you are wrong on so many levels, and you're going to regret your choices big time."

***

We marched in silence for a while, the sounds of sirens and shouting voices looming in the distance. Natasha's house appeared in front of us—or rather, what was left of it. The building had collapsed from the foundations, demolishing part of the neighboring houses in the process and covering the nearby streets and canals in mountains of rubble, which extended well beyond the embankment. The police had already taped off the area, and the hectic scene reminded me of a busy anthill.

"I have no idea what you did in there, and even less how you managed to get out alive," Carlo commented, shaking his head. "They are saying it was a gas explosion, but I saw everything from afar. The house blasted into a purple flare: it was the weirdest thing ever. I don't think gas explosions look like that."

"In that you are right," I said tersely. "At least the gas part."

He pointed at a narrow street not far away.

"Follow me," he said. I walked behind him, tired and numb under the soggy blanket. My bad cough was back and, if I didn't find a change of clothes soon, I might very well die of pneumonia.

He pointed at a house on the other side of the alley, which must be at least a few hundred years old and showed clear signs of decline. It had a small, aged wooden door facing the alley. Carlo opened it and turned on the lights inside.

"Come in," he said from a dusty hallway.

I glanced in and hesitated. A musty smell was coming from the inside. It must have been empty for a long time.

I tried to tune into my intuition, searching for clues of a trap. The place was absolutely silent, and Carlo stared at me, expectant.

"Are you coming in or not?" he asked with impatience.

I took courage and stepped in.

I followed Carlo along a somber corridor into what must have once been a living room. A large crucifix hung on the widest wall, and I recognized a set of stakes and knives, ordered by size, on a decrepit dresser.

"What's this place?" I asked, taking one of the wooden stakes and weighing it in my hand. It was long and heavier than I had expected. And extremely sharp.

"Just a warehouse for Natasha and her minions to keep old stuff."

"Looks like a vampire hunting museum," I murmured, studying a row of moldy dry garlic garlands which dangled from most lamps.

"Museums are full of outdated things nobody uses anymore, but everything you see here is still perfectly functional." He disappeared into a side room and peeked out of the door, waving at me. "Hurry up. Someone might come any minute."

I left the stake back on the dresser and went after him.

"You should have seen the faces of those tourists when I appeared at the peer pushing Natasha's wheelbarrow and pretending to be a cop…" Carlo was saying, but I stopped listening somewhere around the middle of his sentence, my eyes traveling from the vase full of dusty, dry roses on the bedside table and then to the man lying in an old bed with an ornate headboard.

Clarence lay asleep, and the expression on his face was peaceful now, almost angelic.

"So, here's your Sleeping Beauty, as promised," Carlo said with an impatient huff.

I ran to Clarence's side, pushing aside whole curtains of cobwebs. Then I took his hand, burying my face in his damp, torn shirt, and started to weep aloud on his chest.

Carlo cleared his throat from the doorway and tapped his fingers against the doorframe. I turned to find him still glaring at us, with his arms tightly crossed.

"I'm going outside for a cigarette," he said uncomfortably.

"No, wait! I don't know how to wake him up," I sobbed. "They told me it's a spell, but I don't know what to do about it."

As I spoke, I remembered about Francesca, carrying the weight of a whole building on her very own, and the tears started to run down my cheeks once again.

Carlo frowned. "What spell?"

"I don't know, I think it's called The Silver Cast. Do you know anything about it?" I squeezed Clarence's hand and stood up to face Carlo.

"I've heard about it," he said with irritation. "It used to be a great way to tame vampires who didn't want to cooperate. But I didn't know there were still witches able to cast that one."

"What does it do?"

"It creates a silver cast around the heart, what else? The silver seeps slowly into their bloodstream and keeps them quiet. It poisons them gradually and kills them after a while. It's like a silver stake, only the effects are much slower."

I closed my eyes and took a deep breath. "And how do I reverse it?"

"No idea, I'm not a witch. But, as far as I

know, these creatures are quite tough, and they thrive on other people's life energy, don't they?"

He tilted his chin meaningfully toward my neck and bit his lower lip, making me feel oddly self-conscious.

"Oh, okay," I said, as a rush of warmth flooded my cheeks.

"Yeah, that might do the trick." Carlo averted his eyes. "I guess I'll leave you alone now. I'm not sure I have the stomach to watch this. I'll be outside if you need me."

***

Clarence rested with his arms over his heart. The water had washed away the blood and grime from his face, but his nose appeared slightly too angulous, and his cheeks more sunken than usual. He wasn't breathing, but his closed eyelids twitched faintly when I sat down by his side.

"It's me, Alba," I told him.

I removed the bandage from my hand and studied the cut: it was deep and still hurt. As soon as I opened my hand, the wound started bleeding again. A few crimson drops gathered over my palm, and I wiped them with the tip of my finger. I smeared the blood over his blue lips, turning them a shocking carmine color.

He took a deep breath but didn't move.

"Wake up, Clarence," I whispered, trying to shake his shoulders. I barely managed to nudge him.

I tried again. And again.

I pressed my finger against his lips, hoping he would smell the blood and wake up, but he didn't react. He just lay there, lifeless and oblivious to my efforts.

What if Carlo had been wrong?

I decided not to consider such grim possibilities just yet.

What if my blood wasn't good enough? It smelled horrible, didn't it? Was that the problem? Had he been just polite when he said it didn't bother him? What was I going to do?

Desperate, I licked the blood off the wound and bent over Clarence to kiss him.

I approached him slowly, letting my lips softly brush against his; hoping he would respond to my kiss. I softly tracked the contour of his mouth, pausing over the ridge of his upper lip.

Suddenly, his eyes flung open, crimson and glimmering, and he yanked the back of my head, tangling his fingers in my hair, in a way very much unlike the Clarence I knew. He licked the blood off my lips, then stared at me for a second before pulling me toward him with inhuman strength and sinking his sharp fangs on my neck, with such passion and need that I shrieked, startled by his abrupt reaction. My whole body shook with a mixture of panic and passionate elation as the pain gave way to pleasure in a matter of seconds.

He snarled and held me against his chest, drinking deep until a glimpse of realization finally reached his eyes and he sat up, a dismayed expression on his face.

"Alba?" he said, looking around in confusion. "Where am I? What happened?"

The color had returned to his cheeks, although it had probably left mine in the meantime. I let out a sigh of relief, not before stepping back and slightly away from him, my knees shaking with a mixture of rapture and shock.

"It's fine," I said, my voice quivering. "You woke up. You woke up… don't worry."

"I'm… I'm sorry," he stuttered, staring at my neck with horror. "I didn't know it was you. I thought I was dreaming. I was… I didn't…"

"*Shh.*" I put my finger to his red lips. "It's okay."

I hugged him, pressing my cheek against his and letting my warmth extend to his skin.

Carlo appeared in the doorway. He must have heard my scream, because he arrived carrying a large stake and a hammer.

"Everything alright here?" he barked.

I nodded and covered the bites with one hand as I urged him with the other one to lower the stake. He left it on a dresser by my side. "In case you change your mind," he mumbled.

"No, everything is great." I grinned. "Your idea worked."

"Awesome," he said without much conviction, his eyes settling on Clarence's blood-stained lips. "I can't say I'm exactly happy to hear that, but I hope I gained your trust now."

"I guess you did," I answered slowly.

"We can't stay here," he said, eyeing Clarence with disgust. "It's not safe. Come with me to the car, I know a place where we can stay in for a couple of days, until you decide what to do."

"Okay, just give us a minute, will you?" I said.

"Yeah, okay, but hurry up." Carlo turned his back to us and left the room. When I thought he was already gone, he peeked once more into the bedroom, addressing me like Clarence wasn't even in the room, "And tell Sleeping Beauty that, if he ever tries to bite me again, I'm turning him into vampire dust, will you?"

Clarence's eyes flashed, but I silenced him with a warning glance, aware of the vast vampire hunting arsenal available in the adjacent room.

I nodded to Carlo. "I'll tell him," I answered, and waited for his steps to fade.

"You scared me," I said, sitting back on the edge of the bed.

"Forgive me," he whispered. His eyes were back to a subdued shade of maroon, with no traces of light in them. "I… I was not myself." He stood up, but his legs faltered, and he had to hold onto the dresser. "Actually, I was, and that is the problem."

Clarence caressed the stake, forgotten on the chest of drawers, and lifted it pensively.

"I love all versions of you," I said quietly. "You should know that."

He sighed and kissed the top of my head without saying a word.

"You scared me because I thought you would never wake up again," I clarified. "Otherwise, I'm fine. I just didn't expect such an enthusiastic… greeting. You didn't hurt me. I was just a bit surprised."

He smiled with bitterness. "Thank you for being you," he said. "Sincerely. I promise this will not happen again. If it does, feel free to use this on me while I sleep." He handed me the stake. "I reckon the witches taught you to?"

"No, they didn't. They think I'm a disgrace." I shrugged, then left the stake where it had been. "It's okay if it happens again, just… give me a little warning first, will you? I don't think Sleeping Beauty bit Prince Florimond like that in the fairy tale."

"I don't think the good Fairy Hippolyta looked like Carlo, either," he commented.

We looked at each other and snorted.

"Come on, let's go," I told him, "the good Fairy Hippolyta must be getting impatient out there."

Clarence took a tentative step but stumbled against the dresser once again. I extended my hand and offered it to him. "Let me help you."

"I'm too heavy for you," he protested, reluctant to take it.

"Give me some credit," I retorted. "I got you out of Natasha's house, didn't I? I can hold you if you need me to. I'm stronger than I look."

He wrapped an arm around my shoulders.

"As always, you are right," he said with a

nod, sniffing the tender spot behind my ear as we left the dark bedroom behind. "Walking together is so much easier."

Epilogue

We sailed the highway, swift as an arrow, possibly the oddest crew which ever traveled the Northern Italian roads: a vampire-hunting corrupt policeman, an inept witch wrapped in a damp blanket and a puzzled, hungry vampire; the three of us sharing a red and slightly too small Alfa Romeo, on our way to Tuscany's undulating hills.

Carlo's family property was located on top of a steep slope, overlooking vast rows of vineyards. He told us they usually rented the house to tourists, but it was vacant when we arrived. The property manager, a kind and discreet neighbour, had already changed the sheets and was waiting for us with hot coffee, bread and jam when we parked on the driveway right before sunrise.

I smirked as Clarence fiddled with a teaspoon and pretended to sip his coffee, complimenting the housekeeper with flawless politeness. Just in case, I held his arm to keep him from leaping on the housekeeper's neck. It was obvious from his clumsy behavior that he was still thirsty and confused, but the blue tinge to his skin was gone, replaced by a slightly more human-looking, albeit sickly pallor. For some reason, he didn't seem to remember much from the moment he had been captured by the witches until he woke up to the taste of my blood on his lips.

"I can't stay," Carlo said, once the kind neighbor went back home. The car ride had been awkwardly silent, mostly because Carlo refused to talk to Clarence and vice-versa. As for me, I was just thankful they hadn't tried to kill each other. "I'm booking a flight for this evening and going back to Emberbury." He threw me a sidelong glance. "What about you?"

I watched the steam rise from the coffee cup between my hands. "I'd like to remain in Italy, at least for a couple of days, until I find out what happened to the others. If you don't mind us staying here a little longer."

Carlo nodded, watching the vineyards from the old-fashioned kitchen window, and handed me a bunch of keys. "Okay. Stay as long as you want. Give the keys to Maria before you go, and feel free to call me when you get back." He scribbled his phone number on a piece of scrap paper, which reminded me that I had no operative phone at all.

"I'll see," I answered. "Thank you for everything," I added, not sure whether thanks were in order after all our ups and downs.

"See you in Emberbury," Carlo said, and slammed the door behind him.

"Hopefully not," Clarence muttered, and I smiled at him, relieved to have him back.

***

The next day, the neighbor lent me her van, and I drove to the village to get myself a new phone. The first thing I did was try to ring up Alice in case she had news about Francesca, Julia and Ludovic, but she was unavailable. After that, I called Minnie and finally spoke to my daughters, who were happy and well. On my way back to the villa, I bought cheese, cookies and vegetables from a stall by the road and devoured half of my haul during the ride.

I found Clarence in the wine cellar, where he had made himself a cozy nook in a trunk to spend the day away from sunlight.

"Any news?" he asked me as I reached the end of the stairs.

I shook my head. "No. I can't reach Alice to ask her about Natasha." I took a seat on the stool next to him. "But Katie and Iris are okay."

"That's nice to hear," he said, rubbing my back fondly, although his wrinkled forehead gave away his concern.

"Natasha said Julia and Ludovic had been relocated to France," I told him, remembering our conversation in Venice. "But Francesca…"

He held his head in his hands over the wooden bar counter but remained silent. I had explained to him everything that happened while he was unconscious, and some of his memories seemed to be seeping back, blended with bizarre dreams and visions.

"I can't believe I might not see her again." He avoided my eyes and stared at the mosaic on the wall, lost in his recollections. I rested my head in the crook of his neck, allowing him time to grieve, and he let out a deep breath.

"She was always so brave. Much more than I," he breathed into my hair.

"She *is* really brave," I corrected him. "More than all of us combined."

We remained silent for a while, sharing a turmoil of unspoken, grim reflections.

"I'm sure there's still hope," I said, squeezing his hand.

"And Julia. And Ludovic," he continued, in a distraught tone. "Just when I found out they were still alive, I lost them again."

"We'll find them."

I stood up and placed my hands on his shoulders, trying to massage his rock-hard back with my healthy hand. It was more difficult than it seemed at first sight. He placed his hand over mine with affection and gave me a faint, appreciative smile.

"You should go back to Emberbury and check on your daughters. Talk to Elizabeth, too," he added with a sad tinge in his voice. "She will know what to do."

I thought about my phone conversation with Minnie. She had found it strange that I hadn't answered for so long, but I had lied about losing my phone, and she had believed me. For a Harvard graduate, she wasn't the sharpest knife in the drawer. But judging by the pictures she had sent me, the girls were doing well in her charge. Still, I missed them so much.

"Maybe you're right," I answered. "But what about you?"

"I'll leave right after you. As soon as I feel good enough to withstand the crossing."

I swallowed, wondering when that would be. He looked livelier this morning, and I prayed the Silver Cast spell had been reversed for good. But what if he changed his mind and disappeared for weeks once again, just like he had done a few times before? He lowered his gaze, possibly reading my mind, and made the stool swivel so we were facing each other.

"I know what you are thinking," he said, "but I have learned a lesson out of this." He caressed my cheek with his thumb. "I'm not leaving you again. Ever. I promised you that night, when you were a ghost. And I promise you now that you are not."

I closed my eyes, too overwhelmed to answer.

"Unless, that is, you are already fed up with this old, indecisive vampire and his whims," he added, cupping my face in his hands.

"Who ghosted me and then bit me," I pointed out with a tiny simper. "Twice, to be precise."

Clarence tilted his head and glanced away, looking embarrassed. "Sorry about that. I'll make sure it doesn't happen again."

"Don't worry, I have seen worse," I teased him, and his eyes glimmered dangerously.

He stood up and started to study the intricate glass mosaic which adorned the wall behind us.

"It's spectacular, isn't it? What do you think?" he asked me with a half-smile, brushing the tip of his finger against the soft glass tiles.

"Are you trying to change the subject?" I admonished him.

"No." He chuckled and vaguely vampire-blushed. "Fine, perhaps I am. Do you really want to continue that route? Alone and locked in a remote cellar with a thirsty vampire?"

"*Hm.*" *Did I?* I was quite weak myself after everything that had happened. As suggestive as his offer might sound, it would have to wait.

I turned to the mosaic.

"Maybe you're right. So, if you want my honest opinion about this… *piece of art*, it's not the ugliest I have seen, but…" I stopped mid-sentence.

"But what?"

"I don't know. I never understood the appeal of mosaics. You first shatter a bunch of perfectly usable tiles, spend days putting them together like a puzzle, and end up with a picture made out of mismatched shards. Isn't the whole thing a bit ridiculous? The final product looks like a broken vase glued together. It will never be seamless. It will never be… perfect."

"That, it will never be," he agreed, placing a

naughty kiss on the crown of my head. "I agree."

"Then why do you find mosaics so stunning?"

"Because, my dear Isolde," he said dreamily, scooping me into his arms, "the fact that someone managed to put them together after being so broken makes them short of a miracle."

The End

To be continued in book 3, Witches Masquerade

Witches Masquerade

Book 3 of *The Vampires of Emberbury*

Welcome to the Witches' Masquerade, where everyone gets a dance with Death. Follow Alba to a secluded spot in the Pyrenees where she will seek for a long-lost spell which is her only hope of defeating Death. But whose? Hers, Clarence's, or someone else's?

About the author

My name is Eva and I have always lived in a world of magic. Tales of fantasy and sorcery have haunted me since I was a child, which has caused much tripping on my own feet while walking around absorbed in yet another story.

Scan the code to stay in touch:

Acknowledgments

My heartfelt thanks go to everyone who helped me throughout the process of writing and editing this book, and particularly to my beta readers: **Charlie, Kris, Margot, Wendy, Lara and Ksenija**. I love you all and this book is better because of you.
To the ladies of *The Coven*, who were there for me for support and laughs every single day.
I won't name you, so our secret remains so;
but you know who you are.
Also to Elizabeth: thank you so much for editing this novel.

And of course, thanks to you,
who are reading this book,
for following Alba and Clarence's adventures.

Printed in Great Britain
by Amazon